LONESTAR ANGEL

ALSO BY COLLEEN COBLE

Smitten

The Under Texas Skies series
Blue Moon Promise (Available February 2012)

The Lonestar Novels
Lonstar Sanctuary
Lonestar Secrets
Lonestar Homecoming

The Mercy Falls series
The Lightkeeper's Daughter
The Lightkeeper's Bride
The Lightkeeper's Ball

The Rock Harbor series
Without a Trace
Beyond a Doubt
Into the Deep
Cry in the Night

The Aloha Reef series
Distant Echoes
Black Sands
Dangerous Depths

Alaska Twilight
Fire Dancer
Midnight Sea
Abomination
Anathema

LONESTAR ANGEL

COLLEEN
COBLE

THOMAS NELSON
Since 1798

NASHVILLE DALLAS MEXICO CITY RIO DE JANEIRO

Published in Nashville, Tennessee, by Thomas Nelson. Thomas Nelson is a registered trademark of Thomas Nelson, Inc.

ISBN 978-1-61793-423-0

Printed in the United States of America

For Alexa Coble

My perfect angel

1

SILVERWARE TINKLED IN THE DIMLY LIT DINING ROOM OF TWENTY, AN UPSCALE RESTAURANT located inside Charley Creek Inn, a classy boutique hotel. Eden Larson smiled over the top of her glass of water at Kent Huston. He was so intelligent and kind. His blue eyes were filled with intent tonight, and she had known what he had planned from the moment he suggested this place for dinner.

The piano player's voice rose above the music as he sang "Waiting for a Girl Like You." Kent had spoken that very phrase to her often in the year they'd been dating.

"Warm enough?" he asked.

"It's a perfect night."

"In every way," he agreed. "I want to—"

"Kent." She reached across the linen tablecloth and took his hand. "I need to tell you something."

Before he asked her to marry him, he needed to know what baggage she carried. She'd intended to tell him before now—long before. But every time she tried, the pain closed her throat. She wasn't ready to talk about it then, and maybe she wasn't ready now, but he deserved to know.

Kent smiled. "Are you finally going to tell me what brought you to town? I don't really care, Eden. I'm just thankful you're here. I love you."

She wetted her lips. It didn't matter that he said he didn't care. She owed it to him to tell him about her past and the demons that had driven her here to Wabash, Indiana. "Kent . . ." The sense of a presence behind her made her pause.

"Eden," a man said.

Her heart seized in her chest. She'd recognize the deep timbre anywhere. It haunted her dreams and its accusing tones punctuated her nightmares. The deep vibrancy of that voice would impress any woman before she ever saw him.

She turned slowly in her upholstered chair and stared up at Clay Larson, who stood under the crystal chandelier that was the centerpiece of the intimate dining room. "Clay."

How could he be here? He hadn't changed a bit. His hair was still just as dark and curly. His dark blue eyes were just as arresting. And her pulse galloped the way it had the first time she'd set eyes on him.

"I need to talk to you," he said, stepping toward her. "It's important."

Oh, she should have told Kent before now. This was the wrong way for him to discover her past. He was beginning to frown as he glanced from her to Clay, whose broad shoulders and vibrant presence loomed over their table. It was going to come out now. All of it. Her pretend life vanished into mist. What had made her think she could escape the past?

"Who are you?" Kent said. "And what right do you have to interrupt a private conversation?"

"The right of a husband," Clay said, his gaze holding her.

"Ex-husband," she managed to say past the tightness of her throat.

"No, Eden. *Husband*." He held up a sheaf of papers in his right hand.

"What are those?"

"I never signed the divorce papers," he said quietly, just to her. "You're still married to me."

She heard Kent gasp in the silence as the song in the background came to an end. "That's impossible." She stared at Clay, unable to take in what he'd said. "We were divorced over five years ago."

"You sent the papers over five years ago," he corrected. "I just never signed them."

She stared at the blank signature line he showed her. Why had she never followed up? Because she'd been too busy running. "Why not?"

He shook his head. "I had my reasons. Right now, there's something more important to discuss."

"What could be more important?" she asked. Fingers clutched her arm and she turned her head and stared into Kent's face. "I . . . I'm so sorry, Kent. I was just about to tell you."

"Tell me that you're married?" Kent's eyes held confusion and hurt. "I don't understand."

She shook her head. "I'm divorced. Or at least I thought I was. I haven't seen Clay in five years."

Kent's frown smoothed out. "I think you'd better leave," he said to Clay. He scooted back in his chair.

She laid a hand on his arm. "Let me handle this," she said. Anger was beginning to replace her stupor and shock. "Why are you here, Clay?"

"Would you like to step outside so we can continue this in private?" Clay asked, glancing around the room.

Heat flamed in her cheeks when she saw the interested stares from the two nearby tables. "Just go away. We can talk tomorrow."

His firm lips flattened but he stayed where he was. "I've found Brianna, Eden. She's alive."

She struggled to breathe. She searched his face for the hint of a lie but saw only implacable certainty. She shook her head. "That's impossible. She's dead."

Beside her Kent jerked, his eyes wide. She half rose.

"I never believed it," Clay said. "Her body was never found so I kept looking. She's alive, Eden."

She studied his expression. He returned her stare. His face was full of conviction, and she felt a tiny flutter that might be hope begin to stir. "You're serious?"

"I know she's alive. I can't retrieve her alone. I need you to come with me."

"How do you know these things? I don't understand anything."

"I'll explain all of it. But come with me now."

She wanted to believe him, but it was impossible. Had his grief made him delusional? Clay was the most logical, practical man she'd ever met. But what he was saying couldn't be true.

"I need to talk to Kent first," she said.

"I'll wait outside your apartment."

"How do you know where I live?"

"I know everything about you. I always have." He strode away through a gauntlet of interested stares.

She tore her gaze from Clay's broad back and directed her attention to Kent. There would be no tender proposal now. She hated the hurt in his eyes, hated that she'd put it there.

When she reached across the table to him, at least he didn't flinch away. His fingers gripped hers in the same confident way that had first attracted her. "I'm so sorry, Kent."

"You want to tell me about it?"

She didn't want to but she had to. "Clay and I didn't really know one another very well when we married. We met in Hawaii. He was on leave from the air force. He's a photojournalist. Our . . . our fling on vacation resulted in an unexpected blessing."

His brows lifted. "You got pregnant?"

"Yes. Clay wanted to do the right thing. And I wanted to provide the best upbringing for Brianna. I was in love with my daughter the first moment I laid eyes on her." Her eyes misted at the memory. "She was beautiful."

"I'll bet she was," Kent said, his voice soft. "She died?"

Eden nodded. "A kidnapping attempt that went wrong." Oh, she didn't want to talk about it. It hurt too much. Pain radiated from her chest to her throat. She swallowed hard. "Our marriage was all about her, not us. I ran away, unable to deal with his pain and my own." She managed a smile. "But I ended up here in Wabash, where I found Christ. And you. At least something good came of it."

They'd met at New Life, and she knew Kent understood the way her life had changed. He'd become a Christian a few weeks before they met.

Kent's eyes were troubled. "But now he's saying Brianna is alive."

She furrowed her brow. "I can't believe that's true."

Kent's expression grew calm. "Don't you think you'd better find out? If there's even a chance, you have to go with him."

She studied his dear face. While theirs had been no grand passion, they had a special relationship based on mutual respect, faith, and fondness. She'd had every intention of accepting his proposal when it came. His stability attracted her at the deepest level.

She pushed back her chair on the plush carpet. "You're right. Pray for me?"

"You know I will." He stood and walked her to the door, where he paused. "And if you come back to Wabash, we'll see what God has for us then. I think we both want his will."

She lifted her face for him to brush his lips across her cheek. "You're a good man, Kent Huston."

A slight smile tugged his lips upward. "Let me know what happens, okay?"

"I will." She left him at the restaurant and walked across the hotel lobby to the front doors.

Her cell phone rang before she reached the exit. She glanced at the caller ID. Daniel, her foster brother. He'd been in a snit ever since she told him she intended to accept Kent's proposal, and he hadn't answered any of her phone calls since. Well, he could wait himself now. Clay's revelation was too important to interrupt.

Through the glass door she saw Clay standing outside under the old-fashioned streetlight. He was staring at the marquee above the old Eagles Theater.

A forgotten emotion tugged at her heart. Memories vied for

possession of her mind, but she pushed them away and stepped outside. Brianna couldn't be alive. Could she?

Clay stood outside the hotel on the brick sidewalk. Eden's apartment was just down the block, so he had time to admire this pretty town where she had ended up. Victorian-era buildings lined the downtown. Many had been renovated, even the old theater. The historic hotel that housed the restaurant also had a chocolate shop and other specialty stores. Too bad he wouldn't be here long enough to explore.

This was hardly Eden's type of place. He'd thought she would have fled to a big city where she could hide herself in the masses. She liked bright lights and nice clothes. At least she hadn't known he was a Larson when they first met. His family money had nothing to do with their instant attraction that day on the beach.

He reached into his pocket and his fingers touched smooth ceramic. He rolled the necklace around until his fingertips could trace the raised figure of a mother with a child. Clay had given the pendant to Eden when they married, and she had left it behind when she left him. An impulse had made him grab it today. Now that they knew Brianna was alive, maybe it wouldn't be as painful for her to wear again. She'd loved it once, a symbol of the family unit they wanted to build. Because the jewelry was from Colombia, it was a bridge between his two lives.

He heard a sound and turned to see Eden step through Charley Creek Inn's double glass doors. She wore a short skirt with heels and a rust-colored V-neck top that showed off her curves and made her auburn hair glimmer in the streetlight. The sleek glossy locks emphasized her high cheekbones and large turquoise eyes. She stared at him with a million questions in her expression.

"Ready?" he asked.

"I'm ready for some answers."

"Let's go to your place. You'll need to pack anyway." He fell into step beside her.

She stiffened but said nothing as they crossed with the light at Miami Street. He opened the double doors of her building and they entered a foyer dominated by a six-foot-wide staircase. Entering the place was like stepping back into the late eighteen hundreds.

"Nice," he said.

"I'm on the second floor." She led him to her apartment. The living room was spacious with gray-green walls and comfortable furniture. "I need coffee," she said.

He followed her into the kitchen and watched her measure water and coffee into her Cuisinart. When the aroma of coffee filled the kitchen, she leaned against the counter. "Tell me what you know about Brianna."

She seemed not to have considered that Clay might lie, which warmed him. He'd forgotten how beautiful she was, how she stirred his senses and made him forget everything but her.

Clay cleared his throat. "When her body was never found, I couldn't believe that she was dead. I hoped maybe someone had rescued her. I scoured orphanages, checked foster-care places in all the surrounding states, followed every lead. The trail went dead for over four years. Then I got this." He pulled the picture from his pocket and held it out to her.

Eden took it and held it under the wash of light. "Five little girls."

He'd studied it over and over. A row of little girls, all about five.

In the background was a ranch, and a sign beside them read Bluebird Ranch, Bluebird Crossing, Texas. "Look at the back."

She flipped it over. Her eyes widened as she read it aloud. "'Your daughter misses you. You'd better hurry if you want to see her.'" The color drained from her face, and she continued to study the picture. "What is this place?" she whispered.

"It's for kids in the foster-care system. They seem to do a good job with helping children."

Her eyes were pained. "She's been in foster care?"

"At least she's alive, Angel."

"I'm no angel, b-but maybe God has sent an angel to look over our daughter?" Her voice was breathless, just beginning to hold a tinge of hope.

He'd called her Angel the first time he met her in Hawaii. She'd thought it funny at the time. He'd been utterly serious. Her love had seemed so pure, so uplifting. Surely she was an ambassador of God to him. "I believe God has done just that."

She stared at him. "You're a believer now too?"

She'd become a Christian since he'd seen her last. That had been a constant worry for him. He nodded.

She stared at him. "Is it possible?" Her voice trembled and her gaze wandered back to the photo. "Where did you get this picture? How do you know it's not someone playing a nasty trick?"

He'd hoped she wouldn't ask. "I don't. Not for sure. It came in the mail, postmarked from El Paso. I took it to the police and they dismissed it as a joke. They never even discovered the name of the kidnapper, so I didn't expect them to have any leads. But look at the girls, Eden." He watched her study the picture again. "Something in my gut says she's there. Can we afford to ignore the possibility?"

"Who would send this?"

"I always thought the kidnapper who drowned had an accomplice. Maybe the partner sent it."

"Why? To taunt us? And why now?"

There was too much he didn't know. He couldn't let her see any weakness in him though, or she might not come. And he needed her. "I don't know the answer to those questions. Maybe it's a trap. It could be dangerous." He shrugged. "Maybe he wants his money after all. But can we afford to ignore even a slim chance of finding her?"

Eden's head snapped toward him. "I can't quite take it all in," she said.

Her eyes held a yearning that clutched at his throat. He'd felt the same way. "I don't understand what is happening either. Or why he's waited this long to get in touch again. But I have to go, and I need you to help me."

She stared back down at the picture. "Which one is she?"

Eden's beautiful face had haunted his dreams. He realized she was still waiting for an answer. "I don't know. Did her hair turn your shade or mine? We don't have any idea what color her eyes became. They were still blue when she was taken."

He knew the photograph by heart. There was a cute little blonde with blue eyes. Beside her sat a somber brunette with hazel eyes. The laughing one had auburn curls, a dimple, and green eyes. That was the one he was betting money on. A giggling girl with dark skin and large black eyes was next. The last one in the row of girls was a towhead with brown eyes. He'd been a towhead once, so she was a possibility too.

"I need to get a DNA sample from all the girls," he added. "We have Brianna's DNA on record."

"It will take ages to get the tests back," Eden said. She stared at the picture again. "I want to know now." She pushed the photograph back at him. "I'm happy here. Content. I don't know that I believe it, Clay. It might be the kidnapper's partner just trying to hurt us."

He had to make her see the truth. "You trusted me once, Eden. Can you put aside your doubts for a while and go with me on this?"

She glanced at her hands. "My peace has been hard won. I'm afraid."

Her admission made his chest squeeze. All he'd wanted was to protect her and build a home with her. But they'd barely started getting to know each other when their daughter was taken.

"I'm afraid too. But I know she's there. Still, let's say you're right—that someone's playing with us. This is the only shot we've got at finding out the truth. How can we ignore it?"

Eden's lips flattened. She took the picture again. "Where is this place?" She tapped a finger on the Bluebird sign.

"The ranch is near Big Bend National Park."

"I've never heard of it."

"It's in West Texas." He shrugged.

She turned back to pour cream into their coffee. "Why do you need me?"

"The ranch is looking for a married couple to serve as counselors. We'd be working directly with these girls."

She whirled back around to face him. "We'd be spending all our time with them?"

He nodded. "You'll come? I can't do it without you. They want a married couple."

He read the indecision in her eyes. Conflicting emotions of hope and fear flashed through them. "Eden?"

"All right. I'll come."

He closed his hand over her elbow and turned her toward the bedroom. "You need to pack. We'll be gone for several weeks at least. Maybe all summer."

She stopped and tugged her arm from his grasp. "What about my job?"

"Quit. Or take a leave of absence." If he had his way, she'd never come back here again.

She chewed on her lip. "I'll have to quit. They won't be able to get along without me for the summer. Do you have the job description?"

He nodded and dug the ad for the position out of his pocket, then handed it to her. "It's our perfect opportunity to slip in and find out the truth."

"Why can't we just go talk to these people—tell them what is going on?"

"If we waltz in there as strangers, the people who run the camp aren't going to give us the time of day. Their main goal is to protect the children. For all they know, we could be some nutso couple looking to make off with a child or two."

She read the ad, then handed it back. "But what about the police? Won't they help us find the truth?"

"They believe she's dead. The fellow in charge of the case blew me off when I showed him the picture. Once we get down there and assess the law enforcement, we can see if the sheriff is likely to listen."

"I still have a million questions," she said.

He took her arm and propelled her toward her bedroom to pack. "Ask me on the way."

2

CLAY'S "COWBOY CADILLAC" ATE UP THE MILES BETWEEN WABASH, INDIANA, AND BLUEBIRD Crossing, Texas. The last time Eden had been in a truck was the day she left Clay. The odors of horse, grease, and man took her back five years to a place and time she'd worked hard to forget.

She shifted as the memories tried to surface, staring out the window at the orange rocks and shimmering desert that went on for miles. They'd been on Interstate 10 for hours and had seen only one other vehicle. Sage and creosote bushes grew as far as the eye could see. "How far to Bluebird Crossing?"

"Almost there." Clay's voice was gravelly.

He hadn't slept in nearly twenty-four hours. Eden had offered to drive several times, but he'd kept his size-12 boot to the accelerator, stopping only for gas, grabbing food and bathroom breaks when they did. She'd hoped to find out more about his search for Brianna, but his first explanation had been the most complete.

"Why would the kidnapper's partner—if that's who's really behind this—contact you after all these years?" she asked. "I wish we knew that part."

"If we knew that, we might know who they were. And why they'd done it. The police always believed they were illegal immigrants."

"None of it makes any sense."

"No," he said, turning the wheel into a wide curve. "I always thought her kidnappers wanted revenge for that mission I'd been involved in down in Colombia. The money they demanded was the same amount that they claimed was stolen by the officers we got out of the compound."

As a photojournalist in the military, Clay sometimes got involved in dangerous things. During her pregnancy, after they'd been married only two weeks, he was sucked into the rescue operation of two Americans held captive by drug lords. Eden suspected his part was much more intensive than he'd ever told her.

"You've always said that, but the police found no evidence of it. And why would drug lords care about only ten grand?"

"They found no evidence of much of anything," he pointed out. "And I think wanting the money back was an honor thing. At least that's my theory. Besides, the money vanished from our SUV. Someone must have stolen it."

"There were kids hanging around watching."

He shrugged. "I still think an accessory took the money while we were occupied. And now I don't even believe Brianna was in that car that went under the water."

Without warning, images of the day they'd lost Brianna came flooding back. She'd been in her SUV that day, not Clay's truck.

THE SUV SURGED FORWARD WHEN SHE PRESSED HARD ON THE ACCELERATOR. SHE STRAINED to see through the rain sluicing down the windshield. Where was the river? Moisture gathered in her eyes and she blinked it away. Tears would solve nothing.

"Not so fast!" Clay leaned forward in the passenger seat, peering through the downpour. "I think the road turns any second. The pull-off by the riverbank is on the left."

Eden eased up on the pedal. "Do you really think they'll be here with Brianna?" Just saying her baby's name made her throat close and her breasts ache. Twenty-four terrible hours had passed since she last held her six-week-old daughter. Her empty arms twitched with the need to cuddle Brianna, who had given up her first smile the day before she was taken.

"They'd better be there." Her husband's voice was grim. His gun, a big, scary black one, was on his lap as well as the briefcase holding the ransom money. He pointed. "There's the turnoff."

She steered the vehicle onto the gravel path that led to the river. Her vision wavered again. Dratted rain. Opening her mouth to tell Clay she saw the rushing water, she shut it when she saw the other vehicle ahead. Her foot tromped the accelerator to catch the speeding car before she realized she was doing it. The tires spun on the gravel, then caught purchase and propelled the big vehicle toward the Taurus.

"Look out!" Clay yelled.

Too late she realized she was going to ram the Taurus. Her SUV slammed into the car's bumper, and it spun around as it slid down the embankment to the water. The sound of screeching metal filled her ears. The man behind the steering wheel had his mouth open in a scream she couldn't hear as her vehicle shoved the car into the swollen river. The Taurus hit the churning brown water and listed onto its side.

Shoving open her door, she staggered to the edge of the river. "Brianna!" she shrieked into the wind.

The driver pounded on the glass, his panicked face barely visible behind the window. His boot hit the pane and shattered it, and the man clambered through the opening. His head disappeared in the dirty foam. Eden started toward the water, but Clay dragged her back, then dived into the muddy river. She could barely see through the rain. Wading into the water, she tried to paddle after him, but she wasn't a strong swimmer, and the filthy water filled her throat and mouth. Her knees scraped gravel, and she came up gagging. She flung her wet hair out of her eyes. Where was Clay?

She caught a glimpse of his dark head. He'd reached the car, but the current had it as well, and the door handle rolled away from him. He kicked after it, and her heart rose as she saw him wrench open the back door. Water gushed in. He disappeared inside, and she watched with her heart pounding until he exited the rolling car.

He was empty-handed.

SOMETHING TOUCHED HER AND SHE JERKED BACK TO THE PRESENT. STUPIDLY, SHE STARED at Clay's big hand covering hers. The scar on his wrist was another stark reminder. He'd gotten it in the rescue attempt. She became aware that tears coursed down her cheeks, and she swiped her palm across her wet face.

The truck was stopped in a dirt drive. His steady gaze held hers.

"She didn't die in that water, Eden. Don't go there." He leaned over and thumbed away a tear.

She told herself not to react to the warmth of his hand or the gentleness of his touch. How did he know that's what she was thinking about? She could have been crying about anything. "It was my fault," she said.

"It was an accident. It wasn't your fault. It could have happened even if I'd been driving. But I wanted to be ready to play hero."

Her eyes burned and her vision blurred. The next thing she knew, she was sobbing against his chest, her tears dampening his shirt. His arms held her close, and he pressed a kiss against the top of her head. She'd forgotten how safe he always made her feel.

She drew away. Her shiver had nothing to do with his touch. The air conditioner was just too cold, she told herself, until a long-forgotten passion swelled in her. She pressed against him, and his embrace tightened. Would losing her pain in his arms be so terrible? His blue eyes darkened when she lifted her face toward him.

He lowered his head, and she realized what was happening. She couldn't go there again, where passion instead of careful thought ruled. Shoving against his chest with both hands, she tore herself from his embrace.

"I'm sorry," she said in a choked voice. "I'm all right. It's all a little overwhelming."

He gulped in a breath, then nodded and put the truck in drive. A few moments later he said, "We're here."

She leaned forward and drank in the two-story ranch house flanked by a big white barn. It had a hipped roof, and white paddocks stretched as far as she could see. She was surprised to notice a hangar that held a small plane.

A stucco bunkhouse was behind the main building and a newer similar building beside it. She smiled as a child shrieked with laughter, and children were playing jump rope in the grass. Her heart rebounded against her ribs.

Brianna was one of them. But which one?

His gaze on the children, Clay slammed the truck door and stretched out his muscles. He checked his impulse to go directly to the kids.

Eden came around the other side of the truck. She chewed on her bottom lip as she watched the children. She looked out of place in her high heels and short skirt. But very cute. He tore his gaze from her shapely legs.

Eden started toward them, and he caught her arm. "Not yet," he warned. "We're just here about the job, remember? Smile, be professional. We have to get hired first."

"I wish we could just tell them about the situation."

"There's no way they'd let us have access to the girls. Not without a court order. And the police aren't cooperating."

He turned her toward the wide porch attached to the front of the storybook farmhouse. The white stone gleamed in the sunshine. The red door stood partly open past the screen. He could hear a woman's voice on the other side but couldn't make out what she was saying. He put on a smile and rapped on the door.

A pretty brunette came to the door with a welcoming tilt to her lips. "Good afternoon! You must be the Larsons. I'm Allie Bailey." She opened the screen. "Come on in and don't mind the mess. We're still unpacking stuff. A group of older kids arrived this morning."

She led them down the hall, past suitcases disgorging their contents of brightly colored shorts and T-shirts onto the gleaming wood floor. In the living room, a small boy of about three sat in the middle of the chaos, and a girl of about nine with dark curls handed him a cookie.

"These are my two. Betsy and Matthew." Allie lifted the little boy from the middle of the clothes. "Sit here if you're eating a cookie," she said, placing him at the coffee table. She smiled at Clay and Eden. "Have a seat."

Clay glanced around the space and found a chair by the window. The wind blew the scent of hay and manure through the screen. He wiped his brow. "Please excuse our appearance. We drove all night to get here."

Allie's eyes widened. "You came straight from Indiana?"

"We didn't want to miss this opportunity. This is my wife, Eden." He saw Eden stiffen, but she said nothing. "We love kids, and this position is right up our alley."

Allie gestured to the other chair, and Eden settled on it. "Your résumés were pretty persuasive. I've seen some of your photos, Clay, and you can parachute, hang glide, dive, and find your way in any terrain." She laughed. "My husband, Rick, is eager to meet you. He used to be in the military himself and likes to talk about that kind of thing. Plus, we'd love to see you take the kids on some nature outings and teach them photography."

"Sounds great. Is Rick here?" Clay asked.

She shook her head. "He'll be back shortly. He had to run into Bluebird Crossing for supplies. You realize these are small children, though? The hiking trails you will be taking them on are pretty tame compared to what you're used to."

He grinned, already liking the petite brunette. "I'm ready for some tame."

She glanced at Eden. "You're a nurse?"

Eden nodded. "And I'm very organized. I look forward to the challenge and have a special place in my heart for foster kids. I was one myself."

Allie's blue eyes lightened in approval. "Some of these kids really need a woman with your compassion and experience. They've been in rough situations."

He exchanged a glance with Eden. Had their child been one in a tough situation? The thought shook him.

Eden's frozen face cracked into a commiserating smile. Finally. Clay was beginning to think she'd turned to stone where she sat in the chair. And he couldn't blame her. He'd thrown a lot at her in the last day.

"Tell me more about your program," Eden said, her voice surprisingly steady.

Allie nodded. "We get a variety of ages. You would have the five- and six-year-olds. Della and Zeke Rodriguez have the seven- and eight-year-olds that just came in this morning. These kids will be here a month. The group we have coming in after that is older. Teens."

Eden leaned forward. "Your ranch is pretty amazing. How does working with horses help disadvantaged children?"

Allie's smile held a shadow. "Most of the animals here are rescue animals. Some have been neglected and some actually abused. The kids look into the eyes of the horses and find the same misery they are experiencing. It creates a bond that helps them both."

"Amazing," Clay said. He didn't want to think about any child having misery. Especially his own. This was going to be a tough few weeks.

"The kids learn about responsibility and caring for another creature. They discover what giving of themselves is all about." Allie studied Clay's face, then switched her attention to Eden. "Your references had only glowing things to say about both of you. And our mutual friend Michael Wayne sang your praises to the heavens."

He leaned forward. "We really want this job. We brought our belongings with us and can start right away."

Allie blinked, as though taken aback by his forthrightness. "Rick usually makes the final decision, but he already liked what he saw from your résumé. You're hired!" She rose. "Let me show you where to put your things. I'll escort you around the ranch on the way."

Out in the yard, Clay's gaze went straight to the little girls. The redhead caught his eye at once. The color of her hair was like Eden's, gleaming like new copper. The child chased a ball that stopped by his feet.

She stopped and glanced up at him hesitantly. He stooped and picked up the ball, then offered it to her. "What's your name, honey?"

"Katie." She took the ball and stared at him.

"This is Mr. Clay and Miss Eden, Katie," Allie said. "They'll be sleeping in the bunkhouse with you. They're here to help you."

A lump formed in his throat, and he saw Eden take a step toward the girl. He grabbed his wife's forearm. "We'd better go. We'll be seeing you around, Katie."

The child's head dipped, and her gaze went back to the other children.

"Run along," Eden said, her tone brisk. "We'll get to know you all better tonight."

Clay clasped her hand and didn't let go when she tried to tug away. "We're eager to get started."

3

EDEN'S HEELS SANK INTO THE SANDY SOIL AS SHE FOLLOWED ALLIE ACROSS THE SCRUBBY yard. She should have worn flats with her skirt, but when she'd chosen the outfit back in Indiana, she'd needed the extra inches for courage when facing Clay. A pungent odor hung in the air. Mesquite? Sage?

She sneezed and nearly stumbled, but Clay caught her hand and she righted herself. He tried to clutch her fingers but she pulled them free. His touch still ignited something inside her. The sensation was nothing she was prepared to examine. Not now, not ever.

Allie pointed to the newer building. "The other bunkhouse was just finished. Della and Zeke are housed there with the older girls." She pushed open the wooden screen door. "Here we are. It's not a Hyatt, but it's clean and functional."

She led them into a rectangular room that ran the width of the building. Easily forty feet long and fifteen feet wide, the space contained a kitchen and table with benches on one end and a living area on the other. The sofa and chairs had seen their fair share of bubble gum, Little Debbie cakes, and popcorn. An old-style projection TV took up one corner. But everything was spotless, even the plate-glass window that let sunlight stream onto the battered pine floors. The place smelled of lemon wax and an apple-scented candle.

Eden stepped onto the blue-and-white rag rug. "It's very homey."

"We do what we can to make the kids feel loved and wanted here. Let me show you the bedrooms." Allie pointed out the dorm on one side of the hall. Five bunk beds flanked by utilitarian dressers were scattered through the room. There was one queen bed back against the far wall. "We have only one gender here at time."

Eden glanced around and spotted hair ribbons and pink bows. A lump formed in her throat. She wanted to wander the room alone and examine all the little-girl items. Which bed belonged to Brianna? There was a stuffed bear on the closest bed. Its button nose was missing, and the little vest was ragged from the loving touch of small fingers.

She picked it up. "Whose is this?"

"That's Katie's."

The little redhead. The child she'd felt an immediate attraction to. Eden hugged the bear to her chest, then reluctantly placed it back on the corduroy coverlet.

Allie stepped to the door. "Your room is across the hall. There's a monitor so you can hear what's going on in here."

Room. As in one. Eden hadn't thought far enough ahead to consider sleeping arrangements. She stopped in the hall when she saw the king-size bed that dominated the room. Clay nearly ran into her, and his big hands came down on her shoulders to steady them both. She heard him inhale harshly at the same time she did.

She managed a smile at Allie, who had a raised brow. “Nice big room,” she said awkwardly.

Their employer smiled. “There’s a stereo and computer for your use. We’ve got satellite Internet too. Not the fastest high-speed, but better than dial-up. Oh, and cell phone coverage is terrible here. There are only a few hot spots in the county.”

Eden walked the perimeter of the room, peeked into the massive closet, and nodded approval at the two big dressers. “We’ll be fine here.”

“I’ll leave you to unpack, then,” Allie said as a cowboy lugged their suitcases into the room. “This is Buzz. If you need anything, just ask.” She gave a wave, then her sandals slapped against the floors as she exited.

The man’s weathered face cracked into a smile. “Got iced tea in the fridge. Cheese and venison sausage there too if you’re hungry.”

“We’re fine for now,” Eden lied, eyeing the bed.

Buzz backed out of the room. “Just holler if you need anything.” He shut the door behind him.

Eden exhaled. “Well, this is a nice mess you’ve gotten us into.”

He lifted a brow and grinned. “What? It’s a big bed. You stay on your side, and I’ll stay on mine.”

Her glare was lost on him because he turned away, grabbed the biggest suitcase, and heaved it onto the plaid bedspread. He lifted the lid and began to haul her belongings out.

“I’ll do that myself.” She elbowed him out of the way. That spicy cologne was the same one he’d always worn, and the familiarity made her want to lean against him for a moment. But she collected herself. She wouldn't be weak. She had to focus on her daughter.

She kicked off her heels and began to lift her things out. The braided rug was rough on her feet. "Okay with you if I take this dresser?" She pointed to the one on the left side of the bed.

He didn't look at her. "Whatever you want."

Fine. He could give her the cold shoulder if he wanted. She jammed her underwear into the top drawer, then began to hang up her slacks and tops. She glanced at Clay out of the corner of her eye. It would take all her strength to ignore the chemistry between them. And that's all it had ever been.

He turned and caught her staring, but he frowned when he saw her side of the closet. "Is that all you brought? No jeans?"

She wrinkled her nose. "Jeans?"

"I thought by now you would have unbent a little. Everyone wears jeans. It's not a sign of poverty."

What did he know of poverty? He'd never gone to school in jeans that were three inches shy of her ankles and riddled with holes. Not the stylish tears either, but gaping holes that made other girls giggle. When she had finally gotten a decent pair of slacks, she'd sworn never to wear jeans again. And she wasn't about to start now.

An hour later Eden coughed as a cloud of dust kicked up by the horses' hooves enveloped her. The thick red dirt already coated her slacks, and she was sure it was in her hair as well. She sat on the top rail of the corral fence and watched Buzz lead the last horse into the barn. When were they bringing the girls out to meet them? Her insides felt as jittery as the grasshoppers she saw fleeing the cowboy's boots.

Clay touched her arm. "Here they come."

She turned and saw Allie leading the girls from the house toward the corral. The little redhead was first in the line. Clay put his big hands on Eden's waist and lifted her from the fence. She stepped away from him as soon as her flats hit the dirt.

The children reached the scrubby grass beside the corral, and Allie instructed them to sit in a circle. "This is Mr. Clay and Miss Eden, girls. They will be living with you in the bunkhouse. Can you tell them your names?"

The honey-skinned child with cornrows ducked her head. "I'm India," she said, twisting a braided lock around her finger. "I just turned six."

The redhead, Katie, stared directly at them with a curious expression in her green eyes. "I can do a somersault. Want to see?"

"In a little while," Eden said, taken by the child's spirit.

"Can I ride the horse?"

"Tell them your name," Allie said. "Then we'll see about the ride."

"I already did when they got here. I'm Katie," the child said. "I'm India's sister."

Allie smiled. "They've been inseparable since they arrived." She urged a brown-haired little girl forward. "And this is Lacie. She doesn't talk much, but all her shirts are red. Is that your favorite color, Lacie?"

Lacie nodded and puffed out her chest to show her Minnie Mouse shirt.

A blonde with huge brown eyes clung to Allie's leg. "Do you have a dog?" she asked. "My foster mom said I could have a puppy here."

"We have some puppies in the barn you can play with," Allie said. "And Jem is around here somewhere. He's a very nice dog. Can you tell your counselors your name?"

"Madeline," the little girl said. "I'm going to name my puppy Oscar."

Eden smiled at the last little girl. Smaller than the other children, she had her head down. Her mousy brown hair nearly hid her face. "What's your name, sweetheart?"

The child buried her head against Allie's leg. "Paige. I don't want to ride the horses. I'm 'lergic to them."

Allie smiled. "You're not allergic to them, honey. You're just scared. Give it a day or two and you'll find one you love."

"I want to see the puppies now," Madeline demanded. "Miss Casey told us they would be old enough today, and I still haven't seen them."

Allie grinned. "Casey was the previous counselor. She had to leave because her brother was in an accident. The kids are all yours." She pointed to the side barn door. "The puppies are right through there if you want to take the children to see them first. They just got their eyes open. Then you can do whatever activities with them you like. There's a jungle gym set up behind the barn as well as a swing in the hayloft."

Which one of these girls was Brianna? Eden studied each one in turn as they headed to see the pups. She jumped when Clay put his hand on her elbow and leaned toward her to whisper in her ear.

His breath stirred her hair. "Katie looks like you."

"She has red hair. That's all," she said. "Lacie and Paige both have brown hair like yours. Four of them could be Brianna." She'd so hoped one glimpse of the girls would tell her which one was their daughter, but it wasn't going to be that easy.

His hand dropped away and he yanked open the door to the barn. A border collie darted past him and raced toward the house. Eden peered past Clay to the dim interior of the barn. She sneezed at the scent of hay. Dust motes danced in a shaft of sunlight. Was that smell manure? The nauseating scent made her stop dead in the doorway.

Clay glanced at her feet. "I think we'd better get you some boots."

It *was* manure. A patty of brown lay between her and the closest stall. "Boots? I'm a city girl, not a cowboy."

"Alrighty then, city girl. Be careful of the rattlers and tarantulas."

She recoiled when he named the creatures. "You're kidding, right?"

"Dead serious." He pointed to something on the wall.

Peering closer, she realized it was the tail of a snake. The rattling part, she assumed. She shuddered.

"Puppies!" Madeline darted past them to where a border collie lay on a bed of hay. Six round-bellied puppies crawled around her.

"Ooh, too cute!" Eden squatted and scooped up an adorable black-and-white one that had one eye circled in black fur.

"Looks like they're about two weeks old," Clay said.

But he was watching her, not the puppy. Her face heated and she handed the puppy to Madeline. The little girl's wispy hair was so blond it was nearly as white as the little collie's pale fur. Eden resisted the urge to run her fingers through that fine fluff. She'd seen pictures of Clay, and he'd been a towhead as a child.

"This one is mine," Madeline said, cuddling the puppy close. "His name is Spot."

"What happened to naming him Oscar?" Clay asked.

The little girl stared at the puppy. "No, he's a Spot. Oscar is green."

Eden noticed Paige hanging back. "Want to hold a puppy?" she asked.

Paige backed away. "I can't have a dog. I'm 'lergic."

"Well, you can stay here with me, then. Maybe we can get you a fish or something." Eden smiled when the child leaned against her leg. Being around children again was awakening long-dormant feelings of warmth. She watched the other girls romp with the puppies. "Spot can be our group puppy. We'll come and see him often, okay? Because puppies need their mommies to grow up strong and healthy."

Her voice trailed off when the girls looked at her. None of them had mommies, poor kids.

4

EDEN WAS IN THE BATHROOM HELPING THE GIRLS WITH THEIR BATHS. CLAY SAT WITH HIS boots on the scarred coffee table in the TV room. Their first day was under their belt, but it had been too hectic to even think about getting DNA samples. They'd do that tomorrow for sure. He had brought a top-notch kit from a respected lab that law enforcement officers used.

A fist thumped the screen door, and he looked up to see a man in a cowboy hat on the stoop. "Come on in," Clay called.

The man pushed his hat to the back of his head and stepped through the doorway. "You two did a fine job today, Allie said." He held out his hand. "Rick Bailey."

Clay put his feet on the floor and stood, then gripped Rick's outstretched hand. "I've heard a lot about you from Michael Wayne.

And from Brendan Waddell. Michael is looking forward to seeing you again. I'm sure he'll be calling so you can meet Gracie and he can meet Eden."

"I'll track him down if he doesn't."

Rick dropped onto the sofa. "They both gave you a glowing recommendation." The man studied Clay. "Brendan says you helped him out in Colombia."

The awareness in the man's face was caused by more than information about Clay's past career. "Sounds like he's given you more than just my work stats."

Rick's eyes were kind. "He told me about your daughter. I'm sorry."

Clay couldn't hold the man's compassionate gaze. He sighed and glanced out the window. "Thanks." It was a relief to have that bit out in the open.

"Did you ever find out who was responsible?"

Clay shrugged. "Not really." He didn't know the man well enough to confide in him. He picked up the file on the table. "I've been reading about the girls in our bunkhouse. Rough stuff."

Rick nodded, his expression sober. "The things we see could break your heart. This batch of kids is sweet as all get-out, though."

Clay opened the folder. "Looks like Lacie was left outside a Catholic church when she was six months old. In February."

"A puzzle, that one. She'd been well taken care of. Had on a sleeper that came from Nordstrom's. That seemed odd. Her parents were well enough off to buy things at a fine department store but then abandoned her? Something weird about that."

"This was in Dallas?"

"Yep." Rick reached over to pull out a picture of a baby held by a nun. "This is Sister Marjo. She visits Lacie every month, so I hear. She's the woman who found Lacie."

Clay studied the woman's smiling face. "Does Lacie mention her?"

"All the time. The sister is coming here in two weeks while on vacation."

"That's dedication. Getting to this neck of West Texas is like visiting the moon." He flipped to the next child. "Madeline was taken from her mother when the mom was put in a mental hospital. Where is the mother now?"

"Evidently she was released two months ago. She's begun proceedings to regain custody."

Clay winced. "How well is she?"

"Probably not that great," Rick said. "Schizophrenia isn't easily cured. I'm doubtful she can get custody."

"We're quite taken with Katie," Clay said, picking up the picture of the smiling redhead.

"We all are. She lights up a room when she comes in. Her father was shot in a burglary. There were no other family members around to take her, so she ended up in foster care at age three."

"Was she home during the shooting?"

Rick nodded. "She has nightmares about it, though she says she doesn't remember. Several psychologists have tried to get details out of her. The murderer was never apprehended."

"Where's her mom?"

Rick shrugged. "Took off sometime before that and hasn't been in contact."

Clay picked up another paper. "From what I read, India's entire family was killed in a house fire?"

Rick winced. "Horrible situation. She was four. A meth lab explosion."

Clay's own plight began to feel less horrible, somehow, knowing the pain that innocent children endured every day. "Lot of heartache in these kids' lives."

"Too much." Rick leaned over and picked up a picture of Paige.

Clay's heart clenched at the somber expression on her face. Her mousy hair hadn't been washed. Too much misery stared out of those brown eyes. "What's her story?"

"No one really knows. She was a year old and found in a Walmart. There was a video that showed two men leaving her in the toy department."

"Was she—abused?" It was all he could do to force out the question. He wasn't sure he wanted to hear the answer.

Rick shook his head. "No. That was the first worry, but other than being dirty and uncared for, she was healthy."

"How did you know her name?"

"The foster home named her. She's been with the same couple for four years. In fact, they've started adoption procedures. Good family."

Which one was Brianna? Clay had no clue. He was drawn to Katie, but how much of that was simple charisma and personality? And the red hair, of course. His daughter could be any one of the girls except for India. He flipped back through the pictures. Why had he thought this would be so easy?

"Want to meet the other counselors?" Rick asked.

"Sure."

"They're coming here for devotions. We try to do that with all the kids together. I wanted to make sure you were up to it on your first night."

"I can use some of God's Word myself right about now. It's been a wild day. But fun."

Clay watched Rick step to the door and call across the yard. A few minutes later a couple trooped inside with eight girls. The kids were a little bigger than Clay and Eden's charges, calmer somehow, and a little warier.

The couple was in their late thirties. The man looked like a young James Earl Jones, burly and with an expressive face as he smiled and shook hands with Clay. "Glad to have some help here," the man said. "I'm Zeke, and this is my wife, Della."

His wife was beautiful with black hair and dark eyes that held love as she touched the head of a little girl near her. "I caught a glimpse of your pretty wife, Clay. Where is she?"

"She's getting the girls ready for bed." He heard them trooping down the hall. "Here they come." He drank in the sight of the freshly bathed girls. He was already beginning to think of them as his girls.

Eden paused in the doorway and smiled. "Hi. You must be the Rodriguez family."

"We're about to have devotions together," Clay put in.

The day she left him, she shouted that she wanted nothing to do with a God who would take her baby from her. She said she was a Christian now.

When her eager smile came, he wanted to know what had happened in the five years they'd spent apart that had brought her to Christ.

In the shaft of light through the open door, the children were clearly visible. Eden stared at each girl. They slept peacefully, curled together like puppies in the big bed. They'd begged to sleep together, but she doubted they'd stay like that all night. She pulled the door closed, squared her shoulders, and went to find her husband.

She stopped in the hall and gulped. Clay was still her husband. She hadn't allowed her thoughts to wander there much since this race to find their daughter had begun. Was it only yesterday at seven that he'd shown up in her life again? A few hours ago she'd been planning to accept Kent's proposal.

Forcing herself forward, she went down the hall and stood in the doorway to the gathering spaces. An old western starring John Wayne played on the television. The scent of popcorn teased her nose, and she saw Clay in the recliner with his boots off. A bowl was in his lap and a big glass of iced tea was on the table beside him. She knew without sipping it that there would be enough sugar in it to eat the spoon away.

He must have sensed her gaze on him because he jerked his head toward where she stood. Kernels bounced from his lap as he sprang to his feet. "Hey."

"The girls are asleep."

He held up the bowl. "Want some popcorn?"

The smell tantalized her, but the thought of cozying up to him on the couch to share the treat made her shake her head. She chose the chair the farthest away from him.

"Tea?" A grin tugged his lips as he held up his glass.

"I still have a gag reflex."

He took a gulp. "You'll be happy to know I've cut down on the amount of sugar."

"To what? Half a cup?"

His grin widened. "It's what keeps me so sweet-natured."

She squelched the desire to smile. During their very short and tempestuous marriage, he'd always had a way of coaxing her out of a bad mood. Picking up the remote, she shut off the TV. "We need to talk."

"I'm all ears."

"There's no way of knowing which of those girls is Brianna. We need that DNA test as soon as possible."

"I know." He picked up a manila file folder beside him. "I've poured through their histories and even talked to Rick. Any one of them could be our daughter, except India."

She reached for the folder and flipped it open. Katie's smiling face greeted her, and her gut clenched. "I think Katie is Brianna."

His gaze gentled. "She's a little cutie. But don't get your heart set on her. I'm betting Paige is our daughter." He moved out of the recliner and knelt beside her chair. Flipping through the pages, he pointed out Paige's stats. "Look here. She was left at Walmart by two men. Sounds like kidnappers to me."

The infant's photo tugged at Eden's heart. The baby's somber gaze held a light. "No one knows her real name?"

"Nope. But read the rest before you make a snap judgment."

She riffled through the other biographies, then finally closed the file. "You're right. Brianna could be any one of the four. So we really are going to have to wait for the DNA. How long will it take?"

His lips flattened. "Too long. Weeks after these kids leave here."

She desperately wanted to know which of these girls was their daughter. It had been all she could do while bathing them not to press her lips to their damp foreheads. She hadn't wanted to frighten them, though, so she'd been warm but kept an appropriate distance.

"I'll get hair samples from them over the next couple of days," she said. "Can you get them into a priority lab?"

"I can try."

And she knew he would. He had connections. She mentally prepared for what she had to say next. How did she even broach the subject of sleeping arrangements?

"Spill it, Eden," he said.

He grinned, and even though she wanted to glare at him, her lips twitched. She glanced away.

"I already know what's eating you, you know," he said. "But that bed is a king. We'll stuff pillows between us. I promise to stay on my side."

She let out a sigh. "I don't like it, Clay. Our marriage was over a long time ago. It feels—weird." Forcing her gaze up, she stared into his face. "It took me a long time to get over you."

"I never got over you," he said, his voice soft.

Heat flared in her cheeks. "See what I mean? This will never work if you remind me at every opportunity that we were once married."

His eyes narrowed. "We're *still* married."

"So it appears." She still couldn't believe her attorney hadn't made sure everything was final. She struggled to remember how things had happened five years ago. She'd rushed away when Brianna died, and her lawyer had said he'd take care of the details. Something had obviously fallen through the cracks.

But not for long.

"Why did you leave?" he asked. He looked down at his popcorn bowl. "You took off without a word."

She went cold. Admitting she left because his reason for marrying her was gone would only serve to show the chasm between them. But honesty was all that would do now. They had too much at stake to play games.

She held her head high. "Clay, you know perfectly well you only married me because I was pregnant. We barely knew each other. You were gone more than you were home. Once Brianna was gone, there was nothing to hold us together. I needed a clean break."

And she'd barely cauterized the wound. Or was it still oozing blood?

5

SHE COULDN'T STAY IN THE BATHROOM FOREVER. EDEN EYED THE PEACH-COLORED TEDDY SHE wore and shuddered. Why hadn't she checked her suitcase before rushing off on this search? What seemed fine in the privacy of her apartment was indecent here.

She let out a groan and leaned onto the sink. Surely there had to be another way to get to the truth. Why not just tell the Baileys that they thought Brianna was here? They had children. Any parent would be sympathetic to their cause.

But not if it impacted their business. Their mission.

How could she ask them to get involved? The Baileys had been entrusted with the children's welfare. Rick and Allie didn't know her and Clay. The Baileys might toss them out for fear they might kidnap one of the girls. She lifted her head and stared into her own frightened eyes.

She had to open that door and go into the bedroom. This wasn't some stranger she was sharing a room with. This was Clay. He wouldn't hurt her. The problem was, she didn't know how she felt about him. While he'd been absent, she could almost forget their marriage had ever happened. She could push aside the memories of a tiny body cuddled to her breast and the scent of her newborn baby.

The muscles in her throat worked at the memories that surged. Her eyes burned. She would not think about that day. Could not. Straightening, she twisted the doorknob and stepped into the hall and to the bedroom door.

The covers were turned back on the big bed. She focused on the picture above the bed of a tranquil mountain stream. Anything to calm the way her pulse jumped when Clay turned to look at her. His chest was bare and he wore blue pajama bottoms, a concession to her she was sure. In the old days he didn't wear—She cut off the mental image before it could form.

He let out a low whistle. "I assume Kent was to be the recipient of that getup."

She dived for the bed and covered herself with the sheet. "Our relationship was pure, and I'm in no mood for your tone."

He grinned and climbed into the bed beside her. "Want pillows between us?"

"If you promise to keep your distance, you can have the space."

He shrugged. "All I want is to find our daughter."

His words stung more than she'd expected. Not that she wanted him to be making a pass at her. "Why didn't you call?" she asked abruptly. "Rather than just show up. And how did you find me anyway?"

He put his hands behind his head and leaned back on the pillow. "I knew you'd never believe me without seeing the photograph. I've always known where you were. It's not hard to track someone."

He grinned and shrugged. "I tried to get up the nerve to call you when I got the divorce papers, but you'd made your wishes pretty clear."

"Why did you want to reach me then?"

"I wanted to talk you out of it."

She held his gaze. "Why? We were two dumb kids who got caught by our own foolishness. We didn't even know each other very well." They'd had passion between them but nothing more. He'd been in Hawaii on leave and she'd been mesmerized by his good looks and exotic occupation. At least that's what she'd told herself.

"It was more than that and you know it."

She turned away from the intensity in his eyes. "Was it? After Brianna was born, all we did was fight."

"I had to work."

It was a familiar argument. She hadn't wanted to be stuck at home by herself while he traveled the world.

"You blamed me for losing Brianna," he said.

"You blamed me too. You didn't say it, but I felt it."

He raised a brow. "It was my fault, not yours. And you can come up with a dozen other theories, but we both know the kidnappers wanted to punish me for something. So if anyone's to blame, it's me."

She was too tired to argue with him. "Maybe you're right about more than one person being involved." Her next thought chilled her. "What if he's lured us here for a reason?"

"It's a possibility, I admit, but I'm not about to let go of this opportunity to find my daughter. But, yeah, he wants something from us. Money, something. I'm sure he'll make his demands known sooner or later. In the meantime, we find Brianna."

She glanced at him in time to see the muscles in his jaw flex. His determination had never wavered. Why was that? The baby had been a part of their lives such a short time, but he'd never given up hope of recovering Brianna. Against her will, the fact impressed her.

The sheet had slipped from her shoulder, and she tugged it into place. "What could be in this place that would make it worth getting us to come here? Bluebird Crossing is desolate."

"We're close to the Mexico border," he pointed out. "This area is like an open door to the drug cartels. If the culprit who took Brianna is associated with the drug lord I had a run-in with, this would be a convenient place to get access to me. And there are few people, so he wouldn't have to worry about interference."

"So he's got us isolated." She shuddered. "What if he's just saying one of the girls is Brianna? Maybe he wants revenge on you for the man who drowned, and he knew you'd come if you thought our daughter was alive." She didn't want to lose the thread of hope she had, but common sense kept rearing its head.

Clay nodded. "It's possible. It's hard to figure when we don't know who was behind Brianna's kidnapping."

"That envelope containing the picture. It was sent from El Paso. It wouldn't be a problem for a drug lord to send one of his men across the border to mail the letter."

"This whole area has been like a war zone with the violence from Mexico spilling over the border. He'd have no trouble moving around."

She turned off the light and rolled over, facing the window. After a moment, she said softly, "I want her back, Clay. I want to tell her everything and that I love her."

"So do I," he said in the darkness. "And I want to make the man who took her pay."

Though his words seared her, somehow they thrilled her too. And she found she believed every word.

The bunkhouse was quiet except for the crickets that chirped outside the screened windows. The high desert cooled down at night, and Clay had turned off the air to hear the night sounds. He offered to put pillows between them again, but Eden rolled over and offered her stiff back to him, a reminder that she didn't need a physical barrier to keep him in his place.

He shifted in the bed and turned his face toward the window on his side. The pungent odors from the outdoors were a reminder of what he used to be. He'd grown up in the Chihuahaun desert near Terlingua, a place he'd hoped never to see again. Big cities and bright lights were more to his liking now. And though he felt discomfited, he was sure Eden was a bird in the sea.

As he kicked off the sheet, he heard something. A soft slithering sound, like a rope being tugged over the wood. He went on high alert. A snake? His keys were on the nightstand. He threw them to the floor to see if he could elicit any different sound. Like a rattle. But all he heard was the clang of the keys hitting the rug, then a frantic slithering sound. Eden stirred beside him, then her breathing deepened again.

It was definitely a snake, but at least it wasn't a rattler. More likely a patchnose or a bull snake. It would be frightened, but he needed to get it out of the room before Eden saw it and freaked. Unfortunately, he couldn't do it in the dark. He sat up and put his feet on the floor, then flicked on the light. The warm glow chased the shadows from the room. He blinked and glanced around. A snake was coiled about six inches from his foot. He froze when he recognized the familiar markings. A rattler. It hadn't rattled, but then, they didn't always.

The snake was within striking distance, and Clay didn't move a muscle. If Eden moved or made a noise, the thing was likely to bite him. She sighed, and one hand stretched out. The snake's eyes didn't blink, but Clay could tell it had noticed the movement.

"Eden, don't move," he whispered. "Can you hear me? Don't move. There's a rattler by my foot."

She sighed again, and he knew she was sleeping too soundly to have heard his warning. She stirred again, and the snake showed signs of agitation. His best chance was to jerk back his foot, but he knew rattlers. They were lightning fast, and this was a big boy. It might even be able to reach him on the bed.

Wait. The pillow. Could he hit it with the pillow and knock it down? His mouth was dry. Keeping his gaze on the snake, he slowly moved his hand over to grasp the pillow. He threw the pillow and jerked his foot back at the same time. Everything happened so fast that he wasn't aware at first that he'd been bitten. Then a stinging pain radiated from his ankle.

"Eden!" he said, reaching over to grab her arm.

She fought him off. "Don't touch me!"

"Wake up. I need you." He wasn't sure if it was the poison or adrenaline, but his head spun.

She finally sat up in bed. "Clay? What's the matter?"

If he hadn't seen the drops of blood from the puncture wound, he wouldn't have believed it. His ankle stung. "A snake bit me. The phone is on your side of the bed. I need you to call Rick."

Her eyes widened, and the last of the sleepiness in her eyes disappeared. "You've been bitten?"

He nodded. "By a rattler. It's under the pillow on the floor. Don't get out of bed. Just call Rick and tell him what happened. I'm a little woozy. I have to lie down." He flopped onto his back.

She grabbed the phone on the bed stand and called the main house. He listened to her explain the situation to Rick. "He is coming over right away with some men." Her eyes were worried. "How do you feel?"

"My lips are numb," he said, struggling to talk.

"You might be having an allergic reaction. I think it's too soon for venom to be doing anything. I'll call Rick back. Maybe he has an EpiPen." She punched in the number again.

Clay struggled to draw in a breath. His chest felt tight, and his throat seemed to be swelling. Eden was right. The venom shouldn't be having an effect for half an hour, but allergic reactions happened sooner.

The pillow hid the snake, but he could see the reptile's tail sticking out from under it. The tail moved, but the rattle made no sound. So that's why he'd had no warning. He closed his eyes.

6

THE SNAKE'S HEAD EMERGED FROM UNDER THE PILLOW, FOLLOWED BY A LONG, SINUOUS BODY. Eden shuddered, unable to tear her gaze away as the beautiful creature slithered across the floor to curl in the back corner. She touched Clay's damp forehead.

His lids fluttered, then opened. His pupils were enormous. He licked his lips. "Where's Rick?"

"He's coming." A tourniquet wasn't advisable at this point, but she wanted to *do something*.

She heard feet pounding up the walk outside. A few moments later Rick and Buzz burst into the room. Rick wore his boots and jeans, but his shirt was half unbuttoned. He carried a pitchfork. Buzz was behind him with a shovel in his hand.

Rick stared around the room. "Where's the snake?"

She pointed. "There, in the corner. But what about Clay? Did you bring an EpiPen?"

He handed it to her. "You'd better give it to him while we take care of the snake."

Taking the pen, she opened the gray tab, then jammed the tip into Clay's thigh, holding it there for several seconds. Clay flinched but didn't open his eyes. His lips were blue.

Eden dropped the EpiPen and took his hand. It was cold and blue too. "Clay? Stay with me, Clay!" She clutched his fingers and watched the men approach the corner.

It took only moments for them to dispatch the snake. Mumbling under his breath, Buzz carried the snake out on the shovel.

Rick came to the edge of the bed. "He's got a little more color," he said. "What happened?"

"I'm not really sure. I woke up when he said he'd been bitten."

Clay coughed and opened his eyes. The scary whiteness was receding from his skin, and his pupils were looking more normal. His fingers tightened on hers, and he struggled to sit up. Something tight in her chest loosened, and she inhaled deeply, suddenly aware she'd been holding her breath.

"The snake," Clay whispered.

"Is gone," Rick said.

Eden stuffed some pillows behind his back. "You look like you're going to live."

"We still need to get that bite treated," Rick said, withdrawing another vial from his pocket. "I keep antivenom in the fridge."

"Where were you bitten?" Eden asked.

"My left ankle." Clay moved his foot out from where it had been entangled in the sheet. He closed his eyes. "It hurts."

She winced at the puncture wounds crusted over with blood. And even worse at the bruise beginning to travel up his leg. All thought left her. He couldn't die!

"Honey, you're crushing my hand," he said, lifting one lid.

She loosened her grip on him. "Where's the nearest hospital?" she asked Rick.

"Allie called the doctor. He'll come to us."

Eden injected the antivenom into Clay's other thigh. "IV is the best administration, but this will help for now. And the wound needs to be cleaned. I'll do it if you can get me some soap and water. Alcohol too."

Rick nodded and went to fetch the items.

Wheels crunched on gravel outside. "I think the doctor's here," she said to Clay, nearly giddy with relief.

Footsteps hurried toward the door, and Buzz ushered in an older man with hair that stood on end as if he'd gone from the bed straight to the car. He carried an IV bag and pushed a metal stand.

"This must be the patient," he said. Eden climbed out of the way while he got to work on Clay. She was suddenly self-conscious of her skimpy nightwear in the presence of these men, so she grabbed one of Clay's shirts from the closet and slipped into it while the doctor examined the wound. "One side looks dry. I don't think you got a full dose of venom, young man. You're very fortunate."

Rick touched her arm and motioned her back toward the door. "There's something weird about all this," he said.

She walked with him out of Clay's earshot."Weird? We're in the desert. Snakes get inside sometimes, don't they?"

"Not all that often. I've never had a rattler in the house." He put his hand in his shirt pocket and withdrew a piece of paper. "This was on the door."

She took it from his hand and stared at the letter. "'You shouldn't have brought her.'" Wrinkling her forehead, she glanced up at Rick. "What does that mean?"

"I have no idea."

"The kids are too little to do something like this."

He nodded. "Obviously."

"Did any of your other employees want this position?"

"Most of the cowboys have been with me for years, but I just hired Sam a couple of months ago. And I hired an assistant for the cook two weeks ago. There weren't any other applicants for counselor, if you want the truth. No one wants to live this far away from civilization."

The kidnapper. Had he wanted only Clay to come? As far as the kidnapper knew, she and Clay had divorced. "We have to tell Clay about the note."

"I will. But not until the morning, when he's got a clear head."

"Some kind of prank by a teenager from town, maybe?" She knew better, but maybe it would derail Rick's line of thinking. He was eyeing her with a speculative glint in his eyes.

Rick shrugged. "Maybe. It's a weird situation. I don't know what to make of it. Maybe the sheriff will have an idea."

"I hope so." But she mostly hoped Clay could call in some help from his special ops buddy, Brendan. If she had to go to bed every night and wonder what creepy crawlies would slither out to meet her, she wouldn't get a wink of sleep.

And if this had anything to do with Brianna's disappearance, could the children be in danger? She rushed down the hall to check on them.

Clay felt as if he'd been hit by a truck. He blinked until his vision cleared. His leg felt encased in hot tar. When a cool hand touched his forehead, he turned his head toward Eden.

So beautiful. How had he ever let her go? He wanted to reach up and touch her cheek. It would be as soft as Brianna's skin had been.

"How do you feel?" she asked.

"Thirsty," he croaked. She helped him sit up and he practically inhaled the cool water that she offered him. "Where is everyone?" A vague memory of Rick and Allie as well as an older gentleman floated through his brain.

She backed away. "Looking around outside. The doctor had another emergency and had to leave once he was sure you were out of danger."

Her evasive manner sharpened his senses. "What aren't you telling me?"

She bit her lip. "They're looking for whoever put the snake in here."

"Put the snake in here? What do you mean?"

"There was a note on the door. It said, 'You shouldn't have brought her here.'"

His fatigue fell away. He set down the water glass. "It was deliberate?"

She nodded. "I'd bet he was trying to scare me away. I doubt he thought we'd be bitten. How did that happen anyway? A rattlesnake gives a warning."

"Its rattler didn't work." The room felt small and sinister to him now. "What does he want? There hasn't been another demand for money." She didn't have the answers for him, but it helped him to ruminate out loud. "Did anyone check for more snakes?"

"Rick did. The place was clean."

The bed moved as she sat on it. He resisted the urge to inhale deeply of the clean scent of the soap she'd used to bathe the girls. "Why would he care if you came with me? Seems odd."

"I wondered about that too." Her eyes glistened and she blinked rapidly. "I was thinking about what you said about revenge."

"We have no idea what he's planning. Whatever it is, it won't be pleasant."

"Maybe it's all a prank."

He held her gaze. "I wouldn't have interrupted your life for a trick."

The corners of her lips curved. "That leaves me with hope. You consider everything before you jump."

"Except when it came to you," he said, then winced. Had he actually said that? So much for protecting himself.

She looked away. "I always thought you examined what needed to be done and did your duty."

"My feelings for you had nothing to do with duty." Enough of this. He yanked the IV from his arm and swung his legs over the bed.

She grabbed at his arm. "You can't do that! Look at you, you're bleeding."

"The bag is empty. The bleeding will stop. Besides, the doc didn't think I got a full load of venom." He pressed his fingers to his arm. "Got a Band-Aid?"

She sighed but opened the first-aid box beside the bed and withdrew one. Her fingers were warm when she pressed them against his skin. She'd been cold a few minutes ago. He wished he could believe being around him had altered her temperature even one degree.

He jerked on his boots, though every muscle still hurt and his leg throbbed. "Did you check on the girls?"

"Yes, they're sleeping." She followed him into the hall.

He went to the door of the big dorm room and peeked in. The light from the hallway fell on their sleeping faces. He drank in the peaceful scene. Arms curled around dolls and stuffed animals. The air was scented with little girl. He stared until he saw each small chest rise and fall. Reassured, he turned and walked right into Eden.

She grabbed his shirt, and he steadied her. This close, the scent of soap was even stronger. He resisted the impulse to rest his chin on the top of her head. What would she do if he pulled her closer? Probably hit him. His hands dropped away.

"They're all okay."

Her gaze wandered past his shoulder, and she stepped back. "They're so beautiful."

He nodded. "I'm going to go outside with Rick. You keep watch over the girls."

"Do you think whoever tried to hurt us would hurt them?"

"Someone took Brianna once. We have no idea of his agenda."

She clenched her fists. "He won't touch these girls! Do you have a gun?"

"You won't need one. I'll be right outside." He pocketed his hands so he wouldn't touch her again.

Nausea roiled in his stomach. Probably a reaction to the venom. He steadied himself. This stunt wasn't going to keep him from protecting Eden and their daughter. Or the other girls.

7

A CHILL STILL HOVERED IN THE MORNING AIR WHEN EDEN WALKED ACROSS THE SPARSE YARD to the kitchen with five little girls in tow. The scent of maple syrup and pancakes made her steps quicken, and she smiled at the girls to see if they'd noticed. They giggled and skipped along beside her. She hadn't seen Clay the rest of the night, but she'd gotten little sleep. Coffee would wake her up.

India ran ahead of her and pushed open the screen door into the kitchen. "Rita, I'm here," she announced. "I saw some hummingbirds. Do you know they beat their wings fifty times a second?"

An attractive young woman turned with a smile on her face. "My goodness, so fast?" Her blond hair was in braids, as if she'd stepped from the pages of *Heidi*. She wore jeans and a blue blouse that matched the color of her eyes. When she spoke, her voice had a Southern accent that didn't match her appearance. The makeup she wore made her look like a Dresden doll.

"You must be Eden," she said. "Here's your coffee, strong and laced with lots of real cream, just as you like it."

Eden accepted the mug filled to the brim. "Who told you that?"

"Clay."

"He's here?"

"Was," the woman corrected. "He and Rick took off for town. Rick wanted the doctor to take another look at the snake wound."

Eden took a gulp of coffee. It was perfect. "Clay seemed okay? He and Rick were out all night looking for the intruder." She glanced around and made sure the girls were occupied.

"The sheriff came too." Rita turned back to the stove, a mammoth affair that had eight burners. Four of them held skillets with pancakes sizzling in them.

"You're the cook?"

The young woman nodded. "Rita Mitchell. I feed this wild bunch." She ruffled Lacie's hair, and the child hung on to her leg and looked up with clear adoration.

Eden could tell she and Rita were going to be friends. Was everyone in this area so welcoming? "Is Allie gone too?"

Rita nodded. "She had a planning meeting for a missions conference at church. The ladies are coming here for lunch, so you'll get a chance to meet everyone before Sunday."

Eden guided the girls to the table, then returned to seize plates of pancakes. "Is that real maple syrup?"

"Of course. I wouldn't feed my girls anything but the best." The young woman carried more plates to the table. "Eat up, honey. We need to get some meat on your bones. You a model or something?"

Eden's cheeks heated. "I'm a nurse."

Madeline touched Rita's braid when the young woman sat beside her. "Could you braid my hair like that? Then we would be twins."

"I sure can, honey. Or maybe Mrs. Larson can. She's probably better at it than me."

Eden smiled. "I'm not very good at braids. Maybe you could teach me as well."

"Where are you from, Mrs. Larson?"

"Please call me Eden. I'm from Indiana. A little town called Wabash."

"First electrically lighted city in the world."

"How'd you know that?"

Rita shrugged. "My cousin lives in Peru, just down the road a piece."

"Usually no one has ever heard of Wabash."

"The Wabash-Erie Canal. Wabash Cannonball. Lots of interesting things in the area."

Eden took a bite of pancake dripping with syrup. It was magnificent. "You're quite the history buff."

"I'm working on a historical romance set in Indiana. I've been reading up on the area."

"You're an author?"

"Well, not yet. Someday I'll be just as famous as Nora Roberts. Most folks think I'm just a dreamer, but they'll see when my first book is on the shelves."

Eden grinned. "Somehow I believe you can do anything you set your mind to do."

Rita's smile was brighter than the sunbeams gleaming on the

stainless sink. "We're going to get along swell, Eden. I'm glad you're here."

"So am I," Eden said, realizing she meant it. This place was so different from Indiana. The harsh landscape of red rocks and cacti. The sharp scent of creosote and sage in the air. The blue bowl of sky that went on forever. It was a little scary and exhilarating at the same time.

The girls finished breakfast and went off to watch their morning allotment of *Dora the Explorer* on TV. Eden helped Rita and her assistant, Tepin, a Hispanic woman of about thirty, clear the table.

"What do you know of the girls?" Eden asked Rita.

"They're sweethearts, aren't they?"

"They're wonderful. I love them already." Eden smiled. "Any of their families come to visit since they've been here?"

Rita turned on the hot water and dumped Dawn detergent into the sink. "Nope. We don't let them come until the kids have been here at least a week, preferably two. Visits too soon only make them more homesick."

Eden handed her a stack of dishes. "What did you think of that snake showing up last night?"

Rita dumped them into the soapy water. "I think it was blown out of proportion. Snakes get in all the time. One of the hazards of living in the desert." She shrugged. "I saw one in the bushes outside my window just two days ago."

Maybe no one had told her about the note. Eden opened her mouth to tell her, then closed it again. "Any new employees on the ranch right now?"

"Got several new ones. Tepin here. Sam's a new hand. You. I guess not everyone wants to live in the desert."

Before Eden could ask more questions, she saw Clay's truck pull up outside. "Clay's back. I think I'll go see how he's feeling," she said. "I'll be right back."

He should have spent the night in bed, not roaming the rocky hilltops. Clay rubbed his bleary eyes and parked the truck. His leg ached, but he'd popped ibuprofen all night, and the pain was somewhat better this morning. He'd let Rick out down by the barn.

When Clay exited the truck, he turned toward the house and saw Eden running toward him. The sight of her brought him a surge of energy. The morning sun turned her auburn hair to fire. He had to grin at her pumps, so out of place with the jagged rocks of the landscape.

She stopped three feet from him and tucked her hair behind her ears to reveal gleaming diamond earrings. "Find anything?"

"Not much. Just some tire tracks behind the barn, but Rick had no idea how long they might have been there."

"You're pale. You should be in bed."

"I'm fine, really. How are the girls?"

"Watching cartoons. Then we're supposed to take them on a hike." She made a face. "But if you're not up to it . . ." Her eyes were hopeful.

He grinned. "I think we need to teach you to ride first. But you'd need to change into jeans and boots."

She lifted her chin. "Not going to happen."

"You look great in anything, you know."

She flushed. "Want some breakfast? I think there are pancakes left."

"Don't change the subject. What's it going to take to get past that wall, Eden? When you left me, I didn't know you much better than the day we met."

Her eyes narrowed. "I don't know what you're talking about."

She turned toward the house, but he caught her arm. "I'd really like to know the woman past the pretty face and gorgeous hair. What do you want out of life? Who are you, really?"

Her green eyes flashed. "I'm exactly who I seem. It's not my fault if you wanted some kind of wife who hiked the mountains with you. I never pretended to be GI Jane."

"I don't want to change you, but I just want to know you. You were always this perfect woman at the pinnacle of her career. Intelligent and beautiful, but remote. Never rattled for a moment."

"Well, once we find Brianna, you never have to be disappointed in me," she said.

Did her voice quiver? He'd like to think that just once he'd gotten past her defenses. "I was never disappointed in you."

She met his gaze. "Our relationship is over, Clay. All I want is to find my daughter."

"When Brianna was born, I thought your guard was finally starting to slip," he said, tightening his grip on her arm when she tried to pull free. "You were crazy about her."

Tears filled her eyes. "I wish I hadn't given up on her."

"You're too hard on yourself. No one is perfect."

"Except you." Her tears vanished. "The protector and defender of the free world."

"You say that like it's an insult."

"You like being the tough guy who never sheds a tear."

Only because he had wanted to be strong for her. "You think I have no feelings?"

"Do you? You went off quite happily to South America when duty called."

If only she'd seen his internal struggle. But he hadn't allowed it. "The search here in the States was at a dead end." And he'd hoped to find some clue to their daughter's fate.

"I asked you not to go."

She'd done more than that. She'd said if he left, their marriage would be over. And she'd followed through. He received the divorce papers a month after he left. Why *had* he left? Without Brianna to hold them together, he wasn't sure how to make the marriage work. But was it because he couldn't bear to see her leave him? Just the way his mother had done when she left with her lover, without a backward glance at her kids.

He shied away at the thought of his mother. "I had to go, Angel."

She succeeded in pulling her arm free. "I hate that nickname!"

"It suits you." He lifted a brow rather than tell her what it meant to him. "I dare you to change into jeans and boots."

She brushed at an imaginary speck of dust on her shirt. "You know perfectly well I don't own any boots. Or jeans."

"I'll buy you some."

"I'd rather not be beholden to you."

"Where do we go from here?" he asked her. "We both want Brianna when we find her. We've carefully avoided the topic of what happens next."

She gave a shrug. "I suppose we act civilized like everyone else. I'll take custody of her and you can have her every other weekend."

Just what he didn't want. "I don't think so. I want her with me. You can have her every other weekend."

"I'm her mother!"

"And I'm the father who never gave up looking for her." The minute he spoke, he wished he could call back the words.

She swallowed hard. "How did you know, Clay? I'm her mother and I believed she was dead. Why didn't you give up too?"

"I can't explain it."

It had been an intuition deep inside. She thought he had no feelings. The truth was, he had more than he could handle most times. The older he got, the harder it became to maintain his tough-guy, careless facade. He'd accused her of hiding behind a mask. Wasn't he just as bad?

He turned her toward the house. "Let's get chow. My belly is gnawing on my backbone."

When they reached the kitchen, Rita turned with her smile increasing in wattage. "Clay, I kept some pancakes warm for you."

He blinked at the way she batted her lashes. Like she was a Southern belle. Who did she remind him of? That gal who played Heidi maybe. Beside him, he felt Eden tense. She'd always thought friendly women were coming on to him. He wasn't sure where her insecurity came from.

Putting his hand on Eden's shoulder, he guided her to the table. "I could eat a horse."

"I could make you some bacon too," Rita said. She set the stack in front of him, then turned toward the refrigerator.

"No need. These pancakes are plenty."

Rita pulled out a chair across from him and Eden. "Allie said you are a photojournalist. How romantic."

He glanced away from her sappy smile. "Don't let us interrupt your work," he told Rita.

"I can take a break. So you've been to lots of other countries?"

"A few." He shoveled in the food and passed the syrup to Eden.

Allie's voice came from the living room. "Rita, could you come here a moment?"

Rita heaved a sigh and got up. "Call if you want anything more to eat. I'll be happy to fix it." She directed one last smile his way, then stepped out of the kitchen.

"Before you say anything, she's just being friendly," Clay said.

"A little *too* friendly," Eden said. "But I think maybe it's just her way. She was friendly to me too."

He relaxed. "Glad you could see that."

"Besides, we're here only to find Brianna. I have no real hold on you."

That wasn't what he wanted to hear. As far as he was concerned, she could grab hold with both hands and never let go.

8

YOU SHOULDN'T HAVE BROUGHT HER HERE. EDEN HAD BEEN PUZZLING OVER THE CRYPTIC message all day. What possible reason could the kidnapper—or anyone—have for not wanting her here? Was it possible someone intended to harm Clay but didn't want to hurt her? If that was the case, then could that person be someone she knew? Someone who cared about her? The police said a kidnapper was often someone known to the family. In fact, Clay and Eden were suspected for a time of harming Brianna. But detectives interrogated all their acquaintances at great length and filed charges against no one.

The bunkhouse held the scent of the baby powder she'd put on the girls after their baths last night. She settled onto the sofa and grabbed the landline. Daniel should be at home now. They'd grown up together in the same foster home, and he was a true friend and brother. Hearing his voice would calm her jitters. And he'd be happy to hear that her engagement to Kent didn't happen. Her heart hurt when she thought about Kent. She prayed he'd be able to get past the hurt she'd caused him. He deserved to find a woman with a whole heart.

But the phone rang until she was dumped into his voice mail. She left a message with the ranch number and hung up frowning. Would he really still be mad at her about Kent after all this time?

Glancing at her watch, she saw it was time to take the girls on a hike. The mountains were stark and forbidding. Cacti and who-knew-what creepy crawlies would be waiting at every turn. But by the time she retrieved the girls, found Clay, and started up the trail, she was enjoying herself.

India skipped along beside her. "Look, Miss Eden, a yucca. Did you know you can eat the flowers? Buzz told me. Can I taste one?"

"Um, I don't think so, India." Eden exchanged a rueful grin with Clay.

She held Katie and Madeline by the hand as they hiked up the desert mountain where they'd been told they could see into Mexico. The sun was bright and hot on her arms. The landscape was so different from Indiana.

"I'm hungry," Madeline said.

"I have a granola bar in my backpack," Eden said. She stopped and shrugged it off her back. None of the other girls wanted a snack yet, but Madeline scarfed hers down in six bites and asked for another. "I think you have hollow legs," Eden said, handing the little girl another one.

When they reached the peak, they stopped and stared at the

panorama. No people, just endless desert and, in the distance, a ribbon of blue that was the Rio Grande.

Clay set down the picnic basket he carried. She dug into her backpack and pulled out a tablecloth and spread it on the ground. He began to set out the sandwiches and chips Rita had packed for them. When the children finished eating, they began to collect wildflowers.

Clay leaned on his elbow on the tablecloth as he watched them. "They're all so different," he said. "It's fun watching them interact. I've been imagining first one then the other is Brianna."

"Me too," Eden admitted. "Just when I think I have it figured out, I change my mind."

His expression as he watched the girls filled her with warmth. She'd always thought he would be a good father, but he hadn't had the chance to show how good.

His gaze went from the girls to her face. "I don't like the note left on our door last night. There seemed to be animosity toward you in it."

She raised a brow. "I don't think so, Clay. I'm guessing someone wants me out of the way so I don't get hurt. You know how the police always said the kidnapper was likely someone close to the family. Maybe it's someone who likes me and hates you for some reason."

"That would mean he is likely a friend of yours. Or a relative." He shook his head. "I'm not convinced that was the intent of the note, though. I don't want you wandering off alone here. Stick close to me. I'll protect you."

"Just like you protected Brianna?" She wished she could call back the words when his eyes shuttered.

"You still blame me, don't you?" he asked, his voice soft.

She bit her lip. "You knew what you were doing in Colombia was dangerous."

"All my missions are dangerous. And I didn't know that one would be dangerous to my family! You're not without blame either, Eden. If you'd been paying attention that day . . ." He inhaled. "I'm sorry. I didn't mean that."

She blinked at the sting in her eyes. These same arguments were the ones that had sent her fleeing the moment he left the country. And she didn't really blame him. Not anymore. If losing Brianna was anyone's fault, it was hers.

She laid her hand on his. "I'm sorry. I shouldn't have said that. I didn't even mean it. I'd rather fight sometimes than admit the pain I feel."

He studied her expression. "Tell me what's been going on in your life."

Her face heated and it wasn't from the sun. "Just life," she said.

His smile vanished. "You lower the mask for a fleeting second, then slap it right back into place."

Maybe she did tend to be too secretive. She wished she could be more like Allie, laughing and open about her feelings. Maybe it came from being a foster kid. She ached for these five little girls.

"Earth to Eden."

She blinked and smiled. "Sorry, I was woolgathering." Could she let down a small corner of her veil with him? Maybe it was worth a try. "I'm working on being more open, but it's hard for me. Is there something in particular you want to know?"

"I'd like to know how you became a Christian."

"When Brianna . . . died, it was either go crazy or look for meaning. I chose to look for meaning."

His smile came. “And you found it?”

She nodded. “Well, as much as I could in such a horrible situation. I still don’t know why he allowed it, but I came to realize we have no control over bad things. When I got to Wabash, a coworker invited me to church. I just held on to God a day at a time.”

“What about Kent? How did he fit into all this?”

“He helped me start to live again. To begin to think I might do more than get through every day.”

“I would like to have helped you do that.”

She rubbed her head. “I saw the ruins of our hopes everywhere I looked, and it hurt too much.”

“Now here we are.” He smiled and nodded toward the girls. “She’s here. We just have to find her.”

“I hope so. One minute I’m clinging to hope, and the next minute I’m fearful this is a cruel joke. We don’t know.”

“I’m certain,” he said. “Can’t you feel her here, Eden?”

“Maybe it’s wishful thinking.”

He shook his head. “Trust me, Eden. Cling to that hope. We’ll find her.”

He had enough faith for both of them. “I’ll try,” she said.

Clay couldn’t stop watching Eden. He should have seen it right away, that undercurrent of a changed soul. So much for the intuition he’d always thought he possessed. Now that he knew, it was clear to see.

He put his hand in his pocket, and his fingers touched his digital picture viewer. Had she looked at pictures of Brianna lately? Pulling it out, he turned it on, smiling when Brianna's chubby cheeks came into view.

"What's that?"

"I like to look at these," he said. He showed it to her. Brianna was cradled in his hand at the hospital. His hand was nearly as big as she was.

"Oh, Clay," she whispered, her voice full of tears. "I had that picture enlarged and hung it over my bed. On bad days, that's how I imagined her. Cradled in God's hands."

Her insight gave him pause. "And now we know that he's been taking care of her all this time."

She took the viewer and advanced to the next picture. The two of them were staring down at their baby with expressions of awe. In the next picture, they were gazing at one another with love in their faces. His breath caught. He'd forgotten about that one. He hardly dared glance at her, but she didn't go on to the next photo like he'd expected.

"We were so young," she said softly.

"Now we're old and decrepit?"

She shook her head and looked at him. "I didn't mean that. We didn't have any idea what life had in store for us. The pain that was coming our way in a few short weeks."

Tell her. He wanted to say that he'd never wanted her to leave. That he wished he'd been there to comfort her during those dark months after Brianna was taken. He opened his mouth.

"Look, Miss Eden, a tarantula!" India's voice was full of excitement.

Eden broke their eye contact. "Get away from it, India!"

"It won't hurt her," Clay said.

"I've heard those things jump."

"They don't usually bite. It's more afraid of her than you are of it." He pointed to the way the dark blob crawled under a yucca plant.

Eden shuddered and steered the little girl in another direction. "Let's play with the other girls."

But the children preferred to poke at the tarantula. Clay took a stick away from Katie and directed them to a rocky outcropping with a path that appeared safe. "Let's climb to the top."

The children squealed and raced for the top as he and Eden chased them. From the heights, the view of the Rio Grande was even more magnificent.

"People," Lacie said, pointing to about ten people, men and women, hurrying through the desert in single file.

Eden glanced at him with a question in her eyes. "Illegals," he mouthed to her. He could try to call them in, but by the time the Border Patrol arrived, they would be long gone.

"We'd better get back," he said, herding the group back down the trail. "It's almost time for our outing to Big Bend."

9

THE THERMOMETER STOOD NEAR NINETY, BUT THE DESERT BREEZE WAS DRY AND BRISK. THE girls were piled into the back of the Bluebird Ranch van, an older model that was neat and rust-free. Eden sat two seats back with one arm around Lacie and one arm around Katie. She relished the way the girls had taken to her.

Zeke rode shotgun with Clay driving, and Della and Rita were in the back with the older girls. Clay turned into the lot by the park headquarters. The girls chattered excitedly, showing one another their cameras. He'd bought an inexpensive digital camera for each of them.

"Everyone out," he said, opening the van door.

The girls squealed and jostled for the door. Eden counted heads.

Clay led them onto a trail that had vegetation marked. "Here we are. I want you to walk single file. Zeke, you bring up the rear and make sure no one wanders off," he said.

Eden reluctantly let go of the small hands she'd been holding. "Look, there's a roadrunner," she said, pointing to the bird by the agave plant.

The girls all shrieked, and before anyone could show them how to use a camera, the bird ran off into the desert. "I think we need a little lesson first," she told Clay.

He grinned and began instructions on the camera. Eden's eyes glazed over when he started talking about picture composition and where to aim the camera. Her gaze wandered to the high peaks around the park. Though stark, the place was beautiful, but she wouldn't want to be lost in the desert. It could be brutal. She saw something move by her foot and jumped out of the way as a tarantula lumbered by.

Shuddering, she went to stand by Clay. She glanced around, counting heads once more. Wait, there was one missing. She counted again and realized Katie's red hair was nowhere to be seen. "Clay, where's Katie?"

"I told her she could go to the bathroom." He jerked a thumb in the direction of the ranger building.

"Not by herself!" she scolded.

She jogged across the desert to the ladies' room, where she found Katie washing her hands. Eden realized she might have overreacted. This was a family park, and the girl had only gone twenty or thirty feet to the bathroom. But she wanted no snakebites, no run-ins with any of the scary creatures that inhabited this desert.

She took Katie's hand to go back, but the little girl stopped and tugged her fingers free. "I forgot Button!"

Button was the much-loved bear with the missing eye. "Where is he?" Eden asked.

"I left him in the stall." She pointed.

"I'll get him. Wait here." Eden walked to the back stall and pushed it open. The bear was on the floor. Ick. Not very sanitary. She'd have to wash him when they got home. When she returned to Katie, she handed her the bear. "Let's get back to taking pictures."

She pulled on the door handle but it seemed to be stuck. Frowning, she jerked on it again. What on earth?

"You're doing it wrong," Katie said. She grabbed the handle and pushed. It didn't budge.

"Hang on a minute." Eden stooped and peered through the crack in the door. "It appears to be locked. Maybe the janitor locked it accidentally."

But it was the middle of the afternoon. And they'd notified the rangers they were bringing a group of children today. She banged on the door. "Hello," she called. "Can someone let us out?"

She tried to keep panic out of her voice. Being locked in brought back too many memories from her childhood. Was there breathing on the other side of the door? The hair stood on the back of her neck as she listened. "Who's there?"

Silence. She was jumping at shadows. There was no one there. The faint stench of smoke came to her nose. She sniffed again. It was stronger now. Was the place on fire? It was all she could do not to beat on the door in panic.

Katie tugged on her blouse. "Miss Eden, are you all right? You're scaring me."

"I'm fine, honey." Eden picked her up and hugged her. "We'll call to Mr. Clay from the window. He'll come and unlock the door for us."

She retreated to the window and cranked it open. She could see Clay on the trail. He was showing Lacie how to use her camera. "Clay, I need help," she called. She had to raise her voice and repeat it.

His head came up and he turned toward the building. "Eden? Where are you?"

She waved, not sure he could see her in the window. "In the ladies' room. Someone locked the door. I . . . I smell smoke."

He jogged to the building. She heard him at the door, then it opened and he stuck his head in.

"It wasn't locked," he said.

"Well, I couldn't open it." Now that he was here, her courage came flooding back. "Go back out and let me try from in here."

He shrugged and complied. Once the door had closed, she pulled on it and it opened easily. "I know it was locked," she said. "I tried and tried to open it. I saw the lock thrown too." She gave Katie a pat on the behind. "Go join the other girls," she said.

After Katie ran off, Eden sniffed the air again. "Did you smell the smoke?"

"A cigarette." He pointed to a still-smoldering butt perched on the edge of the sidewalk.

"Did you see anyone out here?"

He shook his head. "Were you frightened?"

She hugged herself. "Clay, the door was locked. I know it was."

"A childish prank maybe. There's a group of teenage boys here." He frowned, his gaze intent on her face. "We can't discount it, though." He hugged her. "Stay close to me. I'll be on my guard. Don't be afraid."

Easier said than done, but she kept her mouth shut and followed him back to the children.

Bluebird Crossing was a town with only one eye open. Or so it seemed to Eden that night as she peered through the café window at the sleepy town. She could almost imagine it was the West Texas version of Mayberry. Red-and-white-checkered tablecloths covered the tables, and the decor was vintage fifties. The aromas of enchiladas mingled with those of roast beef and fried potatoes.

"There they are," Clay said when a couple stepped into the café and came toward them. He rose and waved. "Over here."

Eden liked the looks of Gracie Wayne right off. Petite with fine blond hair and a dusting of freckles across her nose, she looked like the girl next door. Her husband, Michael, was military and had the erect posture to prove it. Good looking too. Eden liked the way he guided his wife with his hand at the small of her back. He clearly loved her.

The couple reached the table, and the men shook hands and introduced their wives before they were seated. "Good to get you back here," Michael said.

Back here? Eden glanced at Clay. She'd thought the men knew each other from the air force.

"Feels a little surreal to come home," Clay said. "Thanks for putting in a good word with the Baileys for me."

She should have asked him if the Waynes knew that Brianna was somewhere at the ranch. She'd assumed they didn't, but it was clear that the two men shared a special friendship. There was so much about her husband that she didn't know.

"I hear you have three children," she said to Gracie after the server brought their iced tea.

Gracie smiled. "Jordan, Evan, and Hope. We're a blended family."

Michael grinned. "About to be homogenized." He patted Gracie's belly.

The gentle swell told the tale. "Congratulations! When are you due?" Eden asked, trying to ignore the tiny stab of longing.

Gracie blushed. "Not for four months. The kids are so excited." She leaned her chin on her hand. "How did the two of you meet?"

Eden shrugged. "The usual kind of story. He was a handsome soldier on leave and I was on vacation."

Clay grinned. "Handsome? You thought I was handsome?" He nudged Michael. "I'll bet you can't say the same, buddy."

Michael nodded. "You're so right. She took one look at me and fainted."

"Stop it, Michael," Gracie said, shaking her finger at him.

He grinned and slipped his arm around her. "I'm a lucky man, and I know it."

"You two still act like newlyweds," Clay said. "I hear you're an EMT and own the only helicopter in the county. Rick says you're the go-to guy for everything."

The men started talking about work, and Gracie smiled and shook her head. Watching her and Michael, Eden wished she could feel so relaxed and free with Clay. What had they missed? She'd blamed their distance on his absence, but maybe it was more than that. Maybe it was some fundamental flaw in her. She knew she had walls. Over the years, she'd tried to tear them down, but her defense mechanisms were too strong.

After a pleasant evening, the couples walked outside together. As Eden waved good-bye to her new friends, she found herself tongue-tied with Clay. Did he ever think about what a marriage was supposed to look like?

"Ready to go home?" he asked.

"I need to walk off dinner a bit," she said. He offered his arm, and she took it hesitantly. They strolled the empty sidewalk along closed storefronts. When they stopped in front of the coffee shop, the only place except the café that was still open, she stopped. "Why didn't you tell me you were from around here?"

His easy smile vanished. "You never asked where I was from."

"You didn't think the fact that the kidnapper brought Brianna back to your home area was significant? I thought the location was just a random choice, but it seems it was personal."

"It couldn't get more personal."

"So we basically stepped into the lion's den?"

"I suppose so. But talking about it wouldn't have changed our minds. I'd face anything to get my daughter."

"Our daughter," she corrected.

His lips tightened. "Our daughter." He ran his hand through his hair. "Look, I just didn't want you to worry. It's my job to worry about the danger."

"This is exactly what broke up our marriage!" She turned and ran back toward the truck. She heard his footsteps behind her, but she didn't slow until his hand was on her arm and he pulled her around to face him.

"What do you mean by that?" he demanded.

She was so tired. Tired of fighting, tired of pretending, tired of the mask she always wore. "You always thought about what *you* should do. It was never *us*, what *we* should do. We were two separate people, never one unit. I realized that tonight watching the Waynes."

His hand dropped from her arm. "Maybe so. I wanted to take

my responsibilities seriously. A man isn't supposed to let his wife worry about anything."

"Who says? If they are one, they share everything. The good and the bad. At least that was always my dream. I didn't have the best role models, so I didn't have it all figured out."

"I hate fighting," he muttered. "That's all we seemed to do, and we're starting it again."

"At least we're talking when we're fighting."

He tipped his head and stared at her. "Do you start fights on purpose, then?"

She started to shake her head, then thought better of it. "Maybe I do. There's nothing worse than being ignored." As a child, she'd spent too many nights standing outside in the cold by herself. Or eating a peanut butter sandwich alone.

"I never wanted you to feel ignored. Just protected." He opened the truck door for her. She fastened her seat belt, but he didn't close the door. "Would you like to see where I lived?" he asked.

It was such a small thing, but she didn't miss the trepidation in his voice. She nodded. "Yes."

"It's on our way." He shut the door and went around to his side.

10

HE'D DRIVEN THIS ROAD A MILLION TIMES. CLAY TURNED ONTO THE DIRT DRIVE AND wondered when the grader had last been down it. Darkness was falling quickly, but the moon was bright tonight.

"Are there any other houses back here but yours?" Eden asked.

"Nope. It's a dead end. Which is probably why the potholes are so bad." He hit one and the truck bottomed out and slewed in the road before he straightened it.

Why had he even suggested coming out here? The ghosts had long been laid to rest in his heart. Or had they? Maybe that was it. He needed to confirm this for himself. He turned the truck into the disused lane. Tumbleweeds were strewn around the yard and the drive. His headlamps illuminated several piled against the door, which was half open.

"Looks like vandals have been out here," he said. He parked the truck ten feet from the house and shut off the engine.

She glanced at him. "Are we getting out?"

"Sure." He shoved open his door, but the minute his boots hit the dirt, he wanted to climb back in. The ghosts still lived here.

Eden was beside him before he could change his mind and drive off. She craned her neck to look at the roof, which had a gaping hole in it. "You lived here all your life?"

"Until I was eighteen. I went to college in San Antonio, then joined the air force."

"Where are your parents now? You have two siblings, right?"

So strange that they were only now talking about these things. They'd barely skated the surface of their histories when they were together. "It's been several years since I've seen my sisters. One lives in Boston and the other in Oregon, so we are never together in one place."

"Do your parents live near one or the other?"

He shook his head and advanced to the door. It had once been a grand Santa Fe–style home. There was an interior courtyard that had probably been taken over by snakes and scorpions. It had all fallen into disrepair after being abandoned fifteen years ago.

"So where do they live now?" She followed him.

He kicked the tumbleweeds out of the way and pushed open the door. A frantic rustling noise warned him not to go in. He blocked the doorway with his arm. "Scorpions."

She shuddered and stepped away. "It was quite a place. Sad to see it in such a state."

"Things deteriorate quickly in the desert. By the time I inherited it, it was in sad shape."

"Why didn't your parents sell it?"

"My parents fought all the time and finally divorced. They tried to sell it, but the real estate market this far out is lousy, and my mom wasn't willing to let it go at a loss. So they finally gave up and gave it to us kids."

"Could it ever be brought back, or is it too far gone?"

"It's solid. Well built and stuccoed. The roof would need to be repaired, and some serious pest control done. It would take some time and money." He led her around to the side of the house and pointed. "There's a barn and paddock. A good spring in the back of the property where me and my sisters used to go swimming."

"Your parents?" she asked again. "Where are they?"

He shrugged. "My dad moved to Mexico and hangs out with all the senoritas. Mom remarried Dad's best friend and lives in Florida."

She winced. "I'm sorry. I'm sure that was painful."

"It was okay until I hit sixteen. Then everything was a battle."

"And we repeated that cycle," she said, a ghost of a smile touching her lips.

"There's that," he agreed.

"Do you like the house?"

She studied the house again. "It could be lovely. I imagine there are open beams inside, tile floors." He confirmed this with a nod. "I'd love to see it in the daylight. And without the scorpions, of course."

His fingers found the pendant in his pocket. He wanted to give it back to her, but only when the moment was right.

"Brianna would love it," she said, her gaze drifting back to the yard where a grove of trees surrounded the spring. "So this is your house now? You own it?"

"I do. My sisters signed off on it a couple of years ago. They said they were never coming back here."

"But you weren't so sure?"

"I loved this place once." He wished he'd brought her here in the daylight. But then maybe the mess would look worse. "I might renovate it."

"It would take a lot of money."

He stared at her in the moonlight. "I'm a rich man, Eden."

"You are? Soldiers make that much money?"

He grinned. "I had hazardous-duty pay, but I inherited a lot of money from my grandmother a couple of years ago that I've never touched." He frowned at a movement by the barn. "Who's there?" he called.

He heard rustling and rushed toward the barn. An engine roared to life and a small truck shot from the open door and careened away down the dirt drive. The Toyota barely missed sideswiping his truck. The bed held several people, but it was too dark to make out any features.

"Who could have been here?" Eden asked.

"Probably a coyote hauling illegals," he said.

"Those we saw from the hill?"

He shrugged. "I think I'll take a look."

He jogged back to the truck and got the flashlight out of the glove box. Eden followed close behind, and he could tell by her breathing that she was tense. If he'd had a gun, he would have brought it to reassure her. The beam from the flashlight illuminated discarded clothing, soda cans, and other debris. All the tack that had been hanging on the walls was gone, evidently stolen by the illegals and others who had passed through here.

For a moment he wished he'd kept this place up and never gone off to the military. Would his life have been any different? When he turned to go, he ran into Eden. Smelling the apple fragrance in her hair, he knew he would do it all over again, just for the chance to have met her.

Eden gave each of the girls new hairbrushes to make sure they had uncontaminated DNA samples for Clay to send in. On Wednesday Eden stood at the fence by the corral. Dust swirled in plumes from under the horses' hooves. She coughed and stepped out of the line of fire as best she could, steering the girls toward the fence.

"I want to ride that one." Lacie pointed to a paint horse that was rubbing against the barn siding.

"It's too big," Eden said, instantly regretting it when the little girl's face puckered. "How about the red one?" She pointed to a reddish pony with a sweet face.

The nearest cowboy, Buzz, shook his head. He was covered with red dust. "Don't let her fool you. She's a devil on hooves. She'll try to scrape the kids off her back when you're not looking."

Eden gulped. "I'm not sure this is a good idea."

"The kids love interacting with the horses. And the mares love it too. Don't you, girl?" Buzz patted the paint, which had moseyed over to take a lump of sugar from his palm.

She shuddered when she saw the mare's teeth. "Won't she bite you?"

"Naw. She's gentle." He gave her a final pat. "I'll saddle up the horses. We got two or three I trust with kids this young."

In a few minutes he'd saddled the horses and had them ready to go. She scurried out of the way as he and Clay had the girls take turns on the animals. Their animated faces made her smile.

"Look at me," Katie called. "I want to do a handstand."

Clay shook his head. "No way, kiddo. You stay right in that saddle."

Eden thought the child would cry, but instead she looked relieved. Paige, who never seemed to smile, squealed and waved grandly as she passed Eden's perch on the fence. The child was actually pretty when she was animated. Only Madeline had refused to get on a horse. She played outside the fence with Spot, her puppy.

Eden watched Clay as he interacted with the children. The man was a natural-born dad. He said he wanted Brianna with him all the time. He deserved it too. He'd always believed she was alive somewhere. That showed more faith and hope than she'd ever dreamed he could feel.

Her memory went back to that note on the door. *You shouldn't have brought her here.* Even now the ominous tone made her shiver. They'd heard nothing else. Not a problem in the bunkhouse, not a call. Nothing.

And what about Brianna? The only thing they could do would be to live close together so they could share their daughter. After all she'd been through, Brianna deserved having them both with her.

A family. The thing she thought she'd never have. Not now. What if they stayed together? Oh, the thought was ludicrous. Even if she were willing, Clay wouldn't be. The best they could hope for was an amicable relationship where they put Brianna first. Maybe that would be enough. It had to be, because she didn't have it in her to hope for more.

"Now you, Miss Eden," Lacie called. Her braids bounced on her shoulders as she came past on the horse. Rita had done a good job with the girl's fine hair.

"I don't think so, honey," Eden said.

Before she could react, Clay's big hands were on her waist. He lifted her down from the fence and turned her toward the paint. He smelled of man, dust, and the faint tinge of soap. He'd had a shower after breakfast, but stubble still darkened his chin.

"Smile," he said in her ear. "Don't show any fear. You can do this. The girls expect it."

The protest died on her lips when she saw the girls turn eager faces toward her. She was a role model even if she didn't want to be. "I'm not dressed for it." She glanced down at her shoes and expensive slacks.

"Your clothing will wash." He guided her to the side of the horse. "Put your left foot in the stirrup."

She so didn't want to do this. Her insides were shaky. *Coward. Weakling.* All the name-calling in the world didn't stop her hands from trembling. Dust coated her tongue and swirled around her feet. Her designer shoes wore a layer of red and the stuff tinged her pants as well. She might never get the stain out.

"You're game to try it?" His eyes warmed as they looked her over.

The man was entirely too handsome. And he likely knew the way his touch turned her insides to mush. "You've left me no choice."

Gritting her teeth, she hoisted her left foot into the air and stuck it through the stirrup. Clay's warm hands remained at her waist. They felt much too natural on her. It was as if five years had dropped away into the canyon behind the ranch.

"Now step up," he instructed.

She lifted herself with his help and threw her right leg over the saddle. "I should put the other foot in this stirrup?" she asked, looking down the mare's rounded side. From this vantage point, the horse seemed even bigger. The ground was much too far away. It would hurt if she fell.

"Yes. And take the reins."

"Don't turn me loose!"

"I've got a hold on the bridle." He beckoned Buzz. "Can you adjust the stirrup on that side? They're too long." His fingers brushed her ankle as he lengthened the strap.

The saddle was hard under her bottom and against her inner thighs. Could she even perch here without falling? It felt so precarious. But the girls' faces were avid with excitement and she couldn't disappoint them. Or Clay either, though she hated to admit she wanted to see admiration in his eyes.

He put the reins in her hands. "Hang on to the horn."

The horse took a step, and she lurched, then clutched at the saddle horn. Then the jarring ride smoothed out as Clay led the horse around the corral. The girls clapped as she passed by them. She was doing it! Actually riding a horse. Something she'd sworn never to do. And it wasn't so bad. Not if it made Clay's eyes glow with pride.

11

SHE NEEDED A SHOWER. EDEN SWIPED DUSTY HAIR BEHIND HER EARS AND SQUINTED INTO THE noonday sun. A rumble came from the driveway, and she turned to see a line of cars and pickups pulling up to the house. Two pickups and two cars. She recognized Allie's red compact. Women got out of all the vehicles and started toward the house.

Allie saw her and waved. "Eden! Come join us for coffee," she called.

Though the last thing she wanted was to allow other women to see her in such a disheveled state, Eden could hardly refuse the imperative tone in her employer's voice. She glanced at Clay.

"I'll be here with the girls," he said. "Buzz is going to teach them some roping tricks."

She wished she could stay and watch. The thought of Clay's strong shoulders flexing as he roped a calf intrigued her. *Bad Eden.* That physical magnetism he possessed had gotten her into this trouble in the first place.

"Clay, I'm a mess! You could save me," she said.

He draped an arm around her shoulders. "You look great. The friendships will do you good."

It was as if he knew she needed a bit of encouragement. The embrace was brotherly, but her own reaction was anything but sisterly. She nearly stood on tiptoe and brushed a kiss on those firm lips. Too hastily she tore out of his embrace, then regretted it when she saw his eyes cloud. He thought he repelled her when the very opposite was true.

"I'll be back," she said, keeping her tone distant. She'd rather he didn't know of her attraction.

Everything felt different here. She walked across the sandy yard toward the house. Friendships were usually so superficial in Eden's world. Jealousy was quick to spring up, and coffee dates in Boston where she'd grown up were times of talking about other women, men, jobs, men again, and other women again. The raw land here seemed to inspire close confidences. Maybe it was because survival depended on others.

She already felt herself changing here. Letting down her guard in small ways. Reaching out and wanting to let the inner ice thaw. She heard laughter when she reached the screen door and immediately stiffened, thinking the others were laughing at her dusty appearance. Or were they mocking her designer shoes? Then she made out Allie's voice telling the women about how she'd put sugar in chili the first time she'd made it and Rick had eaten it anyway.

Not many women that Eden knew poked fun at themselves. She pasted on a smile and eased into the back of the living room.

A pretty blond woman with striking blue eyes saw her and smiled. "You must be Eden. I'm Shannon MacGowan. My husband, Jack, and I are next-door neighbors. My, how pretty you are."

"Thanks." Eden wasn't sure what to do with her hands. Or where to sit. When had another woman complimented her? Never in her memory.

These women made her realize how inadequate she was for this job. Their jeans were as natural to them as the sand outside. They'd be able to ride a horse like they drove a car. Facing the vast expanse of wilderness exhilarated them and left her feeling inadequate. They wouldn't have screamed at the sight of the snake the other night. They would have stomped it with their boots. And that tarantula on Tuesday at the park? They would have picked it up and put it in a safe place.

Allie patted the cushion beside her on the sofa. "Sit here and I'll introduce you. You just met Shannon. She's a vet, and her husband owns the biggest ranch in West Texas. And you know Gracie."

Gracie smiled. "I was looking forward to seeing you again."

The last woman was older, probably near sixty. A pair of wire-rimmed glasses perched on her nose, and her sharp eyes looked Eden over. "I'm Julia, also known as Judge Julia. You look familiar."

The woman was a judge. What if she'd seen the write-up in the papers when Brianna was taken? The kidnapping took place in San Antonio—not so far away, given how this area didn't even have its own newspaper.

Eden managed a smile. "I have one of those familiar faces."

"That's not it," Julia said, her eyes narrowing. "It will come to me."

Not if Eden had anything to do with it. She didn't want any law enforcement looking at her and Clay with suspicion again. "What's going on here?" she asked, glancing around the room at the excited faces.

Julia's focus wavered. "Planning the menu for our missions conference at church. We're doing an international dinner. Want to help?"

"I'm not much of a cook."

"I have the recipes for everyone. Pretty easy." The older woman handed her a paper titled "Thai Coconut Chicken."

Eden wanted to hand it back to her, but she didn't dare. The woman might start questioning her again. "Coconut chicken? I'll see what I can do." She glanced at Rita, who came into the room with a tray of coffee and cookies. "Rita might need to help me."

"If it's got coconut in it, you're on your own," the woman said, placing the tray on the table. "I can't even stand the smell." A small pill bottle rolled from her apron, and she quickly retrieved it. She looked a little pale.

"You okay?" Eden asked.

Rita grimaced. "Migraine."

Allie's smile faded. "Go lie down awhile. We can take care of ourselves."

"Thanks, I think I'll do that," Rita said.

Shannon poured herself a cup of coffee and glanced at Eden. "I saw that handsome husband of yours in the corral with the children. How long have you been married?"

Eden started to answer, then checked her initial response of a year. "Six years. We went out to see the house where he grew up. A Toyota went tearing out of the barn."

Julia lifted a brow. "Illegals?"

"That's what Clay thought."

"We've had a lot of problems with that lately," Gracie said. "Drug-lord wars have spilled across the border nearly every week. You're lucky they didn't shoot at you. Where is the house?"

Eden told her. "It was gorgeous once."

Gracie nodded. "I've seen it. Michael showed me when we found out you two were coming. Are you going to live there again?"

Eden glanced at her hands, wishing she hadn't brought up the house. "I don't know. It would take a lot of work to repair it."

"It would be worth it. Lots of room for kids, eventually," Shannon said.

"It was dark, so we didn't get a good look. It's very isolated. Is it safe?"

"With your big husband around, anywhere is safe," Allie said, smiling.

As the conversation went back to food, Eden leaned against the cushions and wondered if she would ever fit into this countryside as well as these women did.

⁂

The little girl was much too quiet. Eden glanced at Lacie sitting beside her, so composed. Her bare feet dangled off the edge of the truck seat, and she didn't tug at the seat belt the way so many children would have. Her hands were folded in her lap, and she stared straight ahead.

Eden had been glad Clay interrupted the women's planning with a child's chewed-up shoe in his hand. Their kind probing had left her uncomfortable. And she wanted to get away from Judge Julia's inquisitive stare.

"The dog didn't leave much of your shoe," Eden said to Lacie. "Shall we look for sneakers or sandals?"

Lacie glanced at her from the corner of her eye and tucked her chin before shrugging. Eden wasn't sure how to draw the little girl out. She'd hoped to learn more about Lacie this afternoon in a private outing to get more shoes.

"I heard Sister Marjo is coming next weekend to see you," Eden said.

Lacie lifted her head and her face brightened. "How many days is that?"

"Ten."

The animation vanished as if wiped away by a giant hand. Lacie dropped her chin again.

"You must really love Sister Marjo."

The little girl nodded, a bob so slight Eden nearly missed it. Lacie crossed her feet at the ankles and turned to stare out the window. The desert landscape rolled out as far as the eye could see. A gleam of white in the distance caught Eden's attention. The truck rounded a curve and she made out the tattered remains of a trailer park. Her gut tightened. She hated the reminder of the life she'd led until she was eight. Though she wanted to avert her gaze as they passed the decaying mobile homes, she had to look. She could almost hear her mother yelling at her.

"GO ON OUT NOW. HE'LL BE HERE ANY MINUTE."

Eight-year-old Eden felt the sting of tears in her eyes and blinked. She was much too old to be whining, according to her mother. "It's cold, Mama."

Her mother lined her eyes with black liquid that made the skin look harsh and thin. "Put on your mittens. You can make a snowman."

"I want to play with my doll." A lady from church had given Eden the baby doll. It wasn't new and had ink marks on the cheeks, but it was the first doll she'd ever owned. And there were clothes to go with it. She could spend hours changing outfits on the doll she'd named Sally.

"Your silly games aren't going to change a thing. Get outside and take the stupid doll with you." Her mother wheeled to glare at her. "He'll be here any minute. Get going before I take a belt to your legs."

Her mother would do it too. Eden slowly went to the only closet in the trailer, a tiny, cramped space in her mother's bedroom. She barely managed to pull down her coat. There were holes in her mittens, and she had no boots, but she knew better than to complain again. When she turned back toward the room, she lost her balance and toppled to the floor. Her forehead thumped the footboard on the bed, and the force of the blow brought tears to her eyes. She pressed her fingers to the spot that was already beginning to bump out.

"Quit crying. You're not hurt." Her mother pulled her roughly to her feet and pushed her toward the door. "You're going to look ugly when your father comes to see you tonight."

The last thing Eden wanted was to be ugly, to see her father's face cloud with anger the way it had when she'd cut her bangs with scissors. Tears spilled down her cheeks. "I want to look pretty for Dad," she said.

"Another reason to go outside and put some snow on your forehead. Now get out of here."

Her mother was pulling on a blue filmy thing when Eden went to the door. "That's pretty, Mama."

Her mother smiled and pirouetted in front of the mirror. "If Mr. Smith thinks so, I might have enough money to get you some pizza tonight. If you're a good girl and stay outside. Now scoot."

Even the thought of pizza failed to lift Eden's spirits. It was scary out at the playground. The big kids threw rocks or made the swing go too high. But there was no persuading her mother, so she put on her coat and went outside.

Snow spit her in the face as she pulled the trailer door closed behind her. As she went down the cracked sidewalk, she saw the car drive up. It was shiny and black. Newer than Eden was used to seeing. The man didn't get out until she was across the street, and she got only a glimpse of his heavy coat and a hat pulled low on his head.

She still had that image of her mother twirling in the mirror when she returned three hours later to find her mother gone, with no trace other than the scent of her face powder still lingering in the bedroom.

EDEN BLINKED AND PUSHED THE MEMORY AWAY. SHE GLANCED AT LACIE AND SAW THE CHILD staring with rapt attention at a trailer near the road. Its green shutters hung askew. Through the gaping front doors, she glimpsed the tattered remains of an orange sofa.

"No one lives there," Eden said.

"It looks like the other one," Lacie said.

"Other one? Did you live in a mobile home once?"

Lacie shook her head. "Sister Marjo takes me to see her niece sometimes. But I'm not supposed to tell the other sisters."

"Why not?"

"Mother Superior doesn't like Sister Marjo's niece. She says she's loose. Does that mean her joints might fall apart?"

No way was Eden going to answer that one. "Where is this trailer park you visit? In Dallas?"

Lacie nodded. "By the park."

Seeing the mobile homes seemed to have unlocked Lacie's tongue. Whatever these visits were, they'd impacted her mightily. "How often do you go?"

Lacie twisted in the seat for one final glimpse of the trailer. "I don't know. Sometimes."

"What's the niece's name?"

"Taylor. She's nice. She kisses my cheek and calls me her little darling."

Was it possible that Lacie was this Taylor's child? "You don't live at the convent, do you?"

Lacie shook her head. "I visit lots. Sister Marjo saved me, so she's 'sponsible for me."

A strange situation. The nun had found her five years ago yet had stayed involved. So maybe Lacie wasn't Brianna.

12

THE SWEET SCENT OF HAY, VERY DIFFERENT FROM THE SMELLS OF EXHAUST AND SMOG CLAY was used to, filled his lungs as he showed the girls how to feed the horses. They giggled and threw flakes of hay at one another. Dust motes danced in the sunlight streaming through the window opening.

He glanced at his watch. Eden had been gone for an hour. Surely she'd be back with Lacie soon. When the horses were fed, he led the girls back to the house to wash up for the meal. He sniffed the air. "Chili for supper, I think."

"Yay!" Madeline said. When the other girls ran on ahead, she slipped her hand into his.

Her fingers closed around his in a confidential way that warmed his heart. Her blond hair bouncing, she skipped along beside him.

He thought she looked a little like the pictures he'd seen of Eden when she was a child, but maybe all little girls were similar.

Her fingers tightened on his when a dented Ford came rolling up the drive. The sun had turned the red paint to a rust color. The back window on the passenger side had been busted out, and a black plastic bag fluttered in the opening. He glimpsed a woman behind the wheel.

Madeline stood stock still, her smile gone. "It's my mother," she whispered. "She's not supposed to come here."

Clay searched his memory. Rick had said Madeline's mom was filing for custody. "She was in the hospital, right?"

Madeline nodded, watching as the car lumbered to a stop. "She was in the loony bin," she said in a confidential tone.

He winced. "She has some mental illness she's fighting," he said gently.

"She scares me. Mom doesn't like her."

"Your foster mom?" Clay watched a woman get out of the car. Even from here he heard the door screech. That old rust bucket was bound for the junk heap soon.

Madeline nodded and hid behind his leg. "Mom said I don't have to talk to her."

"You run ahead inside. I'll talk to her." He watched the little girl run up the porch steps like someone was chasing her. And maybe someone was. He didn't know all the background. Just that the woman had been diagnosed with schizophrenia. If the doctors deemed her well enough to function, there should be no real danger.

He intercepted her determined stride up the walk toward the house. "May I help you?"

About fifty and thin as the fence rail, the woman was dressed in jeans that were stained with what looked like blood but he assumed was red paint. Was that smear of red on her forehead a cross? Her fingers were stained too when she held out her hand to shake his. She was very blond, and it looked natural.

Her grip was strong, almost like a man's. "I am here to get my daughter, Madeline," she said. Her accent seemed to indicate she might be Scandinavian. Her gaze wandered over his shoulder toward the house.

He resisted the urge to step away from the unsavory stench that he thought emanated from her hair. "Get her? Camp won't be finished for another month."

She leaned in and stabbed at his chest with her forefinger. "She belongs to me. You can't stop me from taking her."

"Do you have a court order to allow you to take her? She's not in your custody."

A crafty expression flitted across her face before she hid it. "I am her mother. I have rights." She dug into her pocket. "And I have this." She handed him a wrinkled paper stained with smears of red, blue, and yellow.

Her name was Else Bjorn, so his impression of a Scandinavian accent was correct. He smoothed out the wadded document and scanned it before handing it back to her. "This just says you are filing for custody of Madeline. It doesn't say the custody is granted." Poor woman. He knew the pain of having a child being taken away.

"She is my daughter. You have no right to keep her from me." The woman attempted to brush past him.

He blocked her path. "I'm sorry. I can't allow you to see her. You don't have any visitation rights."

Large tears pooled in her eyes. "Just for a minute," she begged.

"She needs to know her mama loves her. I am fighting for her. Those people put me in jail and are trying to turn her against me."

Was that how she saw it? No way should this woman be out on her own. She couldn't take care of herself, let alone Madeline. Was there someone he could call about this? He'd have to ask Rick or Allie. And as he stared at her, he considered her age. Madeline was five. This woman was at least fifty, unless something other than years had aged her.

"I'm afraid you'll have to talk to the judge about this. You don't want to scare Madeline, do you?"

"Why would her own mother frighten her? She wants to see me. I know she does."

He might have to call the sheriff. Agitation came off the woman in waves. Her pupils were dilated too, and he wondered if she was on any kind of medication for her condition. "Not today," he said in a soothing murmur. "She's eating right now. Talk to the judge and come back when he says it's okay."

Her shoulders slumped and she turned back toward her car. She rummaged inside a moment. "I have something for you." She emerged and wheeled toward him.

A blade glittered in her hand, and her face twisted in a snarl. She leaped toward him with the knife raised over her head. The moment seemed poised in time, almost surreal, as the woman's blond hair flew out behind her and the knife arced toward his chest.

Almost too late, he gathered his wits and dodged to the left. The blade barely missed his shoulder, and he felt the wind of its passing. He twisted back toward her and seized her wrist. She fought back ferociously, baring her teeth and trying to bite his arm. He blocked her and forced the knife from her fingers. The anger drained from her face, and she went limp. He eased her to the ground and yelled for Rick.

While the other man called for the sheriff, Clay watched her, but she never raised her head from her knees as she sat curled in a ball.

Surreptitiously, Eden glanced at the time, then watched Lacie pick up first one shoe then the other. The child had been patient when Eden stopped at another store to buy pajamas that covered her more than the lace teddy she'd been sleeping in. Lacie's eyes had brightened when they stepped into the small shoe store.

"Where do you usually buy shoes?" Eden asked.

Lacie stopped with her hand poised above a pink sneaker. "My foster mom brings them home from Walmart."

"You don't try them on?"

The little girl shook her head. "She measures me. She says she won't take me to the store because all the kids ask for things. That's not fair, though. I've never asked for anything."

Lacie had an odd kind of maturity. Even her syntax seemed advanced to Eden. "Let's try these on," she said, picking up a pair of pink Nikes.

Lacie's eyes widened. "They have the swoosh on them. They cost too much."

"I can afford them." She resolved not to submit the bill to the ranch. "Sit there."

As Lacie clambered onto a nearby bench, Eden's cell phone played "The Voice" by Celtic Woman, which meant the caller wasn't in her contacts list. She clawed the phone from her purse, but it had already rung four times by the time she swiped it on and saw *Unknown* on the screen. For a moment she was tempted not to answer, but what if the caller was Clay and he had his number screened?

She touched *Answer Call* on the screen and put it to her ear. "This is Eden." An electronic noise filled her head. "Hello?"

"I know what you did," the man whispered. The sound of the voice gave her chills. Then she realized there was an electronic device distorting it.

She clutched the phone to her ear and turned her back to Lacie. "Who is this?" she demanded.

He knew what she did. What did that mean?

The voice vibrated with rage. "You'll pay and pay dearly. I took Brianna once. This time will be worse. Much worse. You shouldn't have come."

The kidnapper. The blow nearly doubled her over. "Don't you touch my baby!" she said fiercely.

"How will you stop me?" he sneered.

"What do you want from me? I'll do whatever you say. Just leave Brianna alone."

"Anything, Eden? Really? Would you walk away from Bluebird Ranch right now? Leave Clay behind? I've seen the way you look at him. You still love him, don't you?"

She glanced quickly around the store. Was he here somewhere? Watching her? "No, of course not. I haven't thought of him in five years."

"I didn't think you'd have the nerve to come here with Clay. You're going to wish you hadn't."

The past week had allowed her to put that nightmare behind. "I'm just here for Brianna. Nothing else."

"Prove it. Leave today. Right now."

Everything in her rejected the demand. Not when she was so close. "I'm not abandoning Brianna."

"See? I knew you wouldn't do anything. Now you know too. And you'll have no one to blame but yourself."

She paced on the carpet in front of the shoes. "My daughter is here and I'm not leaving without her." No more trying to appease him. He wasn't going to intimidate her. "What do you want with me anyway?"

The man laughed. "Do you really know who you are, Eden? If you did, you wouldn't be so smug."

She shuddered at the venom in this voice, but no enemy came to mind. "I know who I am. Who are you?"

"Remember, whatever happens, you brought it on yourself."

The click in her ear told her he'd hung up. She put the phone back in her purse and composed herself. Pasting on a smile, she turned back to Lacie. "How do those shoes fit?" she asked in a fake bright tone.

"I think they are good." Lacie had slipped from the bench and was walking a few feet on the carpet. "Can I really have them?"

"Of course. Let me check the size." Eden knelt and pressed on the toes and arch, but her mind raced and her hands trembled. She needed to talk to Clay.

"Do they fit?" Lacie's voice was hopeful.

"They sure do. Let's go pay for them and get back to the ranch. We've already missed dinner."

"We can eat leftovers."

"I think we'll grab some chicken nuggets on the way home. How does that sound?"

The little girl's expression brightened. "We're eating out?"

"I think a little treat is in order," Eden said, forcing herself to be in the moment. The caller was a nightmare, but this time with Lacie was reality. After all, she might be her Brianna.

"I can't eat nuggets, though. I'm 'lergic to wheat. But can I have french fries? And chili?"

"Whatever you like." She paid for the shoes. "Want to wear them?" she asked Lacie.

The little girl nodded. Eden had her sit on a bench, and she slipped on socks, then the shoes. "Now for food," she said.

She ordered their meal to go from the café next door. While she was waiting, she and Lacie stepped next door and bought a large java from Desert Coffee, then returned to the café. When the order was ready, she took Lacie's hand and went out to the parking lot where she'd left the truck. The lot held only a small yellow car. She stared down the street but saw no big black truck.

Was she mistaken about where she'd parked? Maybe it was on the other side of the street? But no, she was sure it was right here.

Lacie ate a fry, then licked her fingers. "Where's our truck? It was parked there." She pointed to the spot where the car sat.

"I know."

Lacie was admiring her shoes. "Maybe Mr. Clay had to borrow it back."

"You might be right." Someone had stolen Clay's fancy truck. He'd be livid. Was it the man who had called her? A chill shuddered through her. He was here. Somewhere close. Watching, waiting to strike.

She pulled out her phone again, then realized she didn't know Clay's cell number. "Let's go see the sheriff while we wait," she said.

Lacie skipped along beside her as they crossed the deserted street to the sheriff's office. Only a receptionist was inside, and the woman told her she'd page the sheriff, who was out on a call. When

Eden stepped back outside, the yellow car was gone, and the truck was right where she'd left it. She saw a flash of yellow and turned to see the car driving away with a teenage boy behind the wheel. Had he taken the truck, or was it a coincidence that he'd parked there?

She took Lacie's hand and walked slowly across the street. When she opened it, a male cologne wafted to her nose, and it wasn't Clay's.

13

It was much later than Clay had expected by the time the tires of his black truck crunched up the gravel drive. He left the girls watching a video in the main house with Rick and Allie's daughter, Betsy, and went out to meet Eden. A fiery sunset backlit the hulking peaks of the surrounding hills, and he glanced around, an odd chill on his spine.

Both doors on the truck opened, and Lacie ran to him. "See my shoes," she said, lifting one for his inspection. "Miss Eden bought them for me. And we had supper out!" Without waiting for his response, she took off for the house. "I have to show the girls!"

He grinned and watched her leap the steps and rush inside. When he turned back toward Eden, he sensed a wariness in her stance. "Something wrong?"

"Someone took your truck for a joy ride," she said. She came around the front of the truck and stopped two feet from him.

"Who?"

"I don't know. I went to report it to the sheriff, and when I came back out, it was back in the space."

He frowned. "You sure you looked in the right space?"

Her face went white. "Yes, I know exactly where I parked it. The spot was empty." She hesitated. "Maybe it was just a kid out for a joy ride. There was a yellow car in the lot too, and it belonged to a teenager."

"Is that it? You seem more upset than the incident would warrant." Even in the gloom, he could see her tremble. He curled his fingers into his palm to keep from reaching out to pull her close.

"I . . . I got a phone call." Her voice shook.

He straightened. "Kent?"

"No, no." Her voice became stronger as anger replaced fear. "It was the kidnapper."

"How do you know it was him?"

"He said he took Brianna once and he could do it again." Her voice began to shake again. "I think he took the truck. To rattle me."

Clay's hands clenched into fists. "He's not getting his hands on her," he said fiercely. "Or you."

"We have to protect our girls, Clay." Her voice was panicked.

"We'll protect them all." He couldn't help but reach out and hold her when he heard her choked voice. She collapsed against his chest. It had been so long, yet she fit there as if she'd never left.

How had he let her go? Fighting for her had seemed pointless at the time. Each of them had been full of recriminations and hurt, and neither had been willing to bend and listen. God forgive him, he'd blamed her too. It shamed him to admit it to himself. He'd been consumed with the what-ifs. What if she hadn't gunned the engine? What if he'd delivered the ransom money alone? What if he'd never gone back to South America? The blame he'd felt toward her had radiated from him, and their fragile relationship had splintered.

"Why is he doing this?" she whispered against his chest. "He seems to be intent on revenge against me."

"Against you, not me?" They'd both assumed the kidnapping had something to do with him. The drug money stolen during the bust. A piece he'd written that had offended someone. Some picture he'd taken that had humiliated a subject.

Sniffling, she pulled away. "He said that whatever happened, I'd brought it on myself."

"Brought what on yourself?"

"I don't know. He asked me if I knew who I really was. Almost as if he knew I'd grown up in a foster home."

"You've offended someone pretty badly. Who could it be?"

"I can't think of anyone."

Her foster brother would know everything. "I bet I know."

"It's not Kent. He's an honorable man. He sent me off without any strings. Besides, someone else sent you the picture. Kent didn't know about us until you showed up."

"I'm not talking about Kent. I'm talking about Daniel. Think about it. He was hanging around the whole time we were married. Commiserating with you about how terrible it was when I flew off to Colombia for that mission. Right there to help when you walked out."

She held his gaze. "Daniel's like a brother. There was never anything between us. We grew up together, for Pete's sake! That feels dirty for you to even say it."

"You're not biologically related."

"He's my brother in every way that counts."

Maybe *she* felt that way, but that didn't mean the slimeball hadn't reveled in their breakup. Clay hadn't trusted him one bit. "How did he take your romance with Kent?"

The flicker of her lids showed her uncertainty. "He didn't say much about it."

"I'm not surprised. You never noticed the way Daniel looked at you. Like you belonged to him. He objected to Kent too, didn't he?"

"What if he did? He was just looking out for me."

"Have you heard from Daniel since you've been here?"

Her frown held confusion. "He called the night you showed up but didn't leave a message. H-He hadn't been accepting my calls."

"What does that tell you?"

"That he would have gotten over it, just like he got over me marrying you. I'm all he has. I should call him again."

"Again? You've tried calling him?"

She frowned and nodded. "Before you showed up and since we've been here. He still hasn't returned my calls, though, which isn't like him."

His insides felt like they were twisted ropes of hot lead. Forbidding her to call the jerk would escalate the tension, but he wanted to tell her to open her eyes. The guy was way too possessive.

"He had the nerve to call me up after you left me," he said, unable to hold it in any longer.

Backing away, she shook her head. "Daniel called you in South America?"

"Sure did. Right in the middle of an interview. Told me you were through with me. Like I didn't know that already."

She batted her eyes and chewed on her lip. "He never told me."

"Of course he didn't. He thought with me out of the picture, he could move in on you. Why didn't he? Or did he try and you were too naive to see it?"

"Well, he tried to kiss me once," she admitted, almost to herself. "I told him it was sweet of him to try to comfort me, but I didn't need that kind of attention. I just assumed . . ."

"You guessed wrong. I bet he's fuming since he found out you ran off with me."

"He'd understand I have to find Brianna." But her lids flickered and she glanced away.

At least she had a few doubts. Crossing his arms across his chest, he glared at her. "If he's so understanding, why hasn't he called?"

"I'm sure he has a good reason."

She was blind where that guy was concerned. "Dinner's getting cold," he said. She walked behind him into the house.

When they stepped into the living room, Paige came rushing toward them. "Mr. Clay, look what I found!" She thrust a yellowed yearbook at him and pointed to a picture of the Spanish Club. "Is that your dad? India says that boy's name is Clyde Larson."

He stared at the photo. "No, it's my cousin." The boy beside his cousin made him squint and take a closer look. *It couldn't be.* "Eden, look here." He thrust the book under her nose. "Who does that look like?"

She leaned over the page and gasped. "It's the kidnapper who drowned!"

"I thought so too. Says here his name is Jose Santiago."

"We need to let the detectives who worked on the case know," she said.

He nodded. "Santiago is a common name, though. It may tell them nothing." But that man's identity might be the clue they needed to figure this all out.

Eden gave the sheriff a statement about the missing truck. She and Clay also showed him the picture of Jose Santiago, and he promised to call the detective about it. He already knew about the snake and the note on the door.

After he left, Eden flounced in the bed. She held the cotton quilt under her nose to blot out the alluring scent of Clay on the other side of the bed. Those moments in Clay's arms when she got home tonight replayed over and over in her head. How natural it had felt. How wonderful. It had taken all her strength to make herself back away. Had he felt anything at all? She doubted it. All he wanted was to find their daughter.

Which was her goal as well. Her only goal.

Clay's accusations against Daniel made her squirm. He'd been like a brother since she was ten. There wasn't anything between them but friendship. Both foster kids, they'd clung together through their growing-up years in the same foster home.

But why hadn't he called? She should call him again. Before she realized it, her bare feet were on the cool hardwood floors. She eased open the bedroom door. Clay's even breathing didn't stop, so she pulled the door shut noiselessly behind her and padded down the hall. The glow of the nightlight lit the path. She hesitated long enough to peek in on the girls. All sleeping.

The clock on the stove glowed the numbers 10:10. After eleven back in Indiana. She went to the sofa and picked up the phone. Sinking onto the cushion, she listened to the call go through. His phone rang five times, and she was trying to decide whether to leave a message or hang up when he finally answered.

"Hello, Eden."

His voice was odd. Cold, detached. Normally, he was happy to hear from her. This man seemed a stranger, not her best friend. "How did you know it was me?"

"I heard you went to Bluebird Ranch. That's what came up on the caller ID."

"Daniel? You sound—odd. Is something wrong?"

"What could be wrong?" Still that remoteness.

"You haven't called."

"You run off with a husband who deserted you and leave me without a word." The words ran together, faster and faster. "I finally got it, Eden. I might be stupid but I finally got it."

She paced in front of the sofa. "What are you talking about?"

"Good old Daniel was always there to pick up the pieces, wasn't he? Well, I'm through being your whipping boy." Passion finally sparked his voice. He was nearly shouting by the time he finished.

"You were never my whipping boy. You're my best friend."

"I showed you in so many ways I wanted to be more than that, Eden. When you decided to marry Kent, I thought I could deal with it. I'd start easing away so I didn't humiliate myself any more than I already had."

To her horror, she realized he was crying. Her throat tightened, and she wanted to weep with him. "I never knew, Daniel. Really. I love you like a brother."

"Brother! I don't want to be your brother. Lover, husband.

That's my role. But you never saw it. You've kicked me for the last time, Eden Davidson."

"Larson," she whispered. "My divorce from Clay was never finalized." Why hadn't she understood all this sooner?

"So I heard. How do you think I felt—to find out from rumors around town? Couldn't you at least have bothered to call me yourself? If I'm your best friend and all."

"I . . . I . . ." She gulped back the tears. "You're right. I should have. Clay told me Brianna was still alive, and everything else just flew from my mind." The strength ran out of her legs, and she sank onto the ground. What had she done to Daniel?

Silence echoed on the other end of the connection. "Brianna? I hadn't heard that one. What kind of trick is he pulling on you now?"

"No trick. She's here. We'll figure it out in just a few more days."

"Then what?" His voice softened, grew lower.

Was he hoping . . . ? Surely not. "Then we try to rebuild our lives. To help her get over whatever has happened to her."

"You're not coming home?" His voice was sharp again.

"Not now. Brianna is all that matters." The reminder of her priorities strengthened her. She rose and leaned against the wall, wrapping the cord around her arm.

"I see. Of course. I was never important. I keep trying to find some way around that truth."

The silence on the other end was so long she thought he'd hung up on her. "Daniel?"

"I'm here." He sighed, a long, drawn-out sound. "I went by your apartment. Doesn't look like you forwarded your mail. Your box was full so I took it inside."

"Thanks." Where was this going?

"There was a letter from the court. I opened it."

"You opened my mail?"

"It looked important."

She couldn't be angry. She'd always shared everything with Daniel. "What was it?"

"Your birth mother is trying to find you."

Of all the things she might have guessed, the thought wouldn't have crossed her mind. "What does the letter say?"

"Just what I told you."

"My birth mom." She couldn't take it in. "What if I don't want to see her?"

"Nothing will proceed unless you agree. I tried to call them to get more details, but the receptionist said you'd have to call yourself. I'll text you the phone number."

Eden couldn't think past the pain squeezing her chest. After all these years, her mother was trying to find her. Why? And did she even want to see the woman after all these years? What good would it do? But even as she tried to talk herself out of it, the desire to ask her mother why she'd been abandoned welled up.

"Send me the number," she said.

"I said I would. Then we're square. Good-bye, Eden. Don't call me again."

The connection broke in her ear. She stared at the phone stupidly. Her best friend was gone. Maybe it was for the best. She'd been so blind. What else was she wrong about? Everything?

14

The moon spilled in through the window as Eden tiptoed back into the bedroom. Her nose was still clogged with tears. As she reached her side of the mattress, the moon went behind a cloud and plunged the room into darkness. Feeling her way, she pulled back the sheet and quilt.

Clay's side of the bed was much too quiet when she eased between the sheets. The springs squeaked and she winced. She was cold, so cold. Mostly because she knew what she was going to do. Tomorrow she would call the office and say she wanted to see her mother. Then what? Did she expect her mother to rush to her with open arms? To ask for forgiveness? And could Eden even give it if her mother asked?

Shivering, she pulled the sheet up to her chin. It was hot outside, but the air-conditioning was too cold. Or else it was stress. Clay's warmth radiated out from him, and remembering how safe she'd felt in his arms earlier, she wished she could curl up against his back.

Clay's deep voice came out of the darkness. "Is your *brother* okay?" His voice was derisive. He rolled in the bed, and the springs protested.

"I . . . I don't know what to think," she said. To her horror, her voice shook. He wouldn't understand her quandary. He'd go see Eden's mom, tell her she was worthless, then never see her again. Good riddance. Eden should feel that way too, but she didn't.

"Hey, what's the matter?" He scooted closer, and his arm came around her. His breath stirred her hair. "Did you have to cover yourself from head to toe?" he asked, a smile in his voice. He didn't wait for an answer. "Tell me what's upset you."

The musky scent of his skin left her motionless when she should have moved away. His warmth seeped into her. He pulled her closer and she didn't protest, though every nerve shouted the danger to her emotions. "I don't want to talk about it."

His fingers tangled in her hair, and he pulled her so close there was no room down the full length of her body. *Danger!*

"It's dark. You can tell me your secrets and I can't see your face." His lips brushed her cheek.

The desire to talk to him swept over her. What could it hurt to unburden her soul? There'd been so few times in her life that she could tell anyone how she felt. Even when they were together before, she was always sure he'd married her because she was pregnant.

What was different now? She couldn't define the difference, but she knew it was there. There was a special bond now that had never existed before. The wariness that had held them apart was gone.

She turned her face against his neck and inhaled. "My mother wants to see me."

His hand smoothed her hair. "So tell her to come down. There's room here in the bunkhouse." His warm chuckle came from the darkness. "I'd like to see your foster mom sharing a bathroom with the kids. She'll be in there and one of them will come flying in yelling at her to get out of the way."

She should laugh, but nothing felt funny. "You don't understand. My real mother."

His arm seemed heavier across her midsection. His muscles hardened too. His hand quit petting her hair. "After all these years?"

She nodded her head, though she knew he couldn't see it. Her throat thickened. She hated to cry. Strength, not weakness, was admirable. "I want to ask her why she abandoned me. But I don't want to face that rejection all over again."

His lips brushed her brow in the darkness. "I'm sorry, sweetheart." His breath stirred her hair, then his lips trailed down the side of her face. "You don't have to see her if you don't want to."

She held her breath and nearly turned her head to press her lips against his. What was she thinking? This was much too dangerous. But she was too languorous to move, her muscles too heavy with desire. They'd always had this chemistry between them. She never should have agreed to this charade. But all her internal protests weren't enough to make her move.

She pulled away a fraction. "I think I want to see her. Is that crazy? She doesn't love me, but I still love her. She entertained men, and those were awful nights. But I also remember the evenings we watched TV and ate pizza together."

"It's perfectly understandable."

"Is it?" she whispered. "To love someone who doesn't love you back?"

"Maybe she realizes her error. She might have found God too."

Was that possible? She'd prayed for her mother. Somehow it made the pain of rejection better. Clay touched her cheek and turned her face toward him. She was helpless to resist him.

"I've missed you, Eden. So much."

His lips trailed across her face to her lips. She couldn't help the way her arms came up and pulled him closer. Why not? They were married. It was perfectly natural. But even as the thought crossed her mind, she heard a tap at the door.

"Miss Eden?" Madeline's voice. "Paige wet the bed and it got on my nightgown."

Clay groaned and his arm fell away. "I thought five was too old to be wetting the bed."

"They're still babies." She felt cold without his arms around her. "I'll be right there," she called, swinging her legs out of bed. It was just as well. Making love to him would have led to endless complications when the time came for their lives to separate.

The bedding had been changed and the girls settled. Clay still detected the faint stench of urine, but the apple candle Eden lit was quickly chasing the odor from the room. The candle's flickering light illuminated five eager faces turned toward where they sat on the edge of the bed with Katie and Paige.

"Sing to us," Madeline demanded. "Do you know 'Amazing Grace'?"

Clay didn't want to look at Eden's expression, but he had to. He'd overheard her singing in the shower a time or two, but she never sang when she thought someone was listening. She was biting her lip as she tucked the blanket under Katie's chin. The air conditioner hummed.

"I know the song," Eden said. "But you need to go to sleep."

"I have to hear it," Madeline insisted. "I tried to play it on the CD tonight, but it's scratched." The other girls chimed in with their pleas as well.

Clay saw Eden physically wilt at the plaintive tones in the girls' voices. "I'll sing with you," he said.

"You can sing it by yourself," she said.

"He can't sing," Lacie said, over in the next bed. "I heard him in the barn today. He sounded like the cow."

Clay grinned. "Just for that, you might have to be tickled." He wiggled his fingers at her, and she squealed and huddled under the covers. He looked at Eden. "I don't think you can get out of it."

She sighed and stared at Madeline's determined face. "Then you have to promise to go to sleep. Mr. Clay and I are tired. It's nearly eleven."

"We will," the girls said in a chorus.

Tension radiated from Eden's slim shoulders, clad in pale blue cotton. He could still feel the texture of her pajamas under his palm from earlier. Probably just as well they were interrupted. She had no intention of working on the marriage. Any entanglement would make the ultimate breakup even more painful. He would not think about how right she had felt in his arms.

"You start," he said. "I'll chime in." He waggled his brows at Paige, who giggled and pulled the sheet up to her chin, then sneezed.

"'Amazing grace, how sweet the sound.'" Eden's voice was a little choked but sweet and even.

"'That saved a wretch like me.'" His raspy voice blended with hers.

"'I once was lost but now am found. Was blind but now I see.'" His eyes stung when he saw the way the girls listened. Did they feel lost as they went from foster home to foster home? Only a couple of them had stayed in the same place. The hunger in their eyes made him want to gather every one of them in his lap and never let go.

And Eden. She'd had the same experience they had. He saw the sheen of her eyes and the way she gulped down her emotion. What would have happened to them all but for God's grace? His gaze met Eden's across the bed as the song ended. The pathos in her eyes told him she saw it too. The hunger for love in these little girls.

"Time for sleep, kiddos," he said. He and Eden made the rounds, brushing kisses across every cheek. "Love you, honey," he told each little girl. The starved way they wrapped their arms around his neck brought a lump to his throat. Katie didn't want to let loose of Eden, and he watched her hold the child close.

He followed Eden back to the living room and dropped onto the sofa. "That was hard," he said. "They need love so badly. Every one of them."

Her eyes were moist when she turned to stare at him. "You love kids so much. Why didn't you just sign the divorce papers and remarry? You could have had two or three more by now."

"God hates divorce. So do I." His voice shook, and he tugged his boots off. There were so many things they'd never told each other about their past and how those things had shaped the person they'd become. "My parents divorced when I was seventeen," he said, wincing when his voice showed his pain. "I always thought it was my fault. They were always arguing about something, and usually it involved me.

Whether I would be allowed to stay out late the night of homecoming. Whether I should have a job. I realize now I was just a convenient excuse to show their dislike for each other."

He glanced up to see sympathy in her eyes. Was there any hope of tearing down the walls between them? He was willing to try.

She sat beside him on the sofa. "You're worried about Brianna and how growing up with us divorced would affect her."

"Aren't you?"

"Of course. She's been in a foster home, without the security and love of her own parents. We don't even know what kind of circumstances Brianna has been in, but looking at the girls' reports, not one has been in a place I'd want our daughter to experience."

He tried to read her expression, but she kept her gaze on the clasped hands in her lap. "Do you still have any hope left, Eden? Hope for that perfect little family we dreamed about once?"

She raised her eyes to his. "Sometimes. But I'm afraid, Clay."

His pulse leapt at her admission. "You think I'm not? I failed you and Brianna once. I want to be here for you both and never let you down again."

Something flickered in her eyes. He wanted to believe it was the beginning of a bit of trust and hope, but before he could nail it down, one of the girls let out a heart-stopping scream.

"Get away, get away!" the child's voice shrieked.

Clay leaped from the sofa and rushed for the bedroom. Eden was right behind him. They spent the next hour soothing Katie from her nightmare, but watching Eden's face, he wondered if she was thinking about what he'd said.

15

EDEN'S EYES WERE BLEARY FROM LACK OF SLEEP. SHE'D TOSSED AND TURNED MUCH OF THE night with the words of the old hymn echoing in her brain one minute and the thought of what she would say to her mother the next. She sat sipping her coffee with Allie and Della at the kitchen table while Rita bustled around clearing away the breakfast dishes. Beyond the window, Clay and the children were out with Rick and Zeke, headed to the corral for another riding lesson.

"I needed coffee this morning," Della said, taking another swig. "One of the girls was throwing up all night." She nibbled on a piece of toast.

"Eden, you're pensive," Allie said, dumping more Cheerios in Matthew's bowl.

Eden felt she didn't know Allie well enough to bare her soul about her mother. Or God. "Paige wet the bed last night. And Katie had a nightmare. By the time we got the bedding changed and all of them settled down again, it was one."

Allie winced. "That was one of our fears when we agreed to take kids this young. We had plastic mattress covers put on all the beds."

"Good decision. She soaked everything. I'll bring the laundry over after a while."

"Tepin will get it," Rita said. "Won't you, Tepin?" she asked the quiet worker who was washing the dishes.

Tepin nodded. "When breakfast is over, I get it."

"I hate to cause you more work," Eden said.

"It is my job," the woman said.

"I want to watch Barney," Matthew demanded. He banged his spoon onto the table and began to slide down from the chair.

"I'll turn on the video," Rita said. "Madeline will be sorry she missed it. And I made her some peanut butter fudge. I was hoping she'd hang around this morning."

"She's glued to Clay," Eden said. "All five girls think he's Superman."

Rita smiled. "I'm making him the hero of my novel. He's enough to make all my readers swoon."

The other woman's focus on her novel was cute. Eden took another sip of her coffee. "The girls have all had such a hard life. It's heartbreaking."

Allie's smile faded. "That was the hardest thing to get used to while running this camp. We love them for a little while and try to make as much difference as we can. Eventually we have to let them go, though. The only way I can get through it is to put them in God's hands."

"Why would he let them go through something so awful?" Eden asked. "I've never figured that out."

Allie's forehead wrinkled. "Life is hard, Eden. For everyone. We all have different challenges to face. All those hardships strengthen our faith and form us, though. I suspect God has great tasks in mind for some of these children. They'll need great grace to accomplish those tasks, so great trials are needed."

Eden frowned. "You believe trials change us?"

"Don't you? Have you ever had a trial that didn't?"

When it was put that way, Eden supposed she hadn't. "Some changes aren't always for the better."

Allie shrugged, then stood and picked up Matthew's bowl. "Only if we allow ourselves to be bitter and resentful over our lot in life. Sometimes we have to ask how we can allow this to make us a better person. There's always a choice in how we react."

Della sat listening quietly. "Was that you I heard singing late last night? I thought it was 'Amazing Grace.'"

Eden smiled. "Madeline insisted. It's her favorite song and she claimed she couldn't sleep without it."

"Sounded to me like you knew the song pretty well."

"I do." Something squeezed in Eden's chest. She stood and walked to the door. "You need me for anything, Allie? I have to make a call."

Allie shook her head. "I'm going to check on Matthew, then take Betsy over to play with Gracie's daughter, Hope."

Rita came back into the kitchen and called after Tepin, who had slipped out the back door. "Bring those soiled linens and don't dawdle. I'm doing laundry today."

Eden grabbed the portable phone from the wall and took it outside, where she settled onto the porch step. The breeze brought the scent of the desert to her nose. Some sweet smell from the wildflowers blooming on the hillside. The purple and yellow blooms fortified her for what lay ahead. She dug the number Daniel had given her out of her pocket and punched it into the phone. Her gut clenched as it began to ring on the other end. The pen in her fingers slipped to the ground and she picked it up.

The phone was answered by a woman with a gravelly voice that made Eden assume she was at least fifty. Or a smoker. Eden cleared her throat. "This is Eden . . . um . . ." Should she say Larson or Davidson? "Davidson," she said. "Eden Davidson. Someone from your office sent me a letter to tell me that my birth mother is asking for contact with me."

"Ah yes, Ms. Davidson. Your foster brother said you weren't interested. If you'll give me your social security number, I'll log in your refusal."

"Actually, I'd like to contact my birth mother."

There was a pause on the other end. The gruff voice softened. "I'm sure she'll be happy. She's been hounding my office for several days. Should I give her your number?"

"Could you give me her number? I'd like to be the one in control of when we talk. I want to make sure I'm alone."

"Of course." The woman rattled off the phone number. "Would you repeat it, please?"

Eden read the number back to her. "Where is the 214 area code?"

"That's right here in Dallas. I have her address as well if you'd like that."

"I would." It would take Eden some time to decide how she wanted her first contact with her mother to go. When she finished writing down the address, she read it back to the clerk as well. "Thank you for your time." She hung up and stared at the slip of paper. Why not call right now?

But she couldn't force herself to punch in the number. In her head, she heard her mother's voice. "*You're going to look ugly when your father comes by.*"

Would her mother have changed? She'd always had beautiful skin. Her hair was red-blond. Men turned to look when she walked by. She'd be much older now.

Eden was afraid. That's what kept her hands in her lap. What if her mother wanted to see her but the mean-spirited comments continued? What possible reason could she have to be looking after all this time?

The riding lesson was over, and Clay turned the girls over to the Rodriguez couple, who would be with them for about an hour as all the children did crafts together. Eden had never shown up, so he went in search of her. When he didn't find her in the bunkhouse, he started for the back door of the ranch house. As he neared, he saw her bright-blue blouse and walked toward her.

She sat on the porch step with her phone in one hand and a piece of paper in the other. Her hair was curled and perfect. She wore immaculate navy slacks and pumps. He'd been sure that she would drop that mask of perfection within a day of hitting the ranch. To find she still clung to her city-girl image confused him. Was there a real person under that smooth exterior? He'd thought so last night.

His boots crunched on a rock, and she looked up. Her eyes were swollen, as though she'd been crying. "You okay?" he asked. "What did your mother say?"

"I haven't been able to bring myself to call her." Her eyes darkened, and her voice trembled. "So many bad memories."

"Yesterday you remembered good ones too," he reminded her.

"In the night it seemed possible that she loved me. Missed me. In the daylight, it seems more likely she wants to yell at me more. Maybe she thinks I ruined her life."

"How could you ruin her life? You were a kid." He dropped beside her on the stoop.

She hunched her shoulders and clasped her knees. "I suppose it doesn't make sense. But nothing about this makes sense. Why would she even want to contact me after all these years?"

"Want me to call her?" The words were out before he stopped to think.

Her head came up to reveal eyes full of hope. "You'd do that? I don't know what to say."

"Give me the phone."

She put the phone into his outstretched hand. "Want me to read you the number?" He nodded, and she read the number slowly.

He listened to the ring on the other end and tried to think how to start the conversation. How old would she be? At least fifty, since Eden was thirty. Unless she'd had Eden as a teenager. Definitely a possibility based on what he'd heard about her.

After five rings, the call was picked up. "Hello." The voice on the other end was male. Pleasant enough, though. Sounded like a man in his fifties or sixties.

"My name is Clay Larson. Eden Davidson is my wife." It felt strange to say the word *wife* when they'd been apart so long. He glanced at the paper Eden held. "Does Nancy Santiago live there?" *Santiago?* He glanced at Eden and wondered if she'd made the connection in her own mind. It was a common name, but the kidnapper's name had been Santiago. Coincidence?

"Oh yes, yes, she does. She has been hoping for this call." The voice grew muffled. "Nancy, Eden's husband is on the phone."

Chills raced up his spine at the excitement in the man's voice. The woman made a smothered exclamation he couldn't make out, but it was clear she'd been hopeful to hear from her daughter. Maybe this wouldn't be a bad thing for Eden. He prayed her mother had changed, that this would bring healing and a new perspective to her.

"Hello?" The woman's voice was eager, almost girlish.

If he didn't know better, he'd think she was as young as Eden. "Hello, Mrs. Santiago. I'm Clay Larson, Eden's husband. She was given this number and told you were looking for her."

"Oh, I have been. For several years now. I'm so glad you called. Can I talk to her?"

He glanced at Eden and mouthed, "She wants to talk to you." When Eden shook her head violently, he spoke back into the phone. "I'm afraid that won't be possible right now. Is there a reason you're looking for her?"

"I'd think it was obvious." The animation was gone from the woman's voice. "She's my daughter. I . . . I didn't do right by her. I'd like to see if she needs anything. Tell her I'm sorry."

Praise God. "That's really good of you, ma'am."

"Can I see her? Maybe it would be better to say everything in person. I wasn't a good mother, Mr. Larson." Her voice broke.

"Call me Clay. And we all make mistakes." He saw Eden tense and look at him with a question in her eyes.

"I hope she can forgive me," the woman said, her voice trailing off.

"I think she will," he said. Eden was going to kill him, but he gripped the phone and made a decision. "Where could we meet?"

Eden shook her head but he ignored her. "We're in Texas too. How about Alpine?"

"That's about a day's drive." Nancy's voice was eager. "We could meet Saturday for dinner."

"That will be fine. I'll research where we might eat and call you back."

"I'll be waiting. Call my cell phone, because we might be on the road. I'll pack immediately."

She gave him her number, and he jotted it down, then hung up. Eden's fists were clenched when he looked at her. "We're meeting her Saturday in Alpine."

"I'm not ready, Clay." Her eyes flashed sparks. "Call her back."

"Some things you just need to face head-on. And this is one of those. I'll go with you."

"You won't leave me alone with her?"

He put his arm around her and she rested her head on his shoulder. "Not for a minute." He pressed his lips against her hair.

"Did she sound . . . eager? What did you think of her?"

"She sounded younger than I expected. How old is she?"

"Forty-nine, I think. She had me at nineteen."

"She seemed contrite over how she'd treated you. I think it will go well, honey. We'll face it together."

It might be the only thing she'd let him do for her.

After dinner, Eden looked at five eager faces, lips stained red from the Popsicles they were finishing. They had plenty of time before bed. "Let's build a tent house," she said.

"You mean we're going camping?" Katie asked, glancing at the darkening sky through the window.

"Sort of. We'll get blankets and build rooms out of them. Each tent can be for different things. You can make up what they're for."

"I want the red blanket!" Lacie said. She ran for the bedroom and returned dragging the red fuzzy blanket from her bed. "My room is for the stuffed animals to live in."

"I want to play," Madeline shouted.

"Hang on, let me get out the blankets," Eden said. She found a stack of linens in the hall closet and carried them to the living room.

In minutes every chair and sofa was draped with blankets, and the sound of giggles made her smile across the room at Clay.

"My room is for princesses," Madeline announced. "I must find a dress for the ball. Do you have one I can borrow?" she asked Eden. "Your pink nightgown would be lovely."

Eden smiled at her serious expression. "It's in my top drawer," she said. Madeline raced off to get her costume. "What's your room going to be for?" Eden asked Katie.

"For Olympic gymnasts. Would you like to see my floor show?" Katie pirouetted across the room, then did a cartwheel and came to a wobbly stop with her arms up.

"Good job!" Clay said. He lifted her to his shoulders and paraded through the room to her tent. "The winner gets to go in first." He set her in front of the opening to her tent room.

Grinning from ear to ear, Katie bowed grandly. "Thank you. I will do another show soon." She dropped to her hands and knees and disappeared inside.

"My room is a hospital," Paige said. "It's for patients with allergies.

No dust mites are allowed inside. I'm the nurse. I think I should take your temperature," she told Clay. "I need a thermometer."

"Use this," he said, offering her a Popsicle stick.

He opened his mouth and she stuck it in. A moment later she pulled it out. "Oh my, you have a temperature. We must put you to bed. Okay?"

"Whatever you say, my nurse." He winked at Eden, then crawled into Paige's tent.

Eden stared after them. Clay's and Paige's eyes looked so much alike, and Paige had that caregiving spirit she was seeing more and more in her husband.

Madeline returned with Eden's pink nightgown trailing around her bare feet. She had stuck bobby pins in her hair in an attempt to get her fine locks into an upsweep. Dark blue eye shadow made her eyes look bruised, but her dimples were flashing.

It was all Eden could do to keep from laughing. "You look lovely, Your Highness," she said. Madeline loved girlie things, just like Eden did.

Oh, which girl was theirs? It was so hard to know. She turned to India. "And what will we do in your room?"

"My room is a Sunday school," India said. "I'm going to teach my dolls about Jesus. Then we can all pray for God to send me a new mommy and daddy."

Eden's eyes filled. The faith of little children put her to shame. She hadn't even asked God what part she ought to play in this situation. All she'd done was follow Clay's lead and come here to find her daughter. What did God expect now that she realized she was still married to Clay?

16

Exhausted from the busy day, Eden sat on the porch of the bunkhouse and watched the storm approach. The night air held a hint of moisture. Lightning flickered off to the west, illuminating the jagged mountain peaks and leaving the scent of ozone in the wind. Storms exhilarated her. She felt alive with the thunder shaking the house and the flashes of lightning burning into her retinas. She was growing fond of this place of extremes.

The screen door slammed and Clay stepped out to join her on the porch. "Della and Zeke are helping with the games, then I told the girls to pick up their blankets and toys." He dropped into the rocker beside hers. "Storm's coming."

Another flash of lightning arced from the clouds to a tree atop a nearby peak. "I'd say it's here."

He straightened and peered up at the display that was nearly overhead. "We should go in. I don't want you struck."

"I love to watch it. We're safe here."

"I don't think so," he said, flinching when a bolt sizzled nearby. "Really, let's go in. It's bathtime anyway."

"In a few minutes." She lifted her face to the cooling breeze. "Thanks for calling my mother today." The generosity of his action still touched her. He'd seen her problem and had moved to help. She stared into the darkness. "I dread Saturday, though."

"I'll be with you. She sounded very nice, Eden. I'm not just saying that."

"Was that her husband who answered the phone?" It was too much to hope that the man was her father. She didn't even remember his name anymore, if she'd ever known it.

"I assume so. Seemed like a stand-up guy. He was as excited as she was."

Excited. Could they really want to see her that badly?

"What do you remember about your father?"

She glanced at him. Was he a mind reader too? "Not much. He came to see me about three or four times a year. They always fought, and he would slam out of the house without even telling me good-bye. I'm not sure why he ever bothered to come. He hardly noticed me."

Another light caught her eye. A car came up the drive, then stopped in front of the ranch house. A man and woman got out and approached the front door. The door to the house opened, and light framed Allie's figure. She gestured toward the bunkhouse. The man and woman turned to look, then started toward them.

"Looks like they're coming back here." Clay stood and stretched. "They'd better hurry. The rain is about to let loose any second."

He'd barely gotten the words out before the clouds opened up. The deluge was worthy of Noah's flood. Eden had never seen rain fall so hard and fast. The couple raced for the steps and arrived gasping and soaking wet.

"Let me get some towels," Eden said.

A basket of towels was just inside the door where she'd left them after dinner. She reached inside the screen door and snagged two. While the couple dried off, she took their measure. The woman had short dark hair in a stylishly layered cut. Large dark eyes. Dressed in Ann Taylor and a pair of red leather shoes. The man wore a navy suit and a crisp white shirt. His blond hair was plastered to his head. Both of them appeared to be in their late twenties.

The man handed the towel back to her. "Much obliged." He straightened his jacket and turned a smile on them. "I'm Tyler Rivers. This is my wife, Christine. We're here to see Paige."

"We're her parents."

"Her parents." It was clear from Christine's tone that she was laying claim to the little girl. And that she loved her.

"The camp prefers to let the girls adjust before visits with their foster parents," Clay put in. "We were told they needed to be here two weeks before there was a visit."

Tyler nodded. "Of course. But it's her birthday tomorrow, and we brought her a gift. Mr. Bailey said it would be all right to see her for a few minutes and give her the present. I have to fly out of town on business tomorrow, and we really wanted her to have her gift."

"If Rick said it was okay, then we're fine with it. Come inside." Clay held open the door for them.

The wave of protectiveness rising in Eden's chest alarmed her. These two were no threat. Was it because she didn't want any of the girls to be attached to someone other than herself? How totally selfish. If she had her way, none of the children would have to go through the abandonment issues she'd experienced. Of course she wanted Paige to be loved. She wanted them all to be cherished.

In the living room, the young girls looked up from their game of Chutes and Ladders. Zeke and Della had brought over their girls too, and there were several different games in progress. Della got up when the couple entered the room and lifted a brow in Eden's direction.

"Mommy!" Paige screamed. She leaped up and ran to throw her arms around Christine.

"Paige's foster parents," Eden said to Della and Zeke.

The woman knelt and picked her up. "I've missed you, honey. Are you having a good time?"

Paige nodded. "I peed the bed last night," she said with great solemnity.

"Oh dear."

"She peed on me!" India said, her voice indignant. "But she couldn't help it, I guess."

Christine's lips twitched. "I can see that would be upsetting," she said.

"How about a kiss for your daddy?" Tyler asked. When Paige reached for him, he took her into his arms and she kissed him with real affection.

Eden glanced at Clay and saw the same raw jealousy in his eyes that she felt. What if Paige was Brianna? Paige had been left by two men in a Walmart. It would rip this family apart to find out she didn't belong to them.

The living room still held the aroma of popped corn. Clay picked up the litter of Popsicle sticks and corn kernels.

"We can't let Paige's birthday go unnoticed tomorrow."

"What do you have in mind?"

Her dimples flashed. "Cupcakes. I'll bake them and you can ice them."

"I'm game if you are." Anything to keep that delight in her face.

He followed her to the kitchen, where she rummaged through the cupboards and found cake mix, a cupcake pan, and liners. Within minutes the cupcakes were in the oven and he put some decaf on to brew.

"I want to show you something," she said, exiting the room.

When she returned a few moments later, she held a tattered photo album. She sat at the table and he pulled out a chair and sat beside her. Even before she opened it, he knew it was pictures of Brianna. He'd probably seen them and, most likely, had copies himself. But when she flipped it open, he was faced with one he didn't remember. In the photo Brianna was peering over the top of his shoulder. She wore a pink ribbon in her thick blond hair.

"That was her first smile," Eden said. "Remember?"

He ran his fingers over the slick surface of the protective sheet. "I didn't see it. She wasn't facing me."

She pointed to Brianna's left cheek. "This is what I wanted to show you. See that dimple? Madeline has dimples."

"Do babies always keep their dimples?"

Her brow furrowed. "I don't know."

The next picture was one with Brianna and Eden. She wore the pendant he'd been carrying around in his pocket, and he put his fingers around it. Maybe now was the time to ask her to wear it again. To consider building their family unit new and fresh.

The phone rang, and she jumped to grab it. "This is Eden." Her smile faded and her fingers went white. "Who is this?"

He leaped up and grabbed the phone. "Who is this?"

An electronic hissing filled his ear, then the dial tone came on. He replaced the phone onto the hook. "Who was it?"

Her laugh was nervous. "I'm probably just skittish. It was likely a wrong number. No one answered."

But the fear in her eyes told him she didn't believe that. And he didn't either.

In the morning Eden's vapors of the night before vanished with the scent of fresh coffee. She poured a cup, then eyed the components of her big project. The ingredients were assembled on the counter. She ticked them off her list: asparagus, chicken, curry powder, snow peas, coconut milk, carrots, onions, jasmine rice. This couldn't be too hard, could it? India and Madeline had begged to help—in fact, all five girls had wanted to help—so Eden compromised by allowing two to help with this trial recipe. The other three would get to help her bake cookies this afternoon.

She studied the recipe. What could she have the girls do that didn't involve a knife? "I need the water and rice measured," she said.

"Me, me!" India shouted, jumping up and down in her chair at the table.

"No, me!" Madeline said, shoving India off the chair.

The little girl hit the black-and-white tile floor but didn't cry. Madeline ran to Eden and snatched the plastic measuring cup from her hand before Eden could reprimand her.

Eden frowned at Madeline. "India gets to measure the rice because you pushed her, Madeline."

The little blonde's face puckered. "But I want to help," she wailed. "She always gets to do things instead of me."

"You can measure the water."

"That's just water." She folded her arms across her chest, and her lip stuck out. "You like India better than me."

"That's not true. I love you both equally. But you can't shove, honey." She put a bowl in front of India. "Measure out two cups of rice," she said. She helped the little girl hold the bag.

"Your turn, Madeline," she said, heading toward the faucet.

"I'm not going to help. She can do it." Madeline slid off the chair and rushed for the back door. Her tear-filled eyes glared at Eden before she focused on the door and began to yank on the knob.

Eden paused. Her first real challenge of discipline. What did she do? "Stop right there, Madeline," she said. She grabbed the little girl's arm and marched her back to the table. Madeline resisted, but Eden lifted her onto the chair. "Time-out. You sit there for five minutes." She walked back to the stove and set the timer. "When this timer goes off, you can get down."

"You're mean," Madeline said, her voice hiccupping in sobs. "I'm going to tell Mr. Clay."

"How do you think Mr. Clay will like the way you're acting?" Eden turned back in time to prevent India from spilling the rest of the rice onto the floor. She was beginning to wish she'd done this job by herself.

Clay stepped into the kitchen from the front room. "Did I hear my name?"

Madeline burst into noisy sobs. "She spanked me," she wailed.

Clay's gaze shot to Eden, and she shook her head. He walked to the table. "I don't think so, Madeline. Did you disobey Miss Eden?"

The little girl buried her face in her hands and sobbed. "You like India better too."

"What's this all about?" Clay asked.

"She knocked India off the chair in a dispute over who got to measure the rice. So I gave her a time-out."

He pulled out a chair beside Madeline. "You don't think you deserve a time-out for shoving India?"

Madeline raised her head. "I wanted to help." She swiped the back of her hand across her face.

"Did Miss Eden spank you? This is your chance to tell me the truth, Madeline. What did we learn in devotions the other night about lying?"

"That lying is as bad as murder," she whispered, staring at her hands.

"So what do you want to tell me?"

Madeline shot Eden a resentful glare. "She *wanted* to spank me."

Eden bit her lip to keep from smiling. Though the situation wasn't really funny, Madeline was determined not to take any blame. The situation was eye-opening. So this was what parenting was all about. It would have been easier to give in, to let her get by with rudeness and talking back. But it wouldn't have taught her anything.

"But Miss Eden didn't, did she?" Clay's voice was gentle.

Madeline looked at the table and not at Clay. "No."

"I'm proud of you for telling the truth. But you need to apologize to Miss Eden for lying about her. And you need to tell India you're sorry you shoved her."

"I won't!" The little girl folded her arms across her chest.

Eden marveled at how well Clay was handling this. As if he'd dealt with five-year-old girls every day. Where did he get that calm firmness? She wanted to tell him not to press Madeline for an apology, but it wasn't the right thing to do. No child should talk back the way she'd done. Just because she was pained that the children had to be in foster care didn't relieve her of the duty to make sure the girls knew right from wrong.

"Then you'll have to go to your room and stay there all morning."

"What about lunch?"

"You can have it when you come out. That is, when you're ready to say you're sorry."

"I'm not ever saying sorry. I'm always the one who has to say sorry, even when it's not my fault!" Madeline's sobs grew wilder.

Eden took a step toward the child, but Clay held up a warning hand and shook his head. She couldn't help a flare of resentment even though she knew her compassion wasn't appropriate right now. How did he know when to be firm and when to back down? She could see where couples might have arguments over discipline, because she was ready to interfere. Madeline's sobs broke her heart. The little girl had been through so much.

She remembered feeling alone and unloved in foster care herself. And maybe just a bit of those feelings were what had catapulted her into full-blown anger with God when Brianna was taken. She thought she deserved better from him, to make up for the things she'd endured. But God hadn't given her any special favors. Just as Clay wasn't giving Madeline a license to disobey.

Eden gave a shake of her head. "No," she muttered.

Clay glanced up, a question in his eyes.

"Nothing," she said. "Just thinking aloud." She stepped to the table and knelt by the little girl. “It’s always easier just to get punishment over with, honey. Can’t you tell India you’re sorry? You could have hurt her.”

Madeline’s lip came out farther. “I’m sorry, India,” she muttered. She glared at Eden. “But I’m not saying sorry to you. I’ll stay in my room forever!”

“That’s enough, young lady.” Clay scooped her from the chair and carried her kicking and screaming out the back door.

Watching through the door’s window, Eden saw them vanish inside the bunkhouse. She was so lucky God had forgiven her for her own stubbornness. Everyone had the same sin nature that deserved judgment.

17

THE HOUSE WAS QUIET EXCEPT FOR THE HUM OF THE AIR CONDITIONER. CLAY RAN A COMB through his hair, still damp from the shower. Eden had been quiet since they punished Madeline. The little girl had gone to bed without telling Eden she was sorry. Not even the thought of a cupcake for Paige's birthday had swayed her determination. He wasn't sure how to handle it next.

"That coconut chicken was pretty good," he said.

"I thought it was a little spicy," she said.

"Zeke ate his weight in it. So did I."

"Maybe it will be a hit at the international dinner." She was brushing her hair. Her hand paused before resuming the strokes. "How long before we get the DNA samples back?"

"Complete profiles will take about six weeks, but I had an idea." He tossed his comb into the drawer and sat on the edge of the bed beside her. "There are paternity and maternity DNA companies. In fact, I sent off a request for the kits and asked they be overnighted. I should have them soon. We could get those back in a few days."

"Days, not weeks? Would they be accurate?"

"I think so. They wouldn't provide a complete DNA strand, but they would tell us if we are the parents to any of the children. We'd have to send in our DNA along with the girls'."

Her eyes were bright. "Let's do it! I can't stand waiting. I'm growing to love all of them." She shook her head. "And that kidnapper is out there. Knowing which child is Brianna might help us figure out who did this. And why."

He nodded. "I dream about it most nights. About telling our daughter we're her parents."

She began to brush her hair again. "Can we do it tomorrow?"

He watched the hypnotic ripple of her hair through the brush. "It will take a couple of days to get it and a couple more for them to receive it. We should have the results within the week."

"And we'll know," she said slowly. "How amazing."

"Then what?"

"We can leave here and pick up our lives again."

He lifted a brow. "And leave the Baileys high and dry?"

Her forehead furrowed. "I didn't mean that. I wouldn't want to hurt anyone, especially not the other girls. We should stay at least until they go home."

"And we have separate lives, and a daughter to share. That's going to take some time to figure out."

She put down the brush, then stood. "I'm tired. We didn't get much sleep last night."

What was she thinking? Was there a chance she didn't want to live apart any more than he did? "No, we didn't."

When he went around to his side of the bed, she was already under the covers with her back to him. He clicked off the light and plunged the room into darkness. But even after he settled into the bed, he knew he'd never be able to sleep without talking to her about what he'd been thinking of.

"Eden?"

"What?" Her voice was sleepy but not impatient.

"I want us to stay married." There, he'd said it. Propping himself on his elbow, he rolled toward her. "Brianna will need all the stability we can give her." *Coward. Tell her you want her, not just Brianna.*

She still didn't answer and remained motionless on her side of the bed. He prayed for her to consider his plea, for her heart to be opened to another chance.

"What if we end up fighting again?" she said softly.

"We've been doing pretty well so far, don't you think? We never had the time to really get to know each other. Now we do."

"We don't know all the challenges yet. I don't want to go through . . ." Her voice trailed away.

What had she started to say? Go through losing him? He wished he could be sure of her feelings. She said nothing for a few minutes.

"Where did we go wrong, Eden?" he whispered. He wasn't sure if she was still awake, or if she'd even heard him.

The sheets rustled, and the line of her silhouette changed as she rolled over to face him. "We weren't suited."

"You think people have to be the same to be suited? What about complementing each other? You like schedules and I teach you to enjoy the moment. I like adventure and you show me the value of family and routine."

The silence lengthened. "We fought too much," she said. "I hated that."

"We were practically strangers." He reached out to touch her cheek. She didn't flinch. "I'll never forget the first time I saw you."

"At the beach in Kauai," she murmured. She leaned into his touch.

"You had on that gold tropical sundress and a killer tan. I thought redheads didn't tan." She'd seemed almost an angel, the way the sun lit her hair and skin.

"It was fake." There was a smile in her voice.

"I should have known."

"It was well done." She fell silent, then said, "You called me Angel."

"You saved me from a lonely life. Or so I'd hoped."

"I thought you were mocking me. I didn't know you thought—"

"You know what drew me first? You were sitting and talking to an old man." She hadn't seemed impatient at all. He'd stood and watched her chat with the old guy for fifteen minutes before he got up the nerve to talk to her.

"We were feeding the birds."

"You were so sweet to him. Not many people pay attention to the elderly."

"I always wanted grandparents."

"You had none? What about your foster mom's parents?"

"They lived in New York, and I saw them once a year. I was always afraid to touch anything in their home. My foster dad's parents died in a small plane crash when I was ten. I only met them once."

He rubbed his fingers over the silken texture of her cheek.

"When you said you'd have dinner with me, I thought I'd died and gone to heaven."

"You were cocky and full of yourself."

They'd packed a lifetime into two weeks. Or so it had seemed. And one night things got out of hand. He'd regretted his lapse of self-control, but when it came to her, he had no sense. It was a truth he'd accepted the minute he saw her again.

The faint glimmer in the room was her eyes. "What did you think when I called to tell you I was pregnant? You were so—cold. I was afraid to ask."

Something about the quiet of the night allowed him to admit it. "I was glad." *Glad*. Such a tame word for the rush of joy that had come over him.

She stiffened. "Glad! How can you say that?"

"I thought I'd lost you. You weren't returning my e-mails. Our phone calls seemed stilted."

"You didn't say anything for what seemed an eternity. Then you just said, 'Well, we'll get married. I'll be there as quickly as I can.'"

He heard the pain in her voice and regretted he'd been the cause. "I wasn't sure how you felt. I wanted to man up."

"Man up," she repeated. "I'd hoped you'd say you loved me. You came right away but you were all business."

How did he tell her he'd been overcome by his good fortune? The words seemed lame now. He should have realized. Why hadn't he? No wonder she'd been so prickly and aloof. It was the only protection she had.

"Then you went on assignment two weeks after we were married. What was I to think but that you were only doing your duty?"

"I had a wife and baby to provide for. I wanted to do right by you both. To be a better father and husband than my dad had been."

"But you told me out at the old house that you're wealthy. So why did you go if you didn't need the money?"

"I only inherited it a couple of years ago."

"I see." There was something in her voice. Panic, fear? He wanted to tell her she didn't have to be afraid.

"I'm sleepy," she said abruptly. She rolled over and presented her back to him again.

Just when he was about ready to tell her he still loved her.

Eden couldn't sleep after that discussion. She lay still until Clay's breathing was deep and even, then rolled onto her back. He might be nostalgic now, but the day they'd set up house together, she'd been sure he blamed her for the pregnancy. There'd been no hiding the fact that he felt trapped.

Her eyes stung, and she threw her arm across them. Their short marriage hadn't had a chance. They'd been virtual strangers and hadn't connected except physically. There'd never been any question about their attraction to each other.

It has taken all this time to get over him. If I even am.

She pushed the insistent thought away. Of course she'd gotten over him. The month he left, she'd known it was over. She wanted to tell Clay why she'd left, but that would mean he would know she loved him. Her pride couldn't stand that.

And it didn't change anything. Not really. When they found Brianna, they would help her adjust, then they would split again. He hadn't uttered a single word of love since reentering her life. They'd been married nine months. And all but a few weeks of that time, he'd been gone. If he'd cared about her, he would have made spending time with her a priority.

She rolled to her side again, willing herself to sleep. Rest would stop this pounding in her chest, this nameless pain that radiated under her breastbone. Closing her eyes, she took a few deep breaths before they popped open again. Maybe warm milk would help.

She eased out of bed, then froze when she heard something at the window. *Scratch, scratch, scratch.* Probably a branch. Then she remembered she was in West Texas. There were few trees here, and none in the yard. The noise came again. Like a long fingernail on a chalkboard. The hair at her neck rippled. All she had to do was step to the window and look out to ease her mind. The cause of the noise had to be something very simple.

"Eden."

The whisper shuddered through her. Clay still slept. The voice came from the side of the house where the window was. For a moment she stood frozen in place. Then she wheeled and leaped back onto the bed.

She grabbed Clay's arm. "Clay!"

He sat up instantly. "What's wrong?"

"Someone is outside the window. He called my name."

He threw back the covers. "Go stay with the girls." He grabbed a flashlight from the top drawer in the chest beside the bed, then jumped up, jerked open the door, and ran into the hall.

She ran behind him and rushed to the girls' room. Her gaze went from bed to bed. They were all sleeping. Her knees went weak and she sagged against the door frame before she shut the door and locked it. She glanced around the room and saw a desk chair. After dragging it to the door, she propped its back under the knob.

She should have called the ranch house. Rick or one of the cowboys would have come running. There was no phone in this room. She went to the window and looked out onto the side of the house where she'd heard the intruder. The storm had passed except for a few stray clouds that shrouded the moon. Puddles glimmered in the few shafts of moonbeam. She didn't see Clay. That alone was worrisome. No intruder either.

She paced in front of the window, stopping occasionally to peer out. Nothing moved other than a jackrabbit that darted from the corner of the house toward the empty corral. No doubt it wished it could glance into the sky to see if an owl soared above. She knew the feeling of waiting for a predator to strike.

When the scratch came at the door, she froze. Had the intruder gained entrance? Had he hurt Clay? Then she heard Clay's soft whisper and ran to move the chair out of the way. When she unlocked the door, he opened it.

"All clear," he whispered. He drew her into the hall and led her to the kitchen, where a light chased away the shadows.

"Did you see anything?"

His jaw hardened. "Footprints outside our bedroom window. Fresh ones."

She closed her eyes and gripped the edge of the table. "So I wasn't dreaming. I didn't think so, but it was so surreal."

"What did you see and hear?"

She straightened and hugged herself. "First I heard scratching. Like a fingernail on the screen. Then someone whispered my name. That was it. I was too afraid to move the curtain and look out."

"Good." He rubbed his bristly chin. "I'm going to have to tell Rick tomorrow."

"Everything?"

"I think so. We have to protect the girls. And you seem to be a particular target."

"Should I call him tonight?"

"No use in disturbing him. There's no one out there now." He stared at her, his eyes intensely blue. "I want to investigate Daniel."

Her gratitude that he was taking this seriously vanished. "There's no need. He would never do anything to hurt me."

"I don't share your confidence."

"He was angry when I talked to him, but it's not him, Clay." She knew her lifelong friend. Her brother. Nothing Clay said would make her believe Daniel would harm her. "What about you?"

"What about me?"

"What if this person wants to hurt you through me?" As soon as she said the words, she realized how ludicrous they were. To hurt him through her would mean he cared. And he didn't.

He pulled out a chair and had her sit down. "I got some hate mail after that incident in Colombia. But this person seems very venomous toward you in particular. While hurting you would hurt me, you'd think he'd send me a warning too."

"Hurting you would hurt me." Did he really care that much? She watched him step to the refrigerator and pull out the milk. He poured her a glass before pouring one for himself. Why had she never noticed how giving he was? The answer came to her quickly. He hadn't been around enough.

18

CLAY'S EYES FELT GRITTY. THE BUNKHOUSE WAS QUIET FOR THE FIRST TIME IN HOURS. ZEKE and Della had taken the older girls on a hike. The younger girls were on an outing with the vet, Shannon MacGowan. She and her husband had two daughters a couple of years older than their girls.

He stopped short in his walk across the spindly grass between the sleeping quarters and the ranch house. *Their girls.* The children had crept into his heart already.

Eden glanced up at him. "What's wrong?"

"Nothing, really. I was just thinking about how often I think of the kids as *our* girls."

She smiled, her face tender. "Me too. I love them so much already."

"You ready to tell Rick and Allie about all this?"

"Do you think they'll kick us out?"

"They might, but I don't think we have a choice now. The girls' safety is too important." He held out his hand and she took it.

They found Allie and Rick in the kitchen still drinking coffee. Rita was nowhere to be seen. Tepin was doing the dishes, her face impassive, as though she were alone.

Rick pushed a chair out with his foot. "Have a seat, friends. You look like a mule dragged you both through a patch of cholla."

Clay pulled out another chair and let Eden take the one nearest Allie. "Didn't get much sleep last night."

"Another bed-wetting?" Allie's dark eyes were full of mischief. "You two are getting broken in right off." She rose and poured them each a cup of coffee.

"I wish it were that benign," Clay said.

Allie sobered and sat back down before glancing at Rick. "You're not quitting, are you?"

"Oh no! We love working with the children," Eden said.

Rick leaned back in the chair with his coffee in his hand. "Then what's up?"

"There was an intruder outside the bunkhouse last night."

Every trace of geniality vanished from Rick's face. He put his coffee down. "What happened? Who was it?"

Clay laced his fingers together. "We don't know, but there's more to our story than we've told you, and it's time we did."

Rick leaned forward in his chair. "What are you saying?" His voice was troubled.

"Five years ago our daughter, Brianna, was kidnapped. She was six weeks old, and we never saw her again." His voice quavered and he cleared his throat.

Allie put her hand to her mouth and her eyes welled. "Oh no! I can't imagine something so awful."

Rick nodded. "I knew that much."

"You never told me?" Allie asked.

"Brendan knows Clay, remember? He told me in confidence." Rick glanced back at Clay. "I can see how the experience would give you a heart for the hurting kids here at the ranch. Is the tragedy related somehow?"

Clay cleared the thickening in his throat and nodded. "Somehow I never believed she was dead."

"I did," Eden put in. "I gave up, tried to move on. Most of the time I thought I was doing a pretty good job of it. Then I'd see a mother with a baby or walk by a zoo and remember all the things I wanted to show Brianna but never got a chance."

Rick's gaze was sober. "So this intruder—?"

"I'm not quite to that part of the story yet. Hang on." This would be the tricky part, convincing Rick to let them stay when they hadn't revealed the real reason they were here. But the Baileys had children. Surely they could understand the lengths a dad would go to for his daughter. Clay glanced at Eden.

She gave a quick nod in his direction and took over the narration. "Clay got a picture a couple of weeks ago."

The wonder of it hit Clay again. He took a quick sip of coffee to swallow down the lump in his throat. "He sent me this." Taking the picture of the girls from his pocket, he slid it across the table to the Baileys.

Allie snatched it up first and stared at the smiling faces. "Our girls?"

Rick took it and studied it as well. "What do the girls have to do with this?"

"Look at the back," Clay said.

Rick flipped it over and looked even more grave. Allie's eyes widened. "So Brianna is alive!" Her voice trembled. She leaned over and took Eden's hand.

Eden squeezed her fingers and smiled. "She is." Her eyes were misty. "Truly a miracle."

Clay pointed at the picture. "One of those girls is our Brianna."

The Baileys froze in place. They exchanged a long glance with each other. Clay couldn't tell if they were judging his motives or the truthfulness of what he'd said.

Rick gave the photograph another stare, then handed it back. "No wonder you were interested in how they came to be here. Do you have any idea which one?"

"I called to get paternity DNA tests sent here. I had planned to wait on the results of full-profile tests, which I sent in after we arrived, but I realized we could get paternity and maternity tests done much more quickly. They would tell us all we needed to know."

Rick's scowl deepened as Clay spoke. "Are you even who you say you are?"

Clay had been expecting the question, and he didn't blame the other man. "I haven't lied about anything, Rick. Both Brendan and Michael vouched for me. I'm laying out everything now."

"The lie of omission is just as great." Rick didn't smile. "You only came here to find your daughter. I'm not okay with that. We're here to help these kids. Most of them have been through things we can't even imagine."

"Would you have hired us if I'd told you all of it?"

"No. I would have thought you were some kind of wackos."

Allie jumped to her feet. "Rick, we have to help them! I realize it would have been better if they'd told us, but—"

"But we wouldn't have hired them," Rick said, his mouth a grim line.

Allie put her hand on her husband's shoulder. "Maybe not. But they're doing a great job with the girls."

"There's more," Clay said. "And what else we have to tell you may convince you that you're right to throw us out. But I pray you won't. Our family's future is in your hands."

Eden clasped her hands together and leaned forward. "He's here. The kidnapper. He scratched on the window last night and whispered my name. In town the other day he called me on the phone and threatened to take her again."

Allie put her hand to her mouth. "Oh, Eden, no!"

"You expected him to be here, didn't you? That this was a trap?"

Clay nodded. "I'd thought he'd want money or something. Instead he seems to be taunting Eden."

Rick stared at Eden. "Is this true?"

Eden nodded. "He said I would have no one to blame but myself. Then he asked me if I knew who I really was. We don't know what that means. But we have to protect Brianna."

"You don't know which of the girls is Brianna," Allie said.

Clay nodded. "We need your help."

Rick rubbed his forehead. He stared at Clay, then Eden. "I'm inclined to make you leave. Your being here puts those kids in danger."

"Rick, no!" Allie cried. "Think how it would be if Matthew or Betsy had been taken. We have to help. Call the sheriff. We can protect them. With us all working together, we'll solve this and reunite a family."

"And if we leave, that leaves Brianna even more unprotected," Clay said.

Rick glanced at his wife and his brow furrowed. "I suppose you're right. And whichever girl is their daughter, she deserves to be with her parents and not in foster care. What can we do, Clay?"

"I think we need to talk to Brendan," he said. A surge of adrenaline hit him now that he had help.

The Reata restaurant almost looked like a house except for the enormous R over the front door. A horseshoe dangled from the loop at the bottom of the R. Eden got out of the truck and walked on shaky legs to the entrance with Clay.

"We're a little early," he said as they stepped inside. He asked the hostess for as much privacy as they could get.

"It's pretty," Eden whispered when the hostess led them through the cowboy-decor room. The walls were painted in mottled warm browns and tans, and the doorway trim was a terra-cotta color. The hostess took them through the restaurant to the patio. Large cowboy murals decorated the side of the building. They were seated at a secluded table under a trellis on the patio. Grasses and yucca softened the surrounding buildings and made an oasis outside.

Eden toyed with her tableware. "Let's go, Clay. We don't have to stay."

"Calm down. It's not going to be as bad as you think." He gave the waitress, a smiling Hispanic woman, their drink order.

A couple stepped through the doors into the courtyard. Eden recognized the woman in an instant. The reddish hair. The slim build. Her mother hadn't even aged that much. She had the beautiful, unlined skin that Eden remembered so well. The peach suit she wore was impeccably fitted, and she wore it with style. The couple paused and scanned the courtyard. Eden sat frozen in place. She couldn't rise, couldn't speak.

Clay glanced at her. "That them?" When she nodded, he rose and beckoned to them.

Her mother's smile was tentative and didn't quite reach her eyes. She followed the man across the terra-cotta tile to the table. "Eden?"

Eden had heard that voice in her dreams. It was softer now, not as demanding. She found her tongue. "Hello, Mom." She cleared her throat and willed herself to stand, to embrace the older woman, who stood with her hands awkwardly in front of her.

Her mother glanced at the man beside her. Tall and distinguished, he appeared to be in his fifties, maybe ten years older than her mother. Or maybe it was the wings of gray at his temples that made him seem older. His mustache held a little gray as well. His genial smile revealed white teeth. Eden focused on his open grin rather than on her mother's pleading gaze. Something about him seemed familiar.

Clay pulled out a chair for her mother beside Eden. "Have a seat."

The breeze sent a familiar scent to Eden. Chanel No. 5. Instantly she was back in her mother's bedroom watching her spritz a liberal amount of the expensive perfume on her wrists and the back of her neck. Why had Eden agreed to this meeting? She should have run the other way. What good could come from this?

The server brought her ice water. She squeezed the lemon into her glass and took a sip. "I assume you're married to my mother?" she asked the man who'd accompanied Nancy.

"I'm sorry," her mother said before he could speak. "I never introduced Omar. We've been married ten years. This is Omar Santiago."

"Pleased to meet you," Eden said. What did she say now? Did she ask how they met or jump right into the reason for the meeting? But no, they should wait for any serious conversation until after they'd ordered their food.

A Don Edwards song played, his gravelly voice singing about cowboys. For a brief instant, Eden even imagined herself in cowboy boots. She shook the nasty image away. Once the server took their orders and left them in peace, she squared her shoulders and glanced at her mother, who smiled back.

"So, Eden," her mother said. "You look well. And your husband is so handsome. I'd like to know about your life."

"Since you walked away and left an eight-year-old by herself?" Eden couldn't help herself. It wasn't the best way to mend fences, but hadn't her mother even wondered what Eden had done when she came home to find her mother gone?

Her mother blanched and glanced at her husband, who took her hand. She lifted her chin. "I'm sorry about that, Eden. What did you do? I want to know the full extent of the damage I caused."

Was she gloating about it? Eden wished the encounter were over and she and Clay were headed home. "When the snowstorm hit, I came back to the house. It was dark. I'd been hiding out in the little playhouse at the park until I couldn't feel my fingers."

Her mother winced and tears pooled in her eyes. She took a sip of water. "I'm so sorry," she said, her voice choked. "Then what?"

Was her mother protecting Omar from the truth? "The trailer was dark. I called your name but stayed in the living room like I'd been told. When you didn't appear by ten, I went to bed. The next morning when I got up, I fixed you breakfast. Toast and jelly, the way you liked it. But your room was empty." Her throat closed and she swallowed hard, remembering the awful moment when she'd seen the empty closet.

She clung to Clay's hand. No good could come from replaying all this. The warmth of his fingers bolstered her courage.

"You saw my clothes were gone?" her mother asked.

Eden nodded. "I didn't know what to do. I didn't have my father's phone number, so I didn't do anything for a few days. I went to school and came home. Eventually I ran out of food, so I went to the neighbor's and asked for some bread. It all came out then. They called the welfare department, and a social worker came and took me away."

Her mother wept, dabbing at her eyes with a wadded-up tissue. Eden watched with a strange detachment. She should feel something, shouldn't she? At least sympathy? Or had all sensation been washed away as the emotions were dredged from her subconscious?

Her gaze caught Clay's, and she glimpsed compassion in the depths of his eyes. For the first time, she wondered how he felt when he realized she'd left him. She felt almost dizzy when she realized she wasn't that different from her mother. No, she hadn't abandoned a child, but she'd run away rather than face any unpleasantness. She looked down at her hands.

Omar motioned to the server. "Bring my wife some coffee, please," he said.

The server acted as though a woman sobbing at the table was an everyday occurrence. She grabbed a pot and a cup from a cart by the door and brought it to the table, then left.

Eden's mom poured half-and-half into the cup, then took a sip.

"I'm sorry. It breaks my heart to know what I did to you." Her eyes were red when she stared at Eden. "How long were you in foster care?"

"Until I turned eighteen." Eden dipped a chip in salsa so her mother couldn't see how upset she was.

Her mother took another gulp of coffee. "W-Were they good people?"

Eden decided she'd been pointed enough about her circumstances. Maybe her mother really was sorry. "Kind and loving." No need to say they had high expectations that had made her a perfectionist. No reason to mention they micromanaged every area of her life. At least she'd had a home and had always felt their love, even if it was conditional.

Her mother fished another tissue out of her purse, a Brighton that looked new. "I was so young."

"You were nearly my age," Eden said. "Hardly a child."

A flush stained her mother's cheeks. She glanced at her husband, who put his arm around the back of her chair and shot a disapproving glance Eden's way. Well, let him. He wasn't the one who'd been abandoned.

Her mother wetted her lips. "Looking back now, it seems the choices should have been easy. I got pregnant with you, but your father was already married. He promised to take care of us, but he seldom sent a check."

"So you became a prostitute." Even to her own ears, the statement was harsh.

Her mother winced. "Hardly a prostitute, my dear. I . . . I had some male friends."

"Who gave you money. I saw them leave it." Eden remembered

the rolls of cash left on the table or on her mother's pillow. Cash that bought them pizza or milk or electricity.

Her mother's eyes welled again, but Eden squelched her flash of sympathy. Her mother's actions might have been bearable if she had done it to keep them together or to feed her daughter. But too many times the cash had gone for pretty dresses or jewelry. Trips to get a manicure or a pedicure. Then she'd just walked away without caring if Eden had food or heat.

Her mother took another sip of coffee. "I thought I had no choice. That you'd be better off without me."

"Which makes no sense. How could an eight-year-old be better off alone, fending for herself?" Clay put in.

Eden glanced at him, heartened by his passionate defense. Did he see how inappropriate her mom's excuses were? But what about her own? She didn't want to see herself in her mother's behavior, but the notion kept popping up.

"Give Nancy a chance," Omar said. "She's trying to apologize for what she did."

The apology had seemed thin to Eden. Was that how Clay saw her own excuses?

When Eden said nothing, Omar rose. "Perhaps we should go," he said, putting his hand on his wife's shoulder.

Eden's mother took his hand. "Sit down, Omar." Her voice trembled. "I've gone about this all wrong. There is no excuse for what I did. All the rationalization in the world doesn't change the fact that I left my child to fend for herself. Without food. Without comfort. Without anything." She caught Eden's gaze. "I hope you can forgive me someday, Eden. I don't think I can ever forgive myself."

With no warning, tears flooded Eden's eyes. A simple, heartfelt apology. That's all she'd ever wanted.

Clay scooted his chair closer and put his arm around her. "You have a tissue?" he asked Nancy, who nodded and passed one to her daughter.

Eden took it and dabbed at the moisture in her eyes. How embarrassing to cry in front of them all. She never cried. She'd sworn never to let someone hurt her like that again. Now here she was, blubbering away.

"Why?" she asked. "What made you think it was okay to leave me? Did I do something?"

"What?" Her mother shook her head. "It was never about you. If I'd thought of you instead of myself, I wouldn't have left. I didn't think I could ever have a life saddled with a child. I was selfish, pure and simple. I rationalized to myself that you'd go to school and tell the teacher. Someone would come."

Eden mopped her streaming eyes again, willing herself to stop. "I never cry," she gulped. "What about my father? I don't even remember his name. It was all so long ago. I can't even remember what he looked like."

Her mother exchanged a glance with Omar. "It was Omar's brother, Hector."

Eden absorbed the news. Maybe that's why the man seemed vaguely familiar. "Where is he now?"

Omar shifted in his seat. "He's a drug dealer in Colombia."

19

SHE'D HANDLED IT BETTER THAN HE DID. THREE HOURS LATER CLAY STIRRED HALF-AND-half into Eden's coffee and slid it across the table to her. The coffee shop was deserted this late. Only a few customers plunked down money for a latte and hurried out into the sunset. The scent of cinnamon and yeast from a bakery down the street was tempting for dessert, but he didn't want to leave her long enough to buy a treat.

"Do you want to see her again?" he asked her.

She sipped her coffee. "No. Maybe." She gave a watery smile. "I don't know."

"You did good, honey. Handled it all with grace."

She dabbed at her eyes. "Hardly. I wish I could quit crying. I hate crying. And what was the point of this? To assuage her guilt?"

Had he ever seen her cry? He didn't think so. She'd screamed and hit things when Brianna was gone. Sobbed hysterically and hadn't slept for days, but her eyes had been dry. "I'd guess so. And to assure herself that you're all right. Maybe you can both move on now."

"Thank you for bringing me. I wouldn't have been able to get through it without you."

At her words, a curl of warmth encircled him. "I wanted to be here for you." He wanted to be there for her forever, not just for a day. Didn't she see that?

She sipped her coffee. "My father is a Santiago. The kidnapper who died was Jose Santiago. What does that mean?"

"A weird coincidence? Santiago is as common a name south of the border as Jones would be in the States." He shook his head. "But you're right, there might be a connection. But why would your father want to hurt his own daughter?"

"None of it has made any sense. Maybe your friend Brendan will have some insight. What time is he supposed to meet us here?"

He glanced at his watch. "Any minute. Rick was picking him up at the airport."

"Amazing that he was willing to come all this way as a favor."

"He saved my hide down in Colombia. I was taking pics of kids in a village along the river. A Jeep full of commandos rolled in and started firing rounds for fun. No good reason. They were laughing and joking while bullets flew. I confronted them. The kids got away and I got thrown in jail."

"Lucky you weren't killed," she said, her eyes huge.

"Actually, they were saving me for sport. My execution by firing squad was going to be in two days." He'd never told her all this. He hadn't wanted her to worry. "Brendan broke me out in the middle of the night."

"How did he know about it?"

"He's special ops. He knows everything." Clay grinned and took a drink of his Americano. "I guess he'd been at a neighboring village and heard about the gringo taking pictures."

"What happened to the pictures?"

"My camera and film were lost. I hated that. I had some really good shots that would have shown the lives these kids lead in drug towns. The only thing I got out with was that pendant I gave you when I got back."

Her eyes widened. "The one with the mother and baby?"

"That's the one."

"You told me a little girl gave it to you in exchange for a piece of hard candy."

"She did. I just didn't tell you the backdrop."

"I loved that pendant." Her voice was wistful. "Where is it now?"

"I've been carrying it around in my pocket."

She gave him a startled look. "How long?"

"Since I jumped in the truck to find you." He reached into his pocket and pulled it out.

Her eyes were soft as she plucked it from his palm. "It's always been special to me."

"I've been wanting to give it back to you, but I wasn't sure you'd take it."

She rubbed the pendant in her hands. "Did the child make it herself?"

"I don't think so. She was only five or six." He wanted to fasten it around her neck, but he waited for a cue from her. "I'm not sure what it's made of. I just like it because it reminds me of the little girl. The design looks pre-Colombian."

"Here, you keep it safe." She started to hand it back to him but he closed her fingers around it.

"It's yours."

She stared at him a moment, then lifted it to her neck and started to fasten the chain. It must have missed the clasp, because it slipped from her fingers and landed on the tile patio. He heard something crack, and when he looked down, the piece of jewelry lay in two pieces.

"Oh no!" She scooped up the nearest piece and it crumbled in her fingers. "I'm so sorry."

He looked at it in her hand and it was different now. Sparkly. "What's that?"

"Wait, it's not exactly broken. A covering has come off." She held out her open palm. Green and gold glittered in her hand.

"Wow." He scooped it up and examined it. "I bet this is worth money. Someone must have covered it over with the other stuff to hide it."

"How exciting!" Her eyes were shining. "Is that jade?"

He looked more closely at the baby. "I think so. And the gold is high quality."

"How would a peasant girl get something like this?"

"She probably didn't know what she had."

A truck maneuvered into a parking space across the street under the streetlight. Two men got out, and he recognized Rick and Brendan. "The reinforcements are here," he said. He stood and greeted the men.

Brendan hadn't changed much in five years. Broad shoulders filled out a casual blue shirt. His khaki pants were a little wrinkled and stained. His dark hair needed a trim, but those brown eyes that missed nothing were sharp and inquisitive.

"I've heard so much about you," Eden said, taking his hand.

"Same here." He squeezed her fingers, then glanced at the pendant on the table. Frowning, he pointed to it. "May I?"

"Sure." Clay handed it to him.

The other man examined it with care. When he turned it over, he inhaled sharply. "What are you doing with a Santiago heirloom? They'd kill to get this back."

Clay wrapped his fingers around the bauble. The trinket was worth so much more money than he'd dreamed, but even more than that, it was prized by a drug family connected to Eden. The cool weight of the jade in his hand convinced him it was real.

He held it up to the light. The veins and color of the jade were exceptional. "Are they looking for this?"

Brendan nodded, swiping a lock of hair out of his eyes. "I heard it was stolen by a rival about seven years ago."

"Stolen?"

Brendan leaned back in his chair. "The Santiago family is a rival of Juarez, that guy you had a run-in with in Colombia."

"Juarez stole it?"

"That's what Hector Santiago claims."

He heard Eden gasp beside him. "Hector Santiago?"

Brendan nodded. "Dangerous guy. He's blamed all the bad luck that's hit his family on its disappearance. Does he know you have it? It's worth more to him than the monetary value. Much more."

"I didn't even know I had it until Eden dropped it. It was covered with this." Clay stooped and pinched a sample of the material that had covered the jewelry.

"So why is it important?" Eden asked.

"It's been in his family for generations. Legend has it that the man who owns it will hold his wealth and power until death. Since it came up missing, his star has been waning." Brendan turned the stonelike substance over in his hands. "Someone took pains to disguise this. Tell me how you got it." He dug a plastic bag out of his pocket and dropped in the remains.

Clay told him how he'd come to have it in his possession. "It was in my pocket the night you busted me out of jail."

"I can tell you now that I'd been in the neighboring town investigating the shooting of someone Santiago thought had this thing. And you had it all along."

Rick came from the coffee shop with two cups in his hand. "Hazelnut latte, extra hot," he said, handing it to Brendan before sitting in the last chair. "What have you found out about the girls?"

"We haven't gotten that far yet." Clay brought him up to speed on the piece of jewelry.

"Is there any way this Santiago could know you have this? Maybe he took Brianna to get it back," Rick asked.

Eden plucked the pendant from Clay's hand. "The ransom demand was for money, not this. I think they're unrelated." Her voice was defiant, and she shot Clay a glance that warned him to say nothing about her father.

Clay held her gaze. "But I never thought money was the real issue. There are a lot of possibilities. I'd always thought they were luring us out into the open for some other reason."

"What about the camera?" she asked, wrinkling her forehead. "What pictures did you take?"

"Like I said, kids, the village." It had been so long ago. Though the trauma of the night in jail was burned into his memory, the village itself had faded into the mists of time.

"No pictures of this?" Rick asked.

"Nope." Clay tried to remember if there were any pictures of the pendant in existence. A dim memory tried to surface, but he couldn't quite grasp it.

"What?" Eden asked.

"Nothing. Let's talk about the girls."

She bit her lip. "Just a minute. We have to tell Brendan and Rick."

"Tell us what?" Rick asked, his face troubled.

"I just met my birth mother after twenty years. She's married to Hector's brother."

Brendan sat upright. "His brother?"

She nodded and exhaled harshly. "Omar. And my mother says Hector is my father."

"Holy cow," Brendan said softly. "This is a strange wrinkle. Where is your dad now?"

"I have no idea. The last time I saw him I was a little girl."

"And you have something he's been searching for a good six years," Brendan said. "That's ominous to me in light of your daughter's kidnapping."

"There's more. We found a picture of the dead kidnapper in an old yearbook at the ranch. His name was Jose Santiago."

"Hector's son."

Clay felt as though he'd been sucker punched. "Brianna's own uncle took her?"

"I . . . I killed my own brother?" Eden's voice trembled. She buried her face in her hands. "Oh, I can't bear it."

Clay scooted his chair closer and put his arm around her. "It was an accident, honey."

She raised a white face. "How could he do something like that? And why not just ask for the pendant back?"

Brendan shook his head. "Makes no sense, does it? I'll see what I can find out." He pulled the file toward him. "These the bios?"

"Yep," Rick said. Then to Clay: "And Brendan brought a copy of everything in the files about the kidnapping. We thought we could compare the two, see if there are any connections." Rick flipped open the file. "Let's look at Madeline."

"We know her mother was in a mental hospital. She showed up here," Clay said. "They look enough alike that I think we can rule her out. She has blond hair just like Madeline. Though she looked too old, it might just be that she's had a rough life."

Brendan pulled the file over to scan it. "In my line of work, you assume nothing." He began to read and his brow furrowed.

"What is it?" Eden asked.

"This makes no sense. The woman who claims to be Madeline's mother had a hysterectomy when she was fifteen, following a car accident. That seems to be what sent her over the edge. She's fifty now. So there's no way she could be Madeline's mother."

"But she came to the ranch," Clay protested.

"Maybe she's another relative, but she's not a mother. Has anyone talked to Madeline about her mother? Or the foster parents who have her? Maybe the mom contacted them and they know something." Brendan made a note.

"I'll do that," Eden said. "She likes to chat with me while I brush her hair. Or rather, she did. She's a little miffed with me since I had to give her a time-out."

"What about the kidnapping?" Brendan asked. "How did this all go down?"

It was going to be painful for Eden to relive it. Clay took her hand. "Brianna was six weeks old. Eden was making cupcakes for my birthday. The baby was sleeping in her room."

"I had the baby monitor in the kitchen," Eden put in, her voice soft. "The dog needed to go out. I stepped outside to put him on his chain. When I came back in, I heard something bang. It almost sounded like the door, but I wanted to check on Brianna first so I ran up the stairs. Sh-She was gone. All that was in her crib was her blanket."

Brendan winced. So did Rick.

"Man, that had to have been hard," Rick said.

"You don't know the half of it," Clay said. "She called me hysterically. I started to dial the police, but before I could, my phone rang. It was the kidnapper demanding ten thousand dollars."

Brendan lifted a brow. "That was all?"

"My thoughts too. He said not to involve the police or we'd never see Brianna again. We had that much money in our account. We were saving to buy a house." He glanced at Eden, hating the pain he saw in her eyes.

"We were supposed to make the exchange at the river," Eden said. "It was all set. But I got in too big of a hurry on the wet roads and rammed into the vehicle. It fell into the water. That was the last time we ever heard from them."

"One body was found but never identified. Until we saw his picture—Jose."

"And then you got that picture of the girls at Bluebird Ranch," Brendan said.

Eden cleared her throat. "I tend to think Lacie might be Brianna," she said, shooting a glance at Clay. "She was left outside a church when she was six months old."

"Dressed in an expensive sleeper," Clay added. "So she came from a wealthy family. Or at least a family that could spend fifty dollars for a clothing item she would only wear a couple of weeks."

"Sounds possible," Brendan agreed. He studied the paperwork on the little girl. "What about this Sister Marjo? Has anyone talked to her?"

"There hasn't been time yet," Clay said. "She'll be at the ranch in a few days."

"You talk to her when she comes and I'll handle Madeline's so-called mother."

His friend knew his stuff. Clay felt empowered just having help. "Katie seems unlikely. Her father was killed in a burglary. The murderer never apprehended. So she had a family."

"Maybe. Let me check into it." Brendan made another note. "Hard to say how he got her. I'll check hospital records and nose around the neighborhood."

"Then there's Paige," Eden put in. "She's also rather likely. Two men left her in the toy department at Walmart." She looked down at her lap. "To be honest, I hope she's not our Brianna. I dearly love her, but her foster parents want to adopt her. She seems to adore them and they're crazy about her. It would hurt them all."

Brendan's gaze softened. "You're a good woman, Mrs. Larson." He read through the report. "I'll see if I can take a look at the Walmart security tape. We'll figure this out, friends. We'll find your girl."

20

THE STREETLIGHTS HUMMED AS CLAY AND EDEN STOOD BELOW THEIR GOLDEN GLOW. RICK would have Brendan in the air by now. Eden turned her face to the night sky, brilliant with stars. Alpine was quiet except for the occasional revving of a car engine on the main street that intersected with this one.

"Ready to go home?" Clay asked, his hand on the small of her back.

Home. How quickly they'd come to think of this starkly beautiful place as home. "Let's sit for a while in the park." She settled on a park bench and watched birds nesting on the trees, their heads tucked under wings. That's how she'd been going through life lately. With her eyes hidden to what was around her. She glanced at Clay. He sat leaning forward with his forearms on his knees. "Thanks for waiting until I was ready to tell them that my father is Hector Santiago. I know he's a bad man, but it somehow felt terrible to be ratting out my own father."

He straightened. "I'm proud of you for telling them. They needed to know. Brendan especially. Otherwise he'd be totally in the dark about what might be going on."

"I had a brother," she said, her voice trembling. "I always wanted a brother or sister."

"I'm sorry, honey. I don't understand why he didn't just ask for the pendant back. I would have given it to him when I found out it was stolen."

She held his gaze. "Would you, really? Knowing he was a drug dealer?"

He sighed. "Okay, maybe not. So if he ordered his son to take Brianna, why didn't he keep her? She was his granddaughter. And why not trade her for the pendant? If he's the kidnapper, he asked only for a paltry ten thousand. That's pennies to him."

"I don't know, but I think I need to talk to him."

"You?" He shook his head. "Way too dangerous. What if this has nothing to do with him but your call attracts his attention? And besides, why would he hate you? The kidnapper seems to have a personal vendetta against you."

She didn't have an answer for him, but the truth he'd pointed out hurt. What could her father possibly have against her? She'd done nothing to him. "I don't even care about why he did it. I'll tell him he can have his pendant if he will go away and leave us in peace."

He chewed on his lip, and she could tell he wanted to believe it would work. And why not? Such a simple solution. He rose and walked the length of several sections of sidewalk before he came back and sat beside her.

"Okay," he said. "But I want to do some investigation first. See what he's up to. I'll have Brendan get Santiago's phone number for us."

"He might oppose our involvement."

"I don't think so. What's it to him if we manage to finally get this madman off our backs?" He pulled out his phone.

"He'll still be in the air."

"He'll have his phone on." Clay dialed the number.

She listened to him explain the situation. It was clear Brendan wasn't happy about it. Clay finally hung up.

"He was ticked," she said.

Clay nodded. "More than I thought he would be. He thinks it's dangerous to contact him."

"It's more dangerous if we don't," she pointed out. "Our daughter is still in danger. And maybe we can find out what he has against me."

"None of us likes it." He paused. "But Brendan is going to get the number. He'll have it for us within twenty-four hours."

And this nightmare might be over. They would identify their daughter and be able to move on with their lives. Clay's arm pressed against hers, and she suppressed a shiver. What would he say if she told him she'd never stopped loving him? He might chalk it all up to God's will. He didn't believe in divorce, he'd said.

Neither did she. But she wanted a man who loved her completely, for herself. Not for some misguided sense of duty. Yes, he'd said he wanted to marry her, that he missed her and was glad when he found out she was pregnant. But how many of his assurances were merely what he thought he was supposed to say?

"Eden?"

His mouth was near her ear, his breath on her neck. If she turned her head, her lips would graze his. But she didn't succumb to the passion burning through her veins. If she did, the heartbreak to come would be too great.

Tell him you want a future with him.

She turned her head and was lost when he slipped his arm around her and drew her close. His lips touched hers, moved to the curve of her jaw and to her ear.

"Tell me what you're thinking," he whispered into her hair.

She let herself mold to him. "I wish I'd had the courage to stay."

"I wish I'd never left you. Neither of us was thinking. What happened when you ran off?"

"Daniel was in Wabash, so I went there. I found a job." She didn't want him to be angry that she'd run to Daniel, so she blurted out the first thing that came to mind. "I spent weeks, months, dreaming that you found me. That you showed up at the door with Brianna in your arms. That was the only way I managed to get by, day by day."

"I should have followed you. Stupid pride got in the way. Then you were seeing Kent."

"That was no grand passion. It was survival."

"I don't think his emotions were heavily involved either."

"No, they weren't. He and I just seemed . . . suitable."

A train blew its horn a block over. A lonesome sound. "That whistle was like me, Clay. Sounding out a lonely note and hoping someone would hear me so I didn't have to be alone. Kent heard it and answered. But that's all it was."

He held her gaze. "I'm glad."

All the girls had freshly washed hair and smelled like Eden's lavender soap, which she'd brought with her. Every female liked fragrance. She'd dried five small heads, then tucked the girls into their beds with a book. Except for Madeline. She sat on the big bed against the wall, as far away from Eden as she could get.

Eden picked up a brush and went to join her. "Want me to brush your hair?" she asked. Madeline had loved having her hair brushed until the day Eden disciplined her. Maybe some cuddle time would end the tension. Eden longed to restore their good relationship. The pain in the child's eyes tore at her.

Madeline didn't look at her, but after a moment's hesitation, she nodded. "If you want." She presented her stiff back to Eden.

"Let's sit at the dressing table." Eden led her to the stool. She wanted to watch Madeline's expressions in the mirror.

Eden released the braids and ran her fingers through to loosen the strands before she began to run the brush through the long blond tresses. "You have such pretty hair. Why do you like so much to have it brushed?"

"Brushing makes it stay pretty."

"It's lovely. Brushing is good for it?"

"My mother used to do it."

Eden slowed the brush, then started again. "When did you see your mother last?"

"I don't know." Madeline closed her eyes, the expression of bliss on her face reflected in the mirror. "I guess I saw her for a minute the other day. She came when she wasn't supposed to. Mr. Clay made her go away."

"How old were you when she . . . went away?"

"I don't remember. Maybe three? I was little."

Eden nodded gravely, smothering her smile. "What do you remember about her?"

"She smelled good. Like flowers. And her hands were soft."

"What color was her hair?"

"It was blond. Like mine."

The blond hair on the woman who had visited the other day might have been dyed. And it wouldn't do any good to ask Madeline how old her mother was. A child had no concept of a parent's age. But Madeline had recognized her mother the other day—unless the person she thought was her mother really wasn't. It was all a muddle.

"She had a little spot right here." Madeline indicated a spot beside her mouth. "She said it was a beauty spot. I liked to touch it."

Eden would have to ask Clay if the woman claiming to be Madeline's mother had a mole by her mouth. "What else do you remember?"

"I had her eyes."

"So, blue eyes?"

Madeline nodded. "She used to sing to me too. She used to sing in the choir in Mexico."

"Mexico?"

Madeline nodded. "That's what she said."

The longer Eden brushed the little girl's hair, the more relaxed she became. Maybe things would be back to normal tomorrow. "Want me to braid your hair for sleep?" she asked, putting down the brush. When Madeline shook her head, Eden smiled. "Time for bed, then. Scoot."

Madeline slid from the chair and Eden patted her behind as she passed. Such darling girls. She felt fulfilled and necessary here. Like what she did mattered. She kissed each of the girls, turned on the

CD of hymns, then flipped off the light and shut the door, leaving a crack that let in a tiny sliver of light.

The heady scent of coffee hung in the air and she followed her nose to the kitchen. "Decaf?"

Clay turned from the pot with two cups in his hand. "Yep. I made it strong, though. And it's freshly ground."

"Smells good." Their hands touched when she took the coffee from him. "I talked to Madeline."

He led her to the living room and plopped onto the sofa. "And?"

She sank beside him on the cushion he'd patted invitingly. "She says her mother had a mole by her mouth. Did you notice a mole?"

He frowned silently for a moment, then shook his head. "No mole. I'm positive."

"She could've had it removed."

"Maybe. But I didn't see a scar either."

"She might have covered it with makeup."

"We can probably get a photo of her."

She took a sip of her coffee. Nice and strong. "I wondered if the woman she remembers from when she was little is different from the older one who came. Madeline seems fond of the memories but frightened of the woman in the yard."

He propped his feet on the battered coffee table. "The kits are on their way."

"It will be such a relief to know. Then we can begin to delve into the background of how Brianna came to be here. That might tell us who is terrorizing us now. I want that man behind bars."

"No more than I do," he said grimly.

She sipped her coffee and studied his expression over the rim of her cup. His comment last night had haunted her. He'd been glad she was pregnant. Glad! When the very thought had terrified her. And her misperception had set the tone of their entire marriage. She'd been sure he felt compelled to marry her, that if he'd had his choice, they never would have seen each other after Hawaii.

What if she hadn't seen anything right?

The DNA kits had been unpacked and spread out on the table. Clay eyed the swabs. "I guess we have to get the samples the way they want them. What do we tell the girls?" He glanced through the window at the children playing in the yard. They were catching lizards.

She took the pitcher of iced tea from the refrigerator and poured a glass over ice, then handed it to him. "We could just tell them we have tests we need to send in. I'm sure they've been to the doctor before. I doubt they'll think anything about it."

"I suppose. One at a time or bring them all in?"

"We'll make it a game with all of them." She shoved open the window. "Girls, would you come in here for a minute?"

The girls left the hapless lizard they'd been chasing and trooped into the kitchen.

"What's that?" Lacie eyed the swabs on the table.

"We're going to see who can do the best job with these swabs," Eden said. She picked one up and held it aloft. "We want you to stick it in your mouth and turn it against your cheek. Like this." She demonstrated, turning the swab against the inside of her cheek. "See if you can get it all wet without sucking on it. You need to push it against your cheek kind of hard but not hard enough to hurt." She finished the sample for herself and popped it into the plastic bag and labeled it with her name.

"I'm going to win!" Katie grabbed the first swab and worked it in her mouth.

The other girls were quick to follow her example. Five minutes later they had five carefully labeled samples. She sent the girls back out to play. "Now you," she told Clay.

He obliged. She labeled his, then slid the samples into the return bag. "Is this even legal?" she asked.

He hesitated. "I'm not sure, to tell you the truth. It wouldn't stand up in a court of law, but I don't think it's illegal. Any father could gather DNA and test a child he's been accused of fathering. I admit, I'd rather do it through the courts, but that will take too much time."

In a few days this nightmare would be over. They'd be able to tell Brianna that she had parents who loved her and wanted her to live with them forever. Eden's eyes misted at the thought.

"Have you thought about how we will tell her?" Clay asked as she sealed the envelope.

"I've thought of little else now that we'll know in a few days."

"And?"

"We have to be careful not to scare her. I'm not sure we should mention the kidnapping. Maybe just say we lost her for a while. Then, when the kidnapper is behind bars, we can tell her the truth."

He nodded. "I've been thinking the same. If Katie happens to be Brianna, she's already dealing with nightmares. We don't want to compound them." Clay's phone rang and he glanced at the screen. "It's Brendan."

She sat down. So much of her past was slamming into her. She wasn't sure she was ready for all of this.

Clay opened a kitchen drawer and rummaged, then produced a pen and paper. "Go ahead," he said.

Brendan must have gotten her father's phone number. Her insides were unsettled. What would she even say when she called? *Hi, I'm the daughter you never acknowledged*. That would go over really well.

Clay disconnected the call. "He got the number."

"I gathered that."

"You look nervous."

She clasped her shaking hands together. "I am."

"I can call for you."

She shook her head. "I need to do this. Maybe there is some sliver of compassion left in his soul for me. I can appeal to him to leave us alone." She didn't remember much about him—just that he was big with black hair and angry eyes.

Clay slid the paper across the table to her. "Tell him to send someone after that pendant and it's all his." He grimaced. "I hate to give it up, though. I liked seeing it on you."

"We'll find something similar," she said.

"All he has to do is leave us alone."

"And tell us which girl is ours," she said, picking up the paper.

"I doubt he knows." He held up the envelope. "This will tell us in a few more days."

She hoped he didn't notice the way her hands shook as she punched in the number. Her mouth was dry as she held the phone to her ear.

"Hola." The man's curt voice was gruff.

The voice turned her insides to pudding. "Is this Hector Santiago?"

"You should have known that before you called, *chica*."

"Don't hang up. Please." She wetted her lips. "Th-This is Eden

Davidson." When silence answered her statement, she thought he'd hung up. "Hello?"

"I am here. What do you want from me?"

"Nothing. I have information for you."

"Perhaps I do not want this information. Especially if there are strings attached. I gave your mother all the money she is getting from me."

"I have something you want."

"Which is?"

"Your missing pendant. The one with the woman and baby."

There was a thump on the other end as though his feet had hit the floor. "You have my pendant?"

A foreboding touched her spine and she shuddered. "I do."

"How is it that you are in possession of this item?"

She was tired of dancing around the truth. He had to know. "My husband has it. We didn't realize its significance in my daughter's kidnapping until yesterday."

The tinkle of ice in a glass came through the phone. "I do not understand."

"I . . . I suspect your son kidnapped my daughter, thinking to get this item back as a ransom once he lured us out for the switch."

"So you killed my son." Irony was in the undercurrent of his words.

"It was an accident." This wasn't going the way she'd thought it would. "Listen, you can have your pendant. We just want to be left alone now. Which child is my Brianna?"

"I know nothing of this matter other than that my son kidnapped a child and died. I never knew what his plan was."

Her hope deflated. Was he lying? "Maybe he wanted to bring the pendant to you as a surprise."

"Perhaps that is so. Thank you for your call. I will send someone to fetch my property."

The phone clicked in her ear. "He hung up." She swallowed hard. "He made no promise to leave us alone."

Clay's face was grim. "He claims to know nothing about Brianna?"

"So he says."

"I'm not sure I believe him."

She chewed her lip. "I don't know for sure, but he appeared to be telling the truth. His son could have been doing it on his own, hoping to gain some favor with Hector. He sounds like a tough and scary man."

"So we're back to square one. But if Hector is the one who has been targeting you, then the harassment will stop."

"Somehow I don't think he's been targeting me. Why scare me? Why not just come and get his property? Kill us if he has to. There is more going on than we know."

"I mean to find out what it is," Clay said. He rose. "I'm going to run these to Rita. She's going to town and can drop them at the post office."

"In a couple of days we'll know which girl is Brianna."

The waiting was almost over.

21

THE BED WELCOMED HER LIKE AN OLD FRIEND, THOUGH SHE DIDN'T EXPECT TO SLEEP WELL. She was beginning to get used to Clay's presence on the other side of the mattress. She waited subconsciously for another scratch on the window or a sinister phone call, but all was quiet.

She was nearly asleep when a shriek tore through the air. She and Clay leaped from the bed at the same time and collided in their haste to get out of the room.

He yanked open the door. "Wait here."

"It's one of the girls!" She followed him down the hall.

When he thrust open the door to the girls' room, light spilled from the hall onto the nearest bed. Katie was sitting upright with her eyes open. Scream after scream tore from her throat.

"Check her."

Eden ran to pull the child into her arms while Clay stepped to the window and peered outside. "It's okay, honey," she said, smoothing the little girl's tangled hair from her face.

Like a monkey, Katie wrapped both arms and legs around Eden. She buried her sweaty face in Eden's neck and burst into tears. Eden rocked her back and forth, shushing her. "I've got you," she said against Katie's hair. "No one will hurt you."

When the child's sobs tapered off, Katie pulled away and a last shudder rippled through her. Eden glanced around to see all the girls sitting up with wide eyes. "Did you see something?" she asked Katie.

Katie shook her head. "I was dreaming. That man came."

"What man, honey?" A nightmare. Her gaze locked with Clay's over the top of Katie's head as he soothed the other girls and they settled back into bed.

"I don't know. Daddy hid me in the closet. But he never came back to get me. The policeman took me away."

"You didn't see the man?"

Katie put her thumb in her mouth and shook her head. She pulled it out shamefacedly, then put her hand in the pocket of her pajamas. "Just his back. I peeked through the keyhole. He had a blue jacket."

Eden hugged her. "It's okay. No one will hurt you."

Katie shivered. "What if he comes back? Maybe he thinks I saw him. But I didn't."

"I don't think he'll be back. Mr. Clay will protect you if he does. I bet he's bigger than that man."

A ghost of a smile lifted the little girl's lips, and she nodded. "He was skinny and not nearly as tall as my daddy."

A little more of a description but still not much. "Could you see his hair?"

She nodded. "It was red like mine. I only 'member because I never saw anyone with my color hair before. Daddy said it was because I came from the angels."

"The angels? What about your mommy?"

"I don't have a mommy." She nestled against Eden's chest. "I want a mommy!"

The words made something nameless swell in Eden's heart. Longing, regret, and pain all mixed to form some emotion that was harder to put her finger on. Maybe *helplessness* was the right word. She'd been caught in a maelstrom and was drowning in all the events that kept slamming her under the water.

"You're a sweet, sweet girl," she whispered against Katie's hair. She inhaled the fragrance of little girl and choked back the lump in her throat. She glanced at Clay. "Anything?"

He shook his head. "Guess it was just a nightmare."

Katie went limp against Eden, and her breathing evened out. Eden reluctantly let Clay lift the child from her arms. On the other side of the bed, Eden pulled back the covers, plumped the pillow, then covered Katie after Clay laid her down. When Eden kissed the soft cheek, she detected a slight smile on Katie's face. Even in sleep, she knew when she was loved.

The other girls were snuggled back in their pillows. She and Clay made another round, comforting each one and bestowing kisses on every face. She would miss this ritual when she was gone from here.

They backed out of the room. "Is that someone at the door?" Clay asked.

She heard the knock then. Not timid, but not loud either.

Authoritative. She followed Clay to the door. The man peering in the window was in his forties. His black hair curled over his collar. He looked dangerous to Eden.

"Are you sure you should open it?" she whispered. "He hasn't seen us yet." But as soon as the words were out of her mouth, Clay flipped on the light.

"Stay here," he said. He crossed the room in four strides and opened the door. "Can I help you?"

"Santiago sent me." The man didn't wait for an invitation but brushed past Clay to stand in the living room.

That was fast. "I'll get it," Eden said. Anything to get away. The man's gaze seemed to see through her cotton pajamas.

She rushed back to the bedroom and snatched up the pendant. Before she took it to the man, she pulled on a robe and tied it. One last time, she ran her fingers over the precious piece and allowed herself to regret that she had to give it up. It had been such a symbol of the family they wanted to build.

He and Clay were silent and tense by the door when she returned. The sooner they got this guy out of here, the happier she would be. "Here it is." She handed him the pendant.

He inspected it, then grunted. "You were telling the truth. I will tell Santiago."

What if they hadn't? Would her own father have murdered her?

Clay could lie and watch her sleep for hours. He propped himself on his elbow and studied the even rise and fall of Eden's chest. So relaxed in sleep. All guards down. Every care eased from her face.

He could only pray turning over that pendant last night would make a difference in the attacks that had been directed at Eden, though she might be right to think there was no connection between the threats and the jewelry. He eased out of bed and went to the kitchen to make coffee. The girls all still slept as well. The late night had worn everyone out. Except for him. He was alert and eager to learn more today from Brendan.

The sun had just begun to peek over the mountain's jagged silhouette when he took his coffee out to the porch. He watched the sun chase the purple shadows from the peaks, exposing the cholla and prickly pear. A blooming cactus or two brought a little color to the hillside. Sipping his coffee, he rocked in the chair. The motion soothed him and let his mind wander. Only God could heal his relationship with Eden. The cracks went deep, and they needed the right foundation.

Boots crunched on gravel, and he saw Rick's familiar form. The other man mounted the steps and dropped into the chair beside Clay. "Want some coffee?" Clay asked him.

"Not that stuff you're drinking. A spoon could stand up in it by itself. I can smell how strong it is from here." Rick grinned and stretched out his legs. "Nothing like early morning for talking with God."

"My thoughts too." Clay felt a real connection with Rick. After rolling his suitcase around the world, Clay didn't have many close friends. His defenses were down with this guy. "Too early to hear from Brendan."

"Actually, I just got off the phone with him."

"That guy ever sleep?"

"He's a panther. Always on the prowl." Rick propped a booted ankle on his knee. "He watched that video from Walmart last night."

"And?"

"The two guys were Hispanic. Maybe Colombian, maybe not. But the interesting thing is that he thought he recognized one of them as a thug who works for Santiago."

Something kicked in Clay's chest. "So Paige is my daughter!"

"Whoa, don't go jumping to conclusions. We don't know that. For one thing, Brendan only thinks it might be him. He's going to run the tape through some programs and see if he can get a definite match."

Clay rubbed his eyes. "This is going to hurt that nice family. We'd hoped for one of the other girls."

"Like I said, don't assume anything." He stared at Clay. "The kidnapper lured you here. Why? He could have taken you out anytime and gotten that pendant, if that's what he's after. Good grief, man, you carried it in your pocket! All he had to do was knock you upside the head and take it."

"I know. Eden seems to be a personal target, which makes no sense. She wasn't even with me in Colombia. Or when I received the picture of the girls here at Bluebird."

"Any idea who might want to hurt her?"

"I had my suspects."

"Had? No longer?"

"Eden called Santiago. He sent a guy to pick up the pendant."

"And you're sure it's over?"

Clay sipped his coffee. "I don't know. Something still feels off about it. Look, there's something we haven't mentioned."

Rick sighed and put his boot back on the floor. "More danger?"

"No, nothing like that. But after Brianna was taken, our marriage fell apart."

Rick's eyes held sympathy. "It happens. Hard to endure so much pain."

"Eden blamed herself. I blamed myself. We blamed each other. Toxic combo. I headed out for a mission, and she wasted no time in ditching me." He hated the derision in his voice.

"I'm sorry."

"Eden filed for divorce. The papers came while I was overseas. I shoved them in a drawer and ignored them. Always thought eventually I'd come back and talk her into trying again."

"And you did."

"Only after I was shoved into it by the picture."

"Bet she was surprised."

Clay wished he could smile at the memory of her shock, but his own had been too great. There she was, about to accept another man's proposal. "I'd always known where she was, but my stupid pride wouldn't let me chase her. I found her in the middle of a marriage proposal."

"But she was still married to you?"

"Yep. But she didn't know it. She'd signed the papers and didn't realize the final decree hadn't been issued. Her attorney had a heart attack and never followed up after he got back to work."

"Hoo-ee, you mean this was one of those scenes like in the movies? You showed up and told her the happy news?"

"At least I got there before she actually said yes." Clay managed a weak smile.

"Bet that was a shock when she saw you."

"I thought she might faint. But I'll give her this—the minute she heard Brianna was still alive, she didn't hesitate. She walked away from the guy and never looked back."

Rick stretched out his legs. “What about him?”

“He let her go. Seemed to think finding Brianna was the best thing for her to focus on.”

“So what’s the problem? She’s resistant to trying again?”

“Bull’s-eye on your first guess, my friend. I’m working on it, though.”

“My wife is pretty perceptive,” Rick said. “She said the other day that it warmed her heart to see the way the two of you look at each other.”

Clay wanted to cling to that encouragement, to hope Eden held some kind of feelings for him besides disappointment and betrayal. “I’m crazy about her,” he said. “From the first time I saw her, I haven’t looked at another woman.”

“She’ll find it hard to resist that kind of devotion.”

“Well, that’s the hope anyway.”

Rick’s stare was speculative. “Where will you go from here when that guy is behind bars and you have Brianna back?”

“Wish I knew. She’s agreed to live together to give Brianna more stability.”

“I don’t know much about the problems in your relationship, but I know one thing,” Rick said, his expression grave. “God can work miracles.”

“That’s what I’m going to need.”

“And that’s what I’ll pray for with you.”

When Rick bowed his head, Clay realized he meant now. God had sent him a prayer warrior right when he needed it.

22

AFTER CHURCH AND SUNDAY DINNER, EDEN WENT WITH ALLIE TO TAKE POSSESSION OF A donated horse. The misery in the old mare's eyes clutched at Eden's heart. "Where'd she come from?" she asked Allie, who was coaxing the animal from the battered trailer with a sugar cube in her outstretched hand. "She doesn't look like she's been fed very well."

Allie's dark eyes flashed. "The way people mistreat their animals makes me furious. I'd like to put this girl's owner in a barn and feed him every three days and see how he likes it."

"Is that what happened?" The horse moseyed toward Eden, and she stepped back, even though she wished she had the courage to touch that rough fur.

"Yes. A neighbor turned him in. Rick talked the guy into letting us have her for a hundred dollars."

"You bought her?"

"It was the only way to save her." The mare finally nibbled at the sugar in Allie's hand, but she flinched when Allie touched her nose. "Easy," she murmured.

"Will she live?" Eden wanted to touch the poor, mistreated thing. She put out a timid hand, then withdrew it.

"I think so. Shannon seems optimistic. This old girl is malnourished, but the right food and some love will fix her right up. We have plenty of both."

"You seem to have an abundance of horses. Do you do this all the time?"

Allie stepped back when the horse meandered away. She wiped her hands on her jeans. "My grandfather had a dream. He saw how abused children responded to mistreated animals. A bond of love helped them both. So he opened this ranch to help children and horses."

"And you've run it ever since?"

"Well, Rick has. I came later." Allie smiled. "I love it here." She glanced at Eden's tan slacks. "There's a really great jeans store in town. Nice selection. We should go shopping."

She couldn't wear jeans any easier than she could shoot someone. Well, maybe she could. She'd been dreaming about jeans and boots. What did that mean? Was she changing? Being here had opened her eyes in some ways. But she wasn't quite ready for jeans.

"Maybe," she said. "I do love to shop. I need to make a call. Do you mind watching the girls a minute?"

"They're fine. Buzz and the guys have them under control. I'll sit right here and oversee." She hopped onto the top rung of the fence.

"Thanks." Eden went to the house, got the portable phone, then settled on the back step. Maybe she shouldn't, but she wanted to tell Daniel what had happened with her mother.

Glancing at her watch, she saw it would be two o'clock back in Indiana. Daniel would be working on his bills this afternoon, maybe watching sports on TV. Sometimes the two of them used to play Monopoly while they ate fudge and popcorn. She missed those days.

The phone rang and rang. She was about to hang up when he finally picked up on the other end. She knew he was on because she heard the TV in the background but he said nothing. "Daniel?"

"I told you not to call me, Eden."

"I know, but I thought you might want to know that I met with my mother," she said before he could hang up.

There was a long pause. "Oh? And why should that interest me?"

His voice was so cold. This was a mistake. "If you're not interested, that's all there is to say. Sorry I bothered you." She hesitated, but when he didn't say anything more, she clicked off the phone.

Her eyes burned. Daniel had been her brother in all the ways that counted. She must have hurt him terribly. Her chest heaved, quick little gasps of air. Daniel was so bitter, so angry. What had she done to him? It was as though she'd worn blinders all her life and didn't see anything clearly.

"Eden?"

She lifted her head at the sound of Clay's voice. "You were right," she said. "Daniel hates me. Hates me!"

He embraced her. "I'm sorry."

She leaned her head into his chest. "I'm not sure why this has hit me so hard."

"What did he say?"

"I called him to let him know I'd seen my mother. Since he gave me the agency's number and all."

"They say there's a fine line between love and hate. He crossed it?"

"It appears so." She leaned into him. His shirt smelled of Downy. She wished she could stay here all afternoon, sheltered by Clay's strength.

He dropped a kiss on her head. "We have that international dinner tonight, right? How about you go do your cooking and try not to worry. I'll look after the girls."

She knew he was right. There was no repairing the damage now. Daniel would get over it or he wouldn't. She went to the kitchen of the main house.

Rita had an apron for Eden and supplies laid out for her. And a pot of coffee on. "You know me too well," Eden told her.

Rita wrinkled her nose. "You'll need all the strength you can get to endure the coconut smell."

Eden grinned, then poured a cup of coffee. "You can leave if it's going to be too painful."

"I'm a big girl. I think you'll need some help." She glanced around. "Where's Clay? I made him some oatmeal-scotchie cookies."

"Those are his favorite!"

"The way to a man's heart is through his stomach."

"You'll have to give me the recipe." Eden turned to her ingredients. "The last batch I made turned out okay, but I have to double it for tonight." Fortified by coffee with cream, she set to work. The rice came out a little sticky, but the chicken mixture looked and smelled right.

She tasted it. "I think it's okay." What a relief. She hadn't wanted to let Allie down. She held up a spoonful. "You can't really taste the coconut."

Rita shook her head. "I'd be able to taste it."

"Are you going to the dinner tonight?" Eden asked.

Rita flipped a blond braid over her shoulder. "I should say! There's a cowboy who works for Jack MacGowan that I have my eye on. I'm not letting one of the other women get ahead of me." She smiled. "Besides, it's good fodder for my novel."

"How's that coming?" Eden had never known a writer.

"I'm halfway through. I got me a book on how to write a romance. I have one of those brooding heroes. One who sweeps the heroine off her feet. Like Clay." She sighed blissfully. "I bet I get a movie offer when it's done. Maybe Clay can land the lead role."

Rita had self-confidence at least. Eden chuckled. "He'd have all the girls after him."

She smiled and put the cover on the dish, then went to find Clay. They had to be at the community center in half an hour. He wasn't at the barn or at the ranch house. Rick told her Clay had asked about a handsaw and suggested she check the shed at the back edge of the property.

The building was on the west side of the back pasture, a dot in the distance from the backyard. Eden followed a crushed-stone path through knee-high scrub and sage to the building. Painted red like the barn, it appeared to be a fairly new addition to the property, about thirty feet square. The door was shut tight but the padlock hung loose. She opened the door and peered inside. It contained tools, a yard tractor, and various gardening items.

"Clay?" she called. The scent of oil and dust made her sneeze. She advanced into the building. "Are you in here?" There was no answer.

The gardening tools hanging on the wall reminded her of when she was a kid. Her foster mother had loved azaleas. There was a small plot of flowers at the edge of their house that held four plants, and her mother deadheaded them and mulched them all summer long. Eden touched a pruning shear, then turned to go.

Strange. She thought she'd left the door open. She twisted the handle and pushed, but it didn't move. Maybe she had to turn the knob the other way. She tried that, but the door still refused to budge. She yanked on it and tried everything she could before she admitted that she seemed to be locked in. Maybe there was another way out. She saw another door at the back and went to try it. It refused to open as well.

And what was that smell? She sniffed the air and the hair stood on the back of her neck. It was cologne, the same smell that had been in Clay's truck after it was taken. "Who's there?" she asked, hating the way her voice shook. "Show yourself."

Was that a scratching sound? Her skin crawled. She had to get out of here. Whirling, she ran to the window on the front of the building. She flipped the latch and tried to raise the sash. It seemed stuck. Maybe she needed to be taller to get better leverage. Grabbing a nearby bucket, she upended it and stepped on its bottom. She shoved the top of the window with all her might but it still wouldn't open. From her vantage point, she realized someone had locked the padlock on the door.

She hopped from the bucket and ran with it to the back window. The back door was padlocked too. She tried to lift the window there and managed to get it up a crack before it stuck again. She smelled gasoline, and the odor began to intensify. The shadows grew deeper too. Was someone hiding behind the tool bench or the yard tractor?

She shrank back against the wall. Would Clay miss her and come searching for her? Maybe Rick would tell him she was out here looking for him. She heard something else. A faint *whoosh*. Then another smell, acrid and noxious, began to overpower the gas. Smoke? Surely not. She sniffed the air again. It was stronger now. No mistaking it. Something was on fire.

A green hose was coiled on the wall. She rushed for it and grabbed it off the hook. Where was the faucet? She frantically looked around the space but saw no spigot. Maybe the hose was simply stored here. The smell was stronger now, and a haze hung in the air. She coughed at the burning in her lungs. There, on the workbench. A crowbar. She grabbed it and ran for the partially open window. With the hook of the crowbar on the bottom edge of the sill, she pried as hard as she could. It went up a bit but still not far enough to squeeze through.

The smoke swirled around her, obscuring her vision even more. The windows were small panes. Standing back a bit, she swung the crowbar at the window. The end of it smashed through the middle pane. The grids were part of the window, not removable. But maybe she could knock them out. She swung the heavy metal bar again and the thin wood popped out. Encouraged, she began to batter the window as hard and fast as she could. Her vision swam and she coughed.

She wasn't going to make it.

23

CLAY WIPED HIS DAMP BROW. HE'D JUST FINISHED CLEANING OUT SOME STALLS. SOME ICED tea would be in order after he returned the saw. He found Buzz in the barn. "Thanks for the saw. Where's it go?"

The old cowboy glanced up from messing with a horse's hoof. "It belongs in the shed out yonder. I just had it up here to work on a fence."

"If you tell me where it goes, I'll put it back."

"Just inside the door to your left are hooks with other tools. Any of those hooks will do." Buzz went back to his chore.

"Be back shortly. The kids will be ready for their rides." Clay stepped outside the barn and squinted at the midday sun that glared down from a cloudless sky. Starting for the outbuilding, he saw a smudge against the sky. Almost simultaneously, he smelled something. *Smoke?* He stared and realized flames were licking at the roof of the building.

"Fire!" he shouted. "Buzz, Rick, the building is on fire!" He saw Buzz exit the barn and run toward him. The cowboy repeated the shout of "Fire!" and Clay put on a burst of speed and ran toward the building. Rick spurted out his door and raced toward him as well.

Clay reached the structure. It was padlocked. Buzz and Rick were only moments behind him.

Rick caught at his arm. "Did you see Eden? She was coming back here to look for you."

The men's gazes locked, and the fear in Rick's face kicked Clay in the gut. "I never came back here. Buzz had the saw." He yanked at the lock. "You have the key?" She couldn't be in there with it locked.

More help spilled toward them. Allie, Rita, Della, Zeke, the other hands. Most carried buckets of water. Rick dug his keys from his pocket and selected a small silver one. He thrust it in the keyhole and twisted. The lock fell open.

Allie reached him. "Where's Eden?" Clay asked her.

Her brows rose. "She was cooking, then came out here to find you. It's time for us to be leaving for the dinner."

Clay's pulse kicked. Then he heard a sound. A choked cry. He yanked the lock from the latch and pulled open the door. Black smoke roiled out. "Eden!" he yelled. He started to run inside, but Rick grabbed his arm.

"It's not safe!" Rick shouted.

Clay jerked out of Rick's grasp and plunged into the building. The smoke was like a living creature. Writhing and hot, it sucked all the oxygen from the air. Soot coated his tongue and throat, insinuated itself into his lungs and ears. The roar of the fire was so loud his own voice screaming Eden's name sounded muffled.

He stumbled over something and fell. Down here on the floor he could breathe a little better, so he crawled forward. "Eden!" he shouted.

His hand touched something yielding and inert. Cloth covering a leg. Eden? He touched a back, an arm, hair. It was her. But which way was out? In the blackness, he couldn't tell. His ears were ringing, and he began to pray for guidance. The fire flared off to his left. The roof screamed and groaned like someone in pain. The ringing in his ears grew louder, then a roof beam crashed down a few feet away. The fire flared higher, and he saw sunlight through the clouds of smoke.

Move, move! He couldn't stay here paralyzed. He needed to go where his toes were pointed. The answer should have been clear immediately. That was the way he'd come. Sliding backward, he dragged Eden's body with him. All he could do was pray he kept going in a straight line back toward the door. He laid his cheek on the hot concrete to rest a moment and try to draw in a bit of oxygen. He thought he heard shouts. Maybe they were close to being out of this nightmare.

Gathering his strength, he began to slide back again. His left foot hit resistance. The wall? "Rick," he croaked. His voice sounded weak and too soft. Rick would never hear him. He licked blistered lips and tried again. "Rick."

A hand grabbed his ankle and yanked. He had just enough strength to hang on to Eden's leg as someone hauled them from the inferno. Moments later he was lying on the hard ground, staring up into an impossibly bright and blue sky. His vision was blurry, but he recognized Rick bending over him.

"Eden," Clay croaked.

"She's out of the building. Allie is taking care of her."

Rick cupped water in his hand and trickled some over Clay's face. He'd never felt anything so wonderful. He opened his mouth and let a bit of the blessed moisture touch his parched tongue. "Does Eden have water?"

"Allie's giving her some."

Clay rolled onto his stomach and got to his hands and knees. "Where is she? Is she going to be okay?" He didn't wait for Rick to answer him but crawled forward a few feet to find his wife. She was lying on her back, but her eyes were open. Her face was wet too. The water Allie had given her had left rivulets in the soot marking her skin.

"Eden," he whispered.

She turned her head and saw him. "You look like you've been playing in mud," she said. Her voice was hoarse.

"How do you feel?"

"Alive." Her hand crept toward him. "You nearly died."

"So did you." Inexplicably, he wanted to laugh.

Her hand crept into his. "You nearly died with me."

"I wouldn't have wanted to live if you'd died." The words were out before he could stop them. And he'd never said anything he meant more.

Clay's words had seared her heart. Could he possibly feel that way? Eden sipped the sweet tea Allie had pressed against her lips in the cool shade of the front porch. Clay was beside her. Her skin felt tight and hot. One spot on her leg was blistered, but not a large enough area to require hospitalization. The doctor had come and gone, leaving aloe cream to help with the burned areas.

Gracie Wayne had come over to take charge of the children and ease their fears while the adults tried to figure out what happened. Firefighters were pouring through the smoking ruins now.

Allie refilled the glass of tea. "Keep drinking," she ordered. "The doctor says we have to keep you both hydrated."

The warmth of Clay's arm against hers was almost painful against her reddened skin, but Eden didn't want to move away.

"What happened?" he asked, his voice hoarse from the smoke. "Do you remember?"

Eden was going to have to tell them about the locks and the cologne she smelled. Her sense of safety vanished. "Someone locked me in and set the fire."

His arm tightened painfully around her. "How do you know?"

"I left the padlock dangling when I went in. When I tried to leave, it was locked. I saw it through the window."

"It was locked when I got there," Rick concurred.

Allie shuddered. "Then what happened?"

"I smelled gasoline, then I heard a *whoosh*. The fire igniting, I suppose. Shortly after that the smoke came. I grabbed a crowbar and tried to bust out the window, but I couldn't get it done before the smoke got so bad that I couldn't breathe. I dropped to the floor so I could get air. That was the last thing I remember until you were giving me water."

Rick was frowning as he stared at her. "I don't think this has anything to do with Clay. You seem to be the only target. First he tried to scare you away, but you didn't go, so he's upped the stakes."

Her chest felt tight, and not just from smoke inhalation. Someone out there hated her so much that he wanted to burn her alive. "But why? I gave him back the pendant."

"Maybe I need to give your father a call," Clay said.

There was something deeper going on. Eden took another sip of tea, even though it was sweeter than she liked. "What if it's not him?"

"What if it is?" Clay countered, scowling.

"We need to investigate all possibilities. Check your background," Rick said. "What were you doing before you got here?"

"I've told you—working as a nurse," she said.

"Let's back up and take another look," Clay said. "How did you meet Kent?"

With their eyes on her, she hated to talk about Kent. "At church. You're on the wrong track there. Kent is a good guy. A friend at church introduced us."

"Was she interested in him?" Allie asked.

"I don't think so." Eden thought back to the church-wide dinner that Kent had come to. Had Molly been interested in him? What exactly had she said? Something about him being the prize sought by all the unattached women. "I suppose it's possible."

"How about hobbies or other activities?" Rick asked.

What could she say? That she collected shoes and purses like some women sought out fresh produce? That she was a professional window shopper? She shook her head.

"What about Daniel?" Clay asked, his voice quiet.

She'd been hoping Clay wouldn't bring him up. Shifting away from him, she straightened and shook her head. "I don't believe he'd try to hurt me."

"You just told me he hated you," Clay said, pulling his arm away.

"Not enough to kill me. I don't believe it."

"Who's Daniel?" Allie asked.

"My best friend. Well, he was. We grew up in the same foster home. He's like a brother."

"He wanted to be more to her, but she never saw it," Clay said, his voice hard.

Could Daniel want to harm her? She thought of his light blue eyes, his genial smile and slim build. "He's not the type. He might be mad at me right now, but he'd never do anything to hurt me. I'm sure of it."

"What's Daniel's last name?" Rick had his pen and paper out again.

Eden pressed her lips together, but Clay told him. She glared at Clay. "This is ridiculous. Daniel wouldn't do such a thing. It takes a really twisted mind to try to torch a building with a person inside."

The problem was, she didn't know anyone that sick.

Clay showered after the children were in bed, but the water on his tight skin was still an agony. He dressed in loose cotton sweats and went to find Eden. She was on the porch swing. Her knees were drawn to her chest and she sat in a ball and looked out toward the remains of the shed.

The swing creaked when he sat beside her. "You okay?"

She put her feet back on the floor. "The burns still hurt a little. I'm sure yours do too." When he nodded, she leaned back against his arm. "But we're still alive. Thanks to you."

Had she even noticed his slip of the tongue when he'd pulled her out? She hadn't said anything about it. He'd meant it, though. Life without her wouldn't be worth living. They swung in companionable silence for several minutes.

"I'm going to call your father," he said, holding up the portable phone.

She shook her head. "Not tonight. I can't take any more."

"I have to, honey. I've been thinking about it for two days. Someone hates you very much to try to burn you alive." His throat tightened and he couldn't say more.

She leaned her head back against his arm. "It is horrible to think about being hated that much."

"I tend to think it's not your dad who's behind this," he said. "But I want to verify it."

He plucked the phone number from his pocket and punched it into the phone. It would be much more pleasant to sit here and smell the apples in her hair, but he couldn't go through another day like this. Refused to go through it again. He'd nearly lost her.

The phone rang on the other end for so long that he thought he would have to leave a message. Then a gruff voice said, "Santiago."

"Mr. Santiago, this is Eden's husband, Clay Larson."

"I received my property back, if that is why you are calling."

"Glad to hear it, but I have something much more grave to discuss with you."

"Yes?"

"Someone tried to kill Eden today. She was locked in a shed and it was set on fire." He heard the guy gasp, then nothing for a moment. "Mr. Santiago? Are you there?"

"I am here. I gave instructions . . ." He went quiet.

Gave instructions to his henchman? So Hector Santiago *was* behind the attacks, even though he claimed to know nothing about

Brianna's kidnapping. "I'd appreciate it if you'd give those instructions again. I fear you have a rogue employee."

"It may be more than that, Mr. Larson. I will do what I can, but the risks to Eden are grave."

Clay's neck prickled. "What do you mean?"

"I can say no more. You will have to guard her carefully."

"At least you care a little about your daughter," Clay said.

"I doubt she is my daughter, but I can't have a rogue—"

"Of course she's your daughter!" Clay saw Eden's eyes widen, and he wished she hadn't heard that. Clay heard a click and stared at the phone. "He hung up on me."

She lifted her head. "He did that to me too. I think he likes the power. He says I'm not his daughter?"

"He didn't seem sure. It sounds like he told whoever was after you to lay off, but the guy disobeyed. I think your father isn't sure he can call him off."

Her eyes went wide. "So he *was* behind it? But why?"

If only he knew. It appeared this was far from over.

24

CLAY SCOOPED UP HAY WITH HIS PITCHFORK AND TOSSED SOME TO THE HORSE IN THE FIRST stall. The sweet scent of the grass blended with the earthy smell of the horse. He liked the combination for some reason. The barn was like a secret friend, living and breathing the odor and life of the horses and the cowboys. Living here on the ranch had changed him in some fundamental ways.

He wanted something different in his relationship with Eden too. He'd thought revealing his heart to her would bring about that sea change. If anything, she'd been a little more aloof the last two days. He'd tried to tell himself it was because she was hurting from her burns, but he wasn't sure that was the reason. Their talk the other night may have made her want to keep her distance.

A shadow fell on the haystack, and he glanced up to see India in the doorway. "Want to help?" he asked her.

She smiled and nodded, coming forward. "I brought Frost some sugar." She dug into the pocket of her jeans and produced two cubes covered with lint.

Her black hair was in cornrows tied with pink bows. Eden loved messing with the girls' hair, and they seemed to enjoy it as well. India's pink top had chocolate on it, and a smear of chocolate frosting dotted the corner of her mouth. Her jeans were getting too short, and he made a mental note to ask Eden to take her shopping.

He leaned on his tool and smiled. "The pitchfork is a little big for you, but you can feed Bluebird some hay when you're done spoiling Frost."

The little girl offered the sugar to the young gelding, then scampered back to where Clay stood. She seized a handful of hay, then held it up to Bluebird, Betsy's horse.

"Are you enjoying yourself here?" Clay asked.

India nodded. "I wish I could stay here forever with you and Miss Eden. I don't want to go back." She sounded forlorn.

The little girl had endeared herself to him in the past two weeks. Always cheerful, always smiling. But sometimes he caught her by herself with a pensive air and tear-filled eyes. She would never tell him the problem, though. He'd often wished she were Brianna, though her nutmeg skin made it impossible. His heart called her his, though.

She shuddered and clasped her arms around herself. "The fire was scary," she said. "I hate fire."

"I'm sure you do, honey. I'm sorry about your parents."

She hopped down from her perch on the fence where she'd been petting Bluebird. Two puppies raced to flop in her lap. "I can't remember my mama's voice anymore." Her voice was choked. "I never wanted to forget it."

He put his hand on her head. "I'm sure she loved you very much."

"Do you think she's looking down from heaven and watching me? The preacher says she is."

They were killed in a meth lab explosion. What were the chances that her parents were Christians? "Did your mama take you to church?"

India nodded. "We went every Sunday. Sometimes at night too. And Mama went to a Bible study across the street."

"How about your daddy?"

"I didn't see him much. He was always working. Sometimes he gave me horsey rides on his back." Her eyes were moist when she glanced up at him. "About heaven?"

"I think your mommy is there waiting for you."

"Mama threw my dad out, you know. She said he was doing bad things in the basement. I guess he was. He came back when she was at work. When she got back, she yelled at him and he slammed the door to the basement. Then she took me to bed and went back downstairs. The boom woke me up."

"How did you get out?" he asked.

"An angel," she said simply, her tone grave.

"An angel?"

She nodded. "He was dressed in a firefighter outfit, but when he carried me out, he disappeared and I never saw him again."

He could see she believed it. And who was he to say it wasn't real? When did he start thinking God would never do something miraculous for him? He brought about miracles every day. He'd saved Brianna when they all thought she was dead. What the kidnapper meant for evil, God had redeemed. Though danger was still out there somewhere, Clay had to trust God was going to see them through this. He'd done it so far.

"Mr. Clay?" India plucked at his shirtsleeve. "You have a funny look on your face."

"I was just thinking about how God takes care of things for us."

"Mama always said that too. And he let me come here. I prayed and prayed for him to take me out of that house."

"What's happening there, honey?" he asked, making sure to gentle his voice.

She was quiet a minute, her small face serious as she worked out what to say. He could see the indecision on her face, in the twist of her mouth and the darting of her gaze from him to the ground.

"There's five of us orphans," she said finally. "Cal and Wanda take their two kids to do fun stuff and leave us home. We usually have soup or peanut butter sandwiches for dinner." She lowered her voice to a whisper. "The older kids say they just took us in for the money."

Clay didn't doubt it. There were great foster parents out there but some stinkers too. The good and the bad mixed up together, as in all of life. He wanted to do something for this little girl. Did she have to go back to that situation? Could Rick make a recommendation that she be moved?

He'd never expected to be so embroiled in the lives of these kids.

Her burns had faded to darkened skin. Eden had avoided talking about anything personal with Clay. She didn't want to rush into anything, the way she had crashed into their marriage. Everything in her wanted to take his declaration of love at face value, but she hadn't been able to handle his frequent absences. What made her think she could endure them any more easily now?

India held Eden's left hand and Lacie held her right. Clay herded the other girls behind them as they hurried toward the store. Madeline wore her princess costume over her jeans. The girls stepped over the weeds sprouting through the cracks in the sidewalk, chanting, "Step on a crack, break your mother's back."

The morbid song brought an image of her birth mother's face to Eden. What was she going to do about her mother's desire to have a relationship? There was no animosity in Eden's heart, just caution. She didn't have the energy to focus on her mother when all she wanted to do was find Brianna and rebuild her life.

India yanked on the store door, and the cool rush of air hitting Eden's face brought her out of her thoughts. "Who's ready to buy jeans?" she asked.

"Me!" Madeline said, shuffling behind her in the plastic heels that went with her costume. "I don't want ones with holes. Can we get some with lace?"

"I'll see what I can do," Clay said, keeping a straight face.

Eden smiled and led the way to the stacks of girls' jeans. She pulled out sizes ranging from fives to sevens. "Let's try some on."

"I want red ones," Lacie said.

"How about a red top? I don't think they make red jeans," Eden said.

"Right here are some," the child said, pointing to a stack of colored jeans.

Sure enough, there were red ones in her size. Eden shrugged and draped two pairs over her arm. "Whatever you want," she said.

She found jeans for all the girls, then realized Clay was missing. When he reappeared, the smug expression on his face told her she wasn't going to like the reason he'd disappeared.

"What have you been up to?" she asked, narrowing her gaze at him.

His grin widened. "Who, me?"

Then she noticed the jeans on his arm. "Oh no."

"Oh yes. You need some too. And some boots." He held up what looked suspiciously like snakeskin boots.

Katie clapped her hands and jumped up and down. "Yeah, we can match!"

"I don't think so," Eden said. But when the girls' pleading faces turned her way, she began to relent. Surely she was adult enough not to care what people thought of her anymore. Who said she had to maintain that old image? She could re-create herself here. With Clay and the girls, she could be herself and not worry that someone might think she was poor white trash.

"It's hard to fit jeans, and I don't have time to try on half a dozen pair," she said.

Clay's smiled turned even more smug. "These will fit. Trust me." He held them out. She held his warm gaze as she took them. "If they don't fit, we'll forget them. I found some with lace for Madeline." He handed a pair of jeans with lace at the hem and on the pockets to the little girl, who squealed and clutched them to her chest.

Eden smiled and ushered the girls into the dressing room. The way he'd gone to the trouble to find them for her touched her in ways she hadn't expected. Clay surprised her at every turn.

After she got the girls fitted, she tried on her jeans. They fit perfectly. The boots fit too. She looked taller and even more slender in the dark jeans and heeled boots. All she needed was a saddle and he'd be putting her in the rodeo.

"I want a style show," Clay called from outside the dressing room. "You all have been in there long enough."

Her cheeks flared with heat when she stepped out of the dressing room and saw the appreciation in his eyes.

"Told you they'd fit," he said. "You look sensational."

A curtsy wasn't appropriate in these clothes, but she did one anyway. "Thank you. They're comfortable."

"Look at me, Mr. Clay," Katie said. She did a handspring across the floor. "Mine are stretchy."

"Very nice," Clay said. He complimented each girl in turn.

Eden marveled at his ability to say the most encouraging thing to each child. He was a born daddy.

25

A TRIP TO A BUFFALO RANCH. WHOSE IDEA WAS THIS? EDEN GESTURED TO THE GIRLS TO board the van. Zeke and Della already had their charges in the back and settled for the drive. Eden's girls were squealing and jumping up and down with excitement as she herded them onto the bus. Rita had come along as well. She wanted to research a buffalo ranch for one of her romance novels.

Allie waved to Eden from the porch. "Phone call," Allie said.

Eden stepped back off the van a moment and motioned for Clay to take over. Peering at the caller ID, she saw it was her mother's number. "Hello, Mom."

"Eden, dear, I wanted to check and see if I might stop by and see you."

"You're still in the area?"

"We've spent the past several nights here in Alpine. I . . . I wanted to give you a chance to adjust before I called again."

Eden found she wanted to see her mother, if only to find out if there was any chance that Hector Santiago wasn't her father. "We are going to Marathon today, to a buffalo ranch. It shouldn't be more than about thirty minutes from you." She gave her mother directions, then hung up and climbed into the van.

"Who was that?" Clay's eyes were shadowed. Neither of them had slept well last night because the girls were unusually wound up from their shopping adventure. "My mother. She's still in Alpine. She and Omar are meeting us at the ranch."

The bus was ready to leave, so there was no more time for a private conversation. As they traveled to the ranch, Eden thought about how to ask what she needed to know. Her mother was bound to be offended if Eden openly doubted her mother could know the identity of her father. The house had been a merry-go-round of men. How could Nancy be certain? Eden needed to know more.

"There they are!" Katie shouted, hopping up and down in her seat.

The buffalo grazed in a fenced meadow. The vanload of kids erupted into squeals. The animals were bigger than Eden expected. They lifted shaggy heads as the vehicle pulled into the driveway and stopped. Clay and Zeke guided the children out for the tour. Pen and paper in hand, Rita trailed behind taking notes.

"Are you all right?" Della asked Eden as she guided the last of her kids to the van door. "You look rather pale today. Are your burns still bothering you?"

"Not bad today. It was just a rough night. I could have taken another day before dealing with a buffalo tour."

"I've been here before. It's rather tame but the girls will enjoy it."

Della followed Eden out of the van, and they joined their husbands and the children at the fence. The girls were on the first rung of the fence, but Clay made them get down as the owner came toward them.

"They're not really buffalo," India said, tossing her black braids. "They're bison. Buffalo are water buffalo."

"How'd you know that?" Eden asked.

"I looked it up."

Though the little girl was only a year older than the others, she seemed much more mature. Eden hugged her and stared at the shaggy beasts.

"They're big and scary," Madeline said. "I don't like them."

Paige sneezed. "I think I'm 'llergic," she whispered. "Can I wait in the van?"

"You're not allergic. It will be fun." Eden pointed toward the sign that explained facts about the buffalo. Or bison, as India had insisted. One of the buffalo watched the girls climbing on the fence. The beast lowered its head and pawed. Eden frowned. "I think that one doesn't like your red shirt, Lacie. Come over here with me."

A man waved and joined them. As he began to tell them about the tour, Eden saw a car pull into the drive.

"They're here," she whispered to Clay. "Can you handle the girls by yourself?"

"Yeah. You'll be okay with her?"

"Of course. I'll catch up as soon as I can. Watch Lacie. That animal doesn't like the red." She walked down the drive to meet the car.

Her mother climbed out of the Lexus with a smile. She wore

a royal-blue sundress that showed her figure to advantage. Omar joined his wife before Eden reached them.

Her mother offered her cheek to Eden. The powder-scented skin brought back too many memories to Eden, and she stepped away as quickly as she could without causing offense.

"Eden, my dear, your face is red and blotchy. Rather unattractive. Did you forget your makeup this morning?"

Eden's cheeks heated. "I was in a fire recently, Mom."

Her mother gasped. "Fire? As in a building on fire?"

"The shed." Eden told her what happened.

Omar put his hand on Eden's shoulder. "Are you saying someone tried to kill you?"

"Yes. And would have succeeded if not for Clay."

Her mother went pale. "Oh my dear, I think I need to sit down."

She always did that. Made everything about her. Eden realized some things would never change even if her mother wanted them to. There was an outdoor patio area on the other side of the drive, and Eden pointed it out. Omar guided his wife to a chair, then went to get her a soda from a vending machine by the building.

"I talked to my father," Eden said as soon as he was out of earshot. "So did Clay."

"Your father? Hector?"

Eden nodded and held her mother's gaze. "He expressed doubts that he was my father."

"Of course he did. What did you expect?" Her mother dismissed Eden's concerns with an airy wave of her hand.

"Mother, I was eight when you left. I remember all the men. How do you know which one was my father?"

Angry spots of red bloomed in her mother's cheeks, but she looked down at her hands for a moment and the color faded. "I suppose I deserve that," she said quietly. She rubbed her hand over her forehead. "I wasn't always the woman you remember, Eden."

And yet, as far back as she could remember, Nancy had been exactly that woman. On Eden's fourth birthday, she'd been sent to her friend's house. She vaguely remembered her mother coming to get her smelling of an unpleasant odor. She later came to know that stench as beer.

When she didn't answer, her mother heaved another sigh. "I was a young girl, impressionable and naive, when I met your father. I didn't know he was married until you were on the way. He was my first real love. And I suppose I never really got over him. I went through a lot of men trying."

For the first time, Eden understood what it might have been like for her mother. "How did you meet him?"

"At a party." She glanced away. "I was young."

"So he knew you hadn't been with anyone else."

Her mother met her gaze. "He knew. Why did you call him?"

"I believe he was behind my daughter's kidnapping."

Her mother gasped. "He was behind Brianna's disappearance?"

Eden stared at her mother. "How do you know my daughter's name?"

"Well, I . . . I—you told me the other day."

Had she? Eden didn't think so.

Her mother smiled, though it was feeble. "What did your father say?"

"Not much. I'm going to try to see him." Eden only said this to see her reaction, and she wasn't surprised when her mother's eyes brightened.

"I'd like to say hello," her mother said. "When are you meeting him?"

"I'm not sure," Eden said. One thing she was certain of—her mother's interest was more than casual.

Clay joined them and draped his arm around Eden's shoulders. "What's going on over here?" he asked, his tone jocular.

"We were just talking about Brianna," Eden's mother said quickly. "Do you have a picture?"

"Sure." Clay dug a USB drive out of his pocket. It was still attached to the digital picture album. "There are some on there."

Her mother fiddled with the frame, then frowned. "These look like men in a jungle."

"Let me see." Clay took it. "You're in the wrong album." He pressed a few buttons, then handed it back. "There she is when she was a month old."

Eden watched her mother's face soften and wished she could believe the older woman really cared.

"I think I'll sleep like the dead tonight," Clay said, yawning. "Neither of us slept worth a darn last night."

Eden had been quiet since the trip to the buffalo ranch. The expression on her face had warned him not to probe until she was ready to talk. Not that there had been much time. The girls had been wild all evening. All they'd talked about was the trip to see the buffalo.

She barely mm-hmmed in response as she got into bed and rolled onto her side with her back facing him. He shut out the light, but the faint moonlight through the window and the green glow from the clock let him see her silhouette. What would she do if he put his arm around her waist, spoon fashion? With every day that passed, he knew he never wanted her to leave him again. Wooing her would take all of his concentration.

Her voice spoke out of the darkness. "Clay?"

"I'm awake." He rolled onto his side, facing her. A mere six inches separated them.

"How much longer is your leave?"

Where had that come from? "Five weeks."

"Then what? Do you know where you'll be sent?"

He should tell her now, but what if it scared her off? When he placed his hand on her waist, she stiffened but didn't move away. "I don't know, Eden. I might not go back."

She rolled onto her back, then to her other side. They were practically nose to nose. "Not go back? What do you mean?"

She was close enough that he could smell her light fragrance. Close enough that he could kiss her if he wanted. "I'm tired of the travel. The excitement has grown old. And Brianna will need me." He wished she would say she needed him too, but he was afraid that was too much to hope for.

"B-But what will you do?"

"I have my inheritance. I could maybe use the money to start a business, but thought about applying for a job at the ranger station too, just to keep busy and do some wildlife photography. I think I'd like that. There's the ranch here we could fix up. It wouldn't cost much to live here."

"Just how much money is in this inheritance?"

He grinned. "Enough to keep you in any style you'd like."

"Really?"

Was she expressing doubt or hope? He couldn't tell without seeing her expression. His hand was still on her waist. He brought it up to cup her cheek. "Really. Think you could stand to have me home every night?"

"I'd like to try," she whispered.

His pulse leaped. He cupped the back of her head and drew her against him. His lips found hers. It was the sweetest kiss in his memory. He drank deep of the promise, hope, and longing in her lips.

She drew away. "You didn't ask me how it went with my mother."

He tried to keep the disappointment from his voice. "I thought you'd tell me when you were ready. You were both a little tense when I joined you."

She scooted a little farther away. "Clay, didn't you think it odd that she knew about Brianna? Did we mention we had a daughter or what happened?"

He thought back, then shook his head. "No. You both talked about the past, about your childhood. There was no mention of the kidnapping or anything. I assumed you didn't want to get into that with her."

"I didn't. But she even knew Brianna's name. I didn't tell her that."

He tensed. That didn't sound right. "What did she say?"

"I told her I suspected my father had something to do with my daughter's kidnapping. She gasped then and said, 'He was behind Brianna's disappearance?'"

He absorbed the information and looked for a logical explanation. "Maybe she looked us up online and ran into the story."

"She knew our name before we met her in Alpine. You introduced us to Omar. So they would have known that first evening. Wouldn't it have been the most natural thing in the world to ask about her granddaughter? To offer condolences?"

"Maybe. But things were awkward anyway. Maybe she didn't want to cause more emotional upheaval." Even to him, the excuse sounded lame.

He raised onto his elbow and stared through the darkness at her. "Eden, do you think it's possible she contacted you because of your father?"

"What do you mean?"

"What if she's involved in this too?" He shook his head. "No, I guess that's crazy."

"What's crazy is that she is married to my uncle. When she couldn't get my father, she settled for his brother. What if they are all in business together?" She bolted upright in the bed. "What if Omar is the one who has been trying to kill me?"

"But why?"

"I don't know." She flopped back onto the pillow. "It's all such a tangle. I have no idea what's going on. But all these things have to connect somehow. I want to know how she met Omar."

"Ask her. When are you going to see her again?"

"I don't know. They're not planning to leave Alpine until at least the weekend."

"I think we need to have another chat with them," he said.

His mind raced through the possibilities. Santiago had what he wanted, so why would anyone want to harm Eden now?

He opened his mouth to discuss it some more with Eden, but the steady rise and fall of her chest told him she'd fallen asleep. Flopping onto his back, he tried to do the same, but it was a long time before he succeeded.

26

CLAY SAT ON THE PORCH SWING WITH HIS ARM AROUND EDEN. "EVERY MUSCLE IN MY BODY aches," he said. "I thought tubing down the Rio Grande with the girls would be a piece of cake. That water was rough."

"I'm about ready for bed," she agreed.

Headlamps swept the front of the main house. A car light came on as the door opened, but he couldn't see who it was from here. Just that it was a woman. She came toward the bunkhouse with purposeful steps.

When she stepped into the glow of the porch light, Eden rose. "Judge Julia! I'm surprised to see you."

The older woman mounted the steps and dragged a rocker around to face them before settling in it. "I heard what happened out here the other night and came to see how you're faring." She looked them over with shrewd eyes in the wash of light. "You both look like something the coyotes fought over."

"Tubing with five little girls will do that to you." He rose and shook her hand. "Clay Larson."

"Judge Julia Thompson." She crossed her jean-clad legs and leaned back in the rocker, looking at Eden. "I remembered, you know. I knew it would come to me."

Clay heard Eden's sudden intake of breath but had no idea what was so upsetting about the judge's statement. "Remembered what?"

"Where I'd seen your pretty wife. And you too." She tapped her nose. "News has a smell to me. Especially crime."

"You know about our daughter?" He doubted the judge was going to go around talking about it.

"I do indeed. The last I heard, the two of you were split. Now here you are. In my county."

He glanced at Eden. How much should they tell this woman? "We're here because this is where our daughter is."

The suspicious glint in the judge's eyes dimmed. "She's alive? I figured the two of you . . ."

"Killed her and tried to cover our tracks?" He'd heard the accusations before, but they stung every time. "I think the investigating detective still believes it."

The judge shrugged. "It's usually a family member. Sad but true."

"I have been looking for Brianna for five years," Clay said. "I never believed she was dead."

"So what's she doing here?"

Clay told her what they knew, including Eden's father's involvement. When the judge heard the name Santiago, her expression grew more sober.

"Santiago's involvement is ominous," she said. "He's behind half the drugs that come through here every year. I sure would like to get him." She studied Eden's face. "Would you be willing to be a lure?"

Clay glanced at his wife. "I don't want her involved in anything dangerous. We have a daughter to raise."

Eden shook her head. "I won't put these kids in danger. If we rile up the situation any further, I don't know what might happen. If he thinks I'm a danger, he might go after all of us with real determination."

"Not if he's in jail," the judge said.

"He's escaped capture many times," Clay said. "I think the risk is too great."

The judge pressed her lips together. "If we can get Santiago and his crew, you'll all be safer."

Eden hesitated. "Maybe so."

He couldn't lose Eden. Not now. "No! I don't want her involved," Clay said.

"I'll have protection for you."

"I've heard that before." But what if Santiago couldn't stop the wheels he'd set in motion? What if the attacker struck again, or evaded capture and came back to avenge Santiago?

The judge steepled her fingers together. "Call your father. Ask to meet."

Eden shook her head. "What excuse can I give?"

"I wish you hadn't already given him that pendant," Julia muttered. "That was your best leverage." She studied Clay's face. "You've crossed tracks with Santiago before, on his turf. Do you have any photos linking him to the drug trafficking? He won't want anything in circulation."

"My camera was taken during that particular mission you're talking about." He shook his head, then an image came to mind. Car keys, flash drive. Eden's mother had mentioned pictures of a jungle, but he hadn't paid much attention. "You know, let me check an old flash drive I have. It's still on my key ring with pictures of Brianna, but there's another folder on it that I haven't looked at in a long time."

He left the women on the porch and went back to the bedroom, where he'd dropped his keys and change. He pulled the drive from the little digital photo album that he'd used to show Eden's mother the pictures of Brianna. He plugged it into the port on his MacBook, and two folders showed up seconds later. He clicked on the unnamed one, and the list of files came up.

Pictures. There were old pictures in the folder. He flipped through jungle scenes. Children playing in the dirt of a small town. These images had been taken the day before the commandos rolled in, firing on the kids, and he'd been thrown in jail for intervening. But was there anything incriminating?

The next picture was of a swarthy man scowling. He stood next to a truck loading stacks of white powder. Santiago? He printed off that picture and three more that clearly showed the contents of the truck. If it was Hector, Eden might recognize him.

⁂

The swing swayed gently as Eden wondered what to say to the judge. The horrid accusations that had swirled around them after Brianna's disappearance brought a lump to her throat. Rumors traveled far. The first time a police officer had accused her of harming her daughter was seared into her memory. Only a lack of evidence had saved them from being arrested. Within a few days the ransom note proved genuine and the police backed off. But it was a painful time. No one stopped eyeing them with suspicion.

"You can stop brooding," the judge said. "If you'd seen what I have, you would have jumped to conclusions too. The way parents treat children is appalling."

Eden started to answer, then checked herself. Her childhood experiences were a confirmation that the judge was right. "I realize our situation wasn't typical. But when you're devastated by loss, then find you're a suspect, it's overwhelming."

The screen door screeched and Clay returned with a paper in his hand. "I hit pay dirt," he said. "You recognize this guy?" He thrust a printout into Eden's hand.

She held it under the porch light and was suddenly eight years old again. "It's my dad," she said.

"I thought so. Santiago is at a village with the drugs."

Julia held the photograph under the light. "It's him," she said. "Tell him you have these. He'll come for them."

Eden's memories crystallized, and she heard his gruff voice telling her to go outside and play while he talked with her mother. She'd always been an encumbrance to both of them. The day her mother left her had been a blessing. She just hadn't fully realized that until now.

The judge glanced at Eden. "Are you willing to try?"

"I don't want the girls in danger," Eden said. "Even if he's captured, what if his men come after us for revenge?"

"Hector's son is dead. His second in command has no interest in family squabbles."

"You don't know that."

Julia shut up and stared at Eden. "You're right—I don't. Not for sure. But don't you have any sense of justice? Don't you want to make sure others are not hurt by this man?"

The judge's questions stung. "Of course I do!" Eden said. "But I'm more concerned about my daughter and the other girls. And he's still my father, in spite of his despicable behavior. The Bible says to honor our parents. He wasn't much of a dad, but the thought of luring him into a trap makes me shudder."

Clay's warm fingers closed around hers. "That's a good point, honey."

"You would protect a man who had no compunction about ordering your death?" Julia demanded. "He would order those girls killed with as little thought. The safest thing is to lock him up where he can't hurt any of you."

"I don't trust that locking him up is the solution."

"We'll make sure the confrontation takes place far from the ranch," Julia promised.

Eden shook her head. "I'm sorry."

Clay's cell phone rang. He glanced at it and raised his brows. "Unknown," he said before he opened it. "Larson here."

She watched his face change, and he mouthed, "Your father." She went still and listened to his side of the conversation.

"I never tried to hide anything from you," Clay said. He listened, then said, "I see. Yes, you've made yourself perfectly clear. Just a minute." He handed the phone to Eden. "He wants to talk to you."

"What did he say?" Eden asked when he didn't explain immediately.

"He seems to know about these pictures. He wants them back."

Eden stared at the phone. "He has this place bugged?" She shuddered.

"He said your mother called him."

"My mother!" Eden collapsed back against the swing. "She would give him ammunition to hurt us more?"

"Apparently so." Clay's voice was dry.

She put the phone to her ear. What did she call him? Father? Mr. Santiago? "Hello," she said, settling for anonymity.

"I did not expect to have to speak with you again. You have been secretive with me."

"That's not true."

"Your mother tells me there are pictures of me. In the jungle. What do you intend to do with them?"

"We just found them. Clay had forgotten that they were on his drive."

"Somehow I doubt the *hombre* did not know this."

"It's true. My mother found them in an old folder. Why did she call you?"

"Money, of course. She does nothing without wishing for cash."

Eden's stomach churned with acid. Her mother had sold them out. "I assume you want the pictures."

"Of course. You will give them back and destroy any copies you have made."

"I told you—Clay just found them. There are no copies."

"See that it remains that way. And what is it you want in return for turning them over to me? I pay my debts."

"You owe me nothing." She glanced at Julia's hopeful face, then looked away. No, she couldn't risk the children. "You're my father."

"So your mother said. I was never certain."

He'd said the same thing to Clay, but was he trying to skirt his responsibilities? Or had her mother lied? Eden had learned never to trust what her mother said. Nancy appeared to have changed, but was it real? "Regardless, there is something I'd like."

"I thought so. Money, I suppose," he said, his voice bored.

"Of course not! I don't want tainted money. I want you to tell me which of these girls is our Brianna."

"Eden, I have not the least idea."

"So you lied to me? You lured us here with a picture and a false claim? You knew about the kidnapping all along, that she was your granddaughter!"

"I did not know everything," he said, his voice grudging. "I never saw the *niña*. Pictures only."

"Who has cared for her all this time?"

"I have no idea. It was not important enough for me to know a name."

Her fingers curled into her palms. His own granddaughter wasn't important. "What were the last pictures you saw?"

"I believe she was two."

Two lost years of Brianna's life. She had to have them. "The last photos I have were when she was six weeks old. So I'll trade you those pictures for these and the original flash drive."

"You are in no position to make demands." His voice held an icy edge.

"You asked what I wanted."

"Very well. I am coming to Texas next weekend. Have the drive ready and on your person at all times."

Her heart sank. She didn't want to see him face-to-face. "You're coming *here*?"

"Business, of course."

"I assumed you would send one of your minions."

"I wish to assure myself that there are no copies. I will be able to see if you are telling me the truth. You are very transparent."

"There's no need for that. I promise you that we will make no copies."

"We shall see."

This was not going as she'd expected. "Where should we meet?"

"I will call you. It is not safe to make prior arrangements."

The phone went dead in her ear. She put her phone down. "He hung up."

"It sounds like he is coming to see you in person?" Julia asked.

Eden nodded. "He's coming, but I don't know when." She may have made the situation worse. In truth, Eden would rather not set eyes on the man. The horror of the fire came to mind again. Her father had been unable to stop it. Would this meddling intensify the danger?

"I'll make sure you're protected," Julia said, her intent gaze on Eden's face.

Eden moved restlessly. "I don't want him anywhere around the girls."

"He won't be," Julia said. "We'll arrest him when he comes."

Eden couldn't see how it could work. "I have a feeling he's used to being careful."

"I don't think he'll be expecting his daughter to turn him over to the cops," Clay said. "The meeting was his idea."

Eden winced. "I'm still not crazy about it."

"He sicced a thug on you, honey," he said. "I don't think you owe him anything."

She stared at Julia. "I guess we have no choice but to go along with it. If I don't show up when he calls, he's liable to do anything." She shuddered at the thought and prayed that the Border Patrol would nab anyone who might be inclined to harm her girls.

The day felt oppressive. Thunderclouds built in the southwest, great banks of roiling clouds that looked like bruises. They were likely in for a big storm. Maybe even hail, according to Allie. The animals were restless too, stomping their hooves in the corral. Allie told Rick she didn't want the girls on the horses when they were so skittish.

Eden sniffed the moisture in the air as she saw the mail carrier stop at the end of the drive. *Please, please, let it be there.* The gravel slipped around under her boots as she rushed to get the mail. The huge box was filled with envelopes. She pulled all of it out and began to go through it as the wind kicked up around her.

Bits of sand pummeled her bare arms, but she barely noticed as her gaze fell on the return address of one of the envelopes. The lab results. There were three more pieces of mail just like it. She quickly sorted the envelopes. Four white rectangular pieces of paper. One of them would tell her which little girl was their Brianna.

She could barely think, barely breathe. Where was Clay? She had to do this with him. He deserved to see it first. He'd never lost hope, never given up. She started for the house as thunder rolled across the desert and hills. Light flickered in the depths of the cloud, and she smelled ozone. While she watched, a sliver of darkness reached down from a rotating cloud. For a moment, she didn't realize what she was seeing. Then it sank in. A tornado!

She started for the house at a run. The tornado was heading

straight for the ranch. "Clay!" she screamed over the sound that intensified around her. The wind howled so loudly it sounded like a train. She saw Allie point, then gather the children to her. They all ran toward the house, then disappeared inside. At least the girls were safe. Allie would take them to the cellar.

Eden struggled to run in the wind. It felt as though she was making no progress. It was these dratted boots. They were still stiff, and it would take too long to sit down and pull them off. Her epitaph would read DONE IN BY NEW BOOTS.

The horses were going berserk. Buzz and the other hands were trying to get them inside the barn, but she wondered if that would protect them. Where was Clay? She screamed his name again, but the wind snatched away the sound of her voice.

Then she saw him. He had a tripod set up at the side of the barn and was busy snapping pictures of the twister as it ripped up cactus and sucked sand into its mouth. Was it larger? She thought so. It roared toward them and she stood, mouth gaping at the destruction.

She glanced back to the barn to see that Clay had noticed her. He was shouting something but she couldn't make out what it was. He grabbed his camera from the tripod, then ran toward her waving his arms. She veered toward him, changing her original course of heading to the house.

They met in the side yard. "Get to shelter!" he shouted. He grabbed her arm and hustled her toward the barn, which was the nearest structure. The side door was shut, but he kicked it open and half dragged her inside as the tornado reached the end of the driveway.

"There's no basement in here!" she shouted above the din of screaming horses and high winds.

He paused and looked frantically around the space. "Under the feed trough!" He thrust her under a heavy wooden bin in the middle stall, then jumped on top of her.

His weight pressed the air from her lungs. Or was it the sudden closeness of the twister that sucked all the oxygen from her chest? She clung to him and listened to his ragged breathing in her ear. The wind roared all around them. She couldn't think, couldn't concentrate on anything but the thought that they were about to die before they found Brianna.

The pressure in her ears began to let up. The sound of a freight train about to run them over suddenly vanished. She drew in a lungful of oxygen. Then another. Breaths came more easily, or they would when Clay got off of her.

He lifted his head and stared into her face. "You okay?"

She nodded. "I think so. We need to get to the girls. They'll be frightened in the cellar."

He rolled off her and helped her to her feet. "We still have a roof on the barn."

She glanced up and saw he was right. "I can't even see any daylight through it."

A child called out, "Mr. Clay!" It sounded like Paige, their fearful one.

In unison, they rushed toward the door and stepped out into blue sky. The ominous cloud was to their northeast now. The twister's destruction stopped about twenty feet from the barn. Then the sparse grass was undisturbed.

"It must have lifted before it hit us," Clay said. "The house is fine too."

She could breathe again. The air was no longer close and thick.

Another miracle. Thankfulness welled in her heart. “God took care of us.”

“He always does.” Clay started toward the porch, but she caught his arm. “Clay, wait.” She showed him the mail in her hands. “The results are here.”

His eyes widened. “The DNA results?”

She nodded, watching his eyes brighten. He’d worked so hard for this moment. And she realized she loved him. Her love wasn’t just physical attraction. His heart was as big as the sky overhead. He might not say things as well as he liked, but the emotion was there. He’d let nothing keep him from finding their daughter.

“I wanted you to open them. You deserve the honor after the way you never lost hope.”

He swallowed hard. “Let’s check on the girls, then go to our room.”

27

FOUR WHITE ENVELOPES. THEY CONTAINED THE NEWS HE'D BEEN SEEKING FOR FIVE YEARS. Clay looked at them spread out on the coffee table. Which one would be theirs? He couldn't even say he had a favorite, that he hoped Brianna was a certain child.

His hand hovered over the first one to his left. "Start with this one?"

The skin on Eden's face was still a little reddened from the fire. Her green eyes widened and she nodded. "Do you have a guess?"

"I think Brianna is Katie."

"I think Paige is our girl."

He raised a brow. "Why Paige? That would cause some difficulties."

She nodded. "And that's why I think it's Paige. This has been so difficult that I can't see it suddenly becoming easy."

"Maybe it's not supposed to be. I'm stronger for the search. I think you are too."

He licked dry lips and picked up the first envelope. Turning it over in his hand, he ripped the flap open and pulled out the folded sheet inside.

Eden leaned over his arm to look. "Well?"

He stared at the probability figure: 0%. "This is Katie's. She's not ours." He showed her the paper.

She dropped the page and grabbed the next envelope. "Check this one."

He ripped it open and glanced at the heading. "This one is Madeline's." He skimmed to the results. "It's a zero too."

"So that leaves either Paige or Lacie. I told you it would be Paige." Her shoulders slumped. "How will we tell that sweet couple that they can't have her?"

He snatched up the next envelope and ripped into it. The waiting was killing him. The faces of the two little girls hung in his mind. He had no preference. They were both sweet kids. "This one is Lacie's."

The results suddenly appeared larger, almost bolded: a 99.97% match. "It's Lacie," he said slowly. "She's our Brianna."

"Lacie?" Eden took the paper from him and scanned it. "I thought it might be her. But she's so quiet. And what about that nun? I thought there would be some mystery to her background. That maybe Sister Marjo was her real mother or something." She clutched his arm. "Oh, Clay, she's our baby. Our Brianna. I want to see her now."

He hadn't dreamed it would be Lacie either. Of all the girls, she hadn't been very high on his list of possibilities. But her quiet strength and sweet nature would fit so well with them.

"When do we tell Lacie?" Her voice vibrated with longing, and when she locked gazes with Clay, pain flared in her eyes. "Can we do it now?"

She didn't seem to be aware she was wringing her hands. He put his hand over hers. "I think we have to wait, honey. We want to handle it right. And we need to talk to the sister."

"But she's ours. Doesn't she deserve to know that? I want to hold her." Her voice was thick.

"I want to tell her too. I'll talk to Rick and Allie about it. We'll let them guide us. Agreed?"

"All right," she said, her voice grudging. "I don't know how long I can hide my feelings. When can we talk to Sister Marjo?"

"She's coming to visit tomorrow. I'll arrange for a private meeting with her." He had hardly assimilated the news. "We've found her. Really and truly."

Something welled inside him—gratitude, disbelief, joy. The emotions swelled until they nearly smothered him. It seemed unbelievable that God would give them this incredible gift. "She's really alive, Eden." He pressed his burning eyes. "Sometimes I thought it was my stubbornness that wouldn't let me see reality. Then I'd get another whiff of hope and keep on looking."

Her touch was tentative on his arm. "You never gave up, Clay. That's the kind of man you are." She turned her head and looked out the window as if the intensity of his gaze bothered her. "It still seems a dream."

"Now what, Eden?" he asked softly.

At least she didn't pretend not to know what he was talking about, though she kept staring at the window. He glanced there himself to see nothing but the rocky hillside in the distance. The silence stretched out, but he wasn't going to say anything until she did. Maybe he was stubborn, but she needed to face the facts and make a decision.

He had to know. "Did you hear what I said after I pulled you out of the fire?"

She sighed and finally turned her head toward him. "I heard."

"I meant it. There's no life without you."

A tiny smile played at the corner of her lips, then she frowned. "We didn't make it before, Clay. What makes you think we can this time? I'm scared."

"You think I'm not?" He raised her hand to his lips and kissed the back of it. "For five years I've felt like a failure. There were so many things standing in our way—our youth, the short time we knew each other. Then losing Brianna. That would harm any marriage."

"Rebuilding from here isn't going to be easy either. Brianna will need a lot of love and support. There may not be a lot of time to focus on our relationship."

"There's always time. How do you think other parents handle it? All these kids want is a family that loves them."

She held his gaze. "I'm a little sad about that. I'd like to keep them all."

He winced. "Me too. It's going to be hard to let them go."

She chewed on her lip. "I hope Brianna will adjust."

"If we show her we love each other and she's an integral part of the family, she'll adjust quickly." There was a question in her eyes, and he knew he had to say the words. "I love you, Eden. I've always loved you. That's the real reason I wouldn't sign the divorce papers."

She inhaled but kept her eyes on him. "I thought I got over you, but I was just deceiving myself in order to get by."

He tried to squelch the leap of joy at her words. There was too much fear in her face. "So what are you saying about us? Are you willing to put doubt aside and forge a new future with me and Brianna? And any other kids who happen to come along?"

She brushed a lock of hair out of her eyes. "I'll try, Clay. That's all I can promise. But if I ever fail my daughter again, I . . . I . . ."

He put his finger to her lips. "We all mess up, honey. It wasn't your fault." He cupped her face in his palm. "I love you so much."

When he moved to take her in his arms, she put her hand on his chest. "Love wasn't enough before, Clay. What guarantee do we have that it will be enough this time?"

"There are no guarantees. We've both learned a lot, though. About each other, about patience, about give-and-take."

She nodded. "I want to try."

He couldn't hold back the grin. "Quit changing the subject. Say it, Angel."

A smile curved her lips, and she didn't pretend not to understand him. "I love you, Clay Larson. I will until the day I die."

The tension in her face drained, and she leaned over and offered him her lips. A gift he was happy to take.

Her eyes looked wide and aware. Eden glanced away from her image in the mirror and spit out the toothpaste. The mint taste cleared her head. She ran a brush through her hair. Her makeup was still on, but she didn't want to take it off. Not tonight.

When she stepped into the hall, she saw Clay through the open bedroom door. He was sitting on the edge of the bed with his Bible in his hand. "Ready?" she asked.

He nodded and put the Bible aside. "Remember, not a word yet."

"I know." Everything in her longed to tell Lacie the truth.

The girls were all on India's bed. It had taken awhile to calm them after the storm, though luckily they'd seen little of it from the cellar. The debris strewn around the yard had frightened them, so she and Clay had tried to make a game out of picking it up. They'd finally prayed with the girls, and the children began to lose their anxiety.

They had a stack of books scattered on the covers. Eden's attention went straight to Lacie. Her Brianna. She drank in the little girl's brown hair. Her light-brown eyes. They were blue the last time Eden had held her. Now that she knew, it seemed her daughter's identity should have been clear instantly. The straightness of her hair was like Clay's. The strength in her chin was her daddy's too. Those cheeks were like Eden's.

"Why are you staring, Miss Eden?" India asked. "Aren't you going to read to us?"

Eden collected her wits. "Of course, honey. You're all so pretty. I had to look, didn't I?"

India giggled. "No one ever calls me pretty."

When Eden sat on the edge of the bed, the little girl leaned her head against Eden's arm. "Want me to take your ribbons out?" she asked.

India nodded. "I like it when you do my hair. It feels good."

Eden exchanged a smile with Clay and saw his attention veer back to the child on her left. Brianna. It was going to be hard not to call Lacie by her real name. The amazement choked Eden. She took the ribbons out of India's hair and released the braids. The black hair sprang from her head in all directions, and Eden began to brush it out. India didn't complain at the tugging.

"What book are we reading tonight?" Clay asked, picking up the top one. "*The Cat in the Hat*?"

"We read that yesterday. Lacie wants *The Story of Ferdinand*."

"Then that's what we'll read tonight. It is your turn, isn't it?" Eden asked, touching her daughter on the head.

Her daughter. Were two words ever more beautifully paired? She hoped Clay could find his voice to read because she wasn't sure she could. She finished India's hair, then Lacie scooted closer. "You want to be next?" she asked. The little girl nodded with a shy smile.

"I'll read," Clay said, his voice husky.

Eden listened to him read the story of a misunderstood bull. Everyone thought Ferdinand was mean, but he'd only been stung by a bee. She smiled as the children gasped and felt sorry for Ferdinand. The intensity in their eyes held her enthralled. When had she last entered into something as completely as they did? Making her marriage work and being a mommy to Brianna were going to take a similar commitment.

She ran her hand along the silken curtain of her daughter's hair. Though it wasn't red, the way she'd thought it would be, it was so beautiful. And hers. Hers and Clay's. They'd made this child together and she bore their imprint in her features. It was right and good that they picked up the pieces and went on. Brianna deserved a whole family. Clay deserved a wife who tried with all her heart. God was telling her what to do, but she was still so afraid.

"Time for prayers, then bed," Clay said, shutting the book.

They held hands in a circle on the bed. Eden clasped India's hand in her right and Madeline's in her left. The girls' eyes were closed and she took the moment to gaze at each one of them. All so individual. All so precious.

Clay shut his eyes. "God, thank you for keeping us safe from the tornado today. Thank you for each one of these girls. Thank you for bringing them into our lives. We love each and every one of them, as we know you do too. Keep them safely in your hands. In Jesus's name. Amen."

"Amen," she echoed. She kissed soft cheeks as she tucked them into bed. Clay shut off the light and closed the door partway behind them. It was too soon to go to bed.

"Want something to drink?" she asked Clay, heading to the kitchen.

"I'll take some tea," he said, following her. "Any of those chocolate chip cookies left?"

She nodded to the cabinet by the sink. "I hid some on the top shelf just for you."

"What a wife." He grinned and opened the door. "In this?" He indicated a plastic container.

"That's it." She took out glasses. "Maybe milk since we have cookies?"

"Sounds good."

Still not ready to face his eyes, she poured milk into the glasses.

"Honey, are you mad about something?"

Heat rushed to her face. "Of course not. I . . . I'm just feeling a little overwhelmed by everything that happened today."

He was smiling, oh so tenderly. She drank in the expression on his face. She wanted to believe his love, longed to put away all doubts. Dropping her gaze, she took a cookie from the container and bit into it. The chocolate hit her taste buds and the sugar gave her courage. She smiled back at him, daring to let her feelings show.

He stopped chewing. "I like that expression in your eyes. Could you look at me like that all the time?"

"Like what?" she asked, allowing her smile to widen.

"Like you might actually love me," he said softly. "I know you said it earlier, but I'm having trouble believing it."

She swallowed the last of her milk, then put down her glass. "I love you, Clay. So much it makes my chest hurt."

The light in his eyes intensified. He stood, reaching out his hand for her to take it. She did, and he drew her close. Before she could say a word, he swept her into his arms and carried her from the room.

28

THE AROMA OF STRONG COFFEE MINGLED WITH THAT OF BACON. EDEN SMILED AT CLAY ACROSS the kitchen table in the main house and prayed Allie and Rick didn't notice any difference. If only she and Clay didn't have things to do today, they could have spent the morning lying in bed and talking about the future. Last night had changed everything.

Rita dropped a skillet in the sink, and the bang roused Eden from her reverie. She rose and went to the coffeepot. "Thanks for making the coffee so strong this morning," she told Rita.

"It's your funeral," Rita said, softening her words with a smile. She pointed to the coffee. "That stuff is going to kill you." She gulped a pill down with water, carried a plate of bacon to Clay. Her smile widened, and she patted his shoulder.

"But what a way to go." Eden hid a smile at the way Clay shifted. She poured cream into the strong brew and carried it back to the table. "We have something to tell you," she said to the Baileys. She'd waited to bring it up until Zeke and Della were gone.

Allie pushed her empty plate away and dabbed at her mouth with the napkin. "What's up?"

"We got the DNA results yesterday." Goose bumps prickled the skin on Eden's arms. What a miracle.

Allie looked at Rick, who was finishing his scrambled eggs. He put down his fork. "Which one is Brianna?"

"Lacie," Clay said.

Allie exhaled. "I thought it would be Katie."

"So did I," Eden said. "But all the other girls were a zero. No chance of them being ours."

"What was the figure for Lacie?" Rick asked.

"It's 99.97 percent," Clay said.

"So, no doubt."

"No doubt," Eden said, nodding.

"Did you tell her yet?" Allie asked.

Eden took a sip of coffee, then shook her head. "We weren't sure how to do it. We don't want her upset. And how should we handle it? Talk to Child Protective Services first?"

Rick tossed his napkin onto the table. "I'll give them a call. I know the director."

Allie's eyes were moist. "Oh, Eden, such wonderful news! No wonder you're glowing this morning. I noticed it right off."

A blush heated Eden's cheeks, and she didn't dare look at Clay. "It feels too good to be true. I looked her over last night. I should have seen the resemblance to Clay right away. For some reason, we thought she'd look like me. But her eyes and chin are Clay's."

"And dark hair like him," Rita put in.

"Exactly. No red hair like mine." Eden tucked a lock behind her ear.

"A little Clay. How cute," Allie said.

"We don't know what the next step is," Clay said.

"I would imagine you'll have to petition the courts for custody and prove you're her parents," Rick said.

Clay frowned, his eyes clouding. "That will take a legal DNA test, I would imagine. We'll have to go to a collection place."

Eden's elation ebbed. "Is there any doubt?"

Clay slipped his arm around the back of her chair and smiled. "No, honey. No doubt. The test is the same, but for the court they want no doubt that the sample wasn't tampered with."

The ardor in his eyes warmed her. And she loved it when he called her *honey*. "When can we get the process in motion?"

"Let me find out." Rick went to the kitchen phone and dialed. He stepped from the room and his voice faded to a dull murmur.

"I really want to tell Lacie," Eden said.

"Maybe it will be allowed. Rick will find out," Allie said. She rose and began to collect the dirty dishes.

Eden stood to help her, though she would rather have stayed with Clay's arm around her. "Sister Marjo is coming today to see Lacie, right? Maybe we can find out more about the way she was found on the church steps."

"She's due here at noon," Allie said, stooping to load the dishwasher.

A crash made both women jump. Eden whirled to see Rita stooping to pick up glass shards on the floor.

"Wet hands," Rita said. "I should have dried them before I tried to carry the glasses." She glanced at Allie. "Have you met Sister Marjo? It's not common for the kids to get visitors. What's that all about?"

Allie stooped to help her pick up the glass. "I'm not sure. I guess she sees Lacie once a month and didn't want to let the tradition falter. The two seem very close."

"So you haven't met her?" Eden asked.

"No. But I feel as though I know her. Lacie talks about her all the time."

Eden turned when Rick stepped back into the kitchen. "Well?"

He went to pour another cup of coffee. "I was right. You'll need to petition the court. And provide the backstory of how your daughter was kidnapped. You'll need to submit to legal testing too."

"How long will all that take?" Clay asked.

"Several months is my best guess. The tests should come back fairly quickly, but you'll need to wait on a court date."

"Can we tell her before?" Eden longed to see Lacie's reaction when she found out she had a real home.

Rick took a sip of coffee. "I wouldn't. It might make the wait unbearable for her."

It was already unbearable for Eden. "She won't have to go back to her foster parents, will she?"

"Maybe. The director was unclear on that point. You can ask for a court date as quickly as possible. This will be an unusual case, so I'm guessing media attention will be strong. That might be enough to get them to move faster on it."

Eden felt like wringing her hands. "I can't bear to have her go back to her foster parents, Rick! Surely there's something we can do."

"Maybe Julia can expedite things," Clay said.

"Of course!" Eden glanced at Allie. "Remember when she said I looked familiar to her? She figured it out. She'd seen the newspaper stories."

"It wouldn't hurt to ask her for help," Allie said.

Eden rubbed her forehead. "We have to get this settled soon. We all deserve to be a family again."

"Let's get it done today," Clay said. "Call the judge."

Eden shrugged and pulled out her phone. "Okay." She placed the call and Julia agreed to help. She told them to come to the clinic and submit a DNA sample at eight thirty, an hour away. This would soon be over.

Horses stomped their hooves in the red dirt. Their tack jingled and glittered in the hot sunshine. Clay squinted into the brilliant blue sky at the position of the sun. Nearly nine thirty. Sister Marjo would be coming soon.

He sensed someone behind him. Turning, he saw Eden moving toward the corral with Madeline by the hand. The little girl kept snatching her fingers from Eden's until finally Eden didn't try to grab them back. What was with the child? All the other girls adored Eden, but Madeline had never fully gotten over her pique of being disciplined. She would warm up for a few minutes, then fall back into her sullenness.

"Hi, girls," he said. "I'm surprised to see you here, Maddie. I thought you didn't like the horses."

"So did I," Eden said, stopping to catch her breath. "She decided she was going to try to pet one today."

Madeline went to grab Clay's hand. "But you have to come with me."

"I won't leave your side," he promised.

He exchanged a puzzled glance with Eden. She'd tried her best to get Madeline to make up with her, but the child refused to so much as smile in Eden's direction. He was a different story, though. She craved his attention.

He let her watch Allie's daughter, Betsy, and the horse Bluebird for a few minutes. Betsy was riding around the barrels in the corral as she practiced for the kids' rodeo coming up in two weeks. "She's good," he said.

Eden joined them at the fence. "Allie says she's even better than Allie was at that age."

Betsy cantered toward them when she completed the course. "Hi, Maddie," she said. "You want to ride Bluebird? He won't hurt you."

Madeline shook her head and buried her face in Clay's leg. He put his hand on her shoulder. "You said you were going to pet a horse today. How about I lift you up? I'll hold you while you do it. That way you won't be afraid."

"No," she said, her voice muffled. "I changed my mind."

It wouldn't do any good to try to force her. "Okay, honey. You can go with Miss Eden back to the ranch house."

"Don't want her. You take me."

Eden's eyes darkened, and he knew she was hurt by the child's behavior. "Okay. But Miss Eden is coming with us."

The three of them walked across the yard toward the house as an older blue truck hauling a horse trailer turned between the fence posts by the road. He stopped and watched the rust bucket approach. "There's a horse in the back," he said.

A young woman got out while the dust from the truck tires was still settling. She wore a petulant expression. Her boots were finely tooled leather, and the cowboy hat she wore looked new too. She stalked to the back of the trailer and threw open the door, then stood looking at them with her hands on her hips.

"Well?" she demanded. "Come get this old bag of bones."

He had to pry Madeline's hand loose from his. "Stay here," he said, nudging her toward Eden.

When he reached the woman, he saw an old horse inside the trailer. Black. The animal's head hung down and there were several sores on its legs. Flies buzzed around the broken skin. Poor thing. "Can I help you?" he asked the woman.

She gave him a haughty stare. "Isn't this the place that takes horses?"

"You're donating him to Bluebird?"

"It's either that or the rendering plant." She grabbed the animal's reins roughly.

"Let me," Clay said. When she shrugged and moved out of the way, he quieted the horse with a soft word and a gentle touch, then led it from the trailer to the gravel. People like this should never own an animal. He clamped his lips against the words he wanted to say.

"He's all yours," she said, striding toward the truck.

"You have a bill of sale or something?" he asked.

She stopped and turned. "You paying for him?"

"No, but I imagine Rick will need proof of ownership."

Her avaricious expression changed to boredom. "I'll sign off on him, then. Just don't expect me to pay for his keep or anything." She reached into the truck and pulled out a paper that she signed and handed over. "Been nice doing business with you."

Clay watched her climb in the truck and pull away. Eden and Madeline joined him. "What a piece of work," he said.

Eden hung back from the horse. "He's been mistreated?"

"Yeah. Looks half starved. And he's got welts on his back from a whip."

"Can we turn her in?"

"I'll have to ask Rick. She should be thrown in jail for cruelty to animals." He glanced down at Madeline and found her staring in fascination at the horse. "I need to name it." He checked the horse over.

Madeline kept her hands behind her back. "That lady was mean to him?"

"Yes. But he has a new home here. No one will be mean to him. We'll make sure he gets lots of food and love. He might like a pat to let him know you like him."

Tentatively, she held out her hand. The horse backed up a few steps, then put his head down. She gave his nose a quick pat. "He likes it!"

Clay grinned. "He sure does. I think you should name him. It's a boy horse."

"His name is Tornado," Madeline said. "He's the same color."

She had a point. The horse was as black as yesterday's storm. "Tornado it is. You're going to have to take charge of him, Maddie. He needs a friend."

She smiled and stepped closer. "Can I feed him?"

"I doubt he'd let anyone else do it. He knows a friend when he sees her." And the horse did seem to know Maddie meant him no harm. He bumped his nose on the little girl's shoulder, and she giggled, then patted him again.

She had a bright smile when she turned back toward the house. "I'm going to tell the other girls," she said.

Clay watched her run up the steps and disappear into the house. "Want to pet him?" he asked Eden.

She hesitated, then touched the horse's nose. Her eyes registered wonder. "It's so soft. Will he bite?"

He shook his head. "He's just glad someone cares." His heart swelled as she murmured soft words to the poor animal. There was so much tenderness in her now that she was dropping her guard.

29

EDEN PULLED THE SHEETS FROM THE BEDS IN THE BUNKHOUSE. THOUGH LAUNDRY WASN'T normally her job, she liked to help out Tepin by at least getting the stuff into a pile. Nancy and Omar were supposed to show up sometime this morning. Too much to do today.

She paused and glanced at the phone. God had been prompting her to call Kent lately. He deserved that much. She picked up the phone and dialed Kent's cell phone number. When she got his secretary, she identified herself and was put through.

"Eden?"

Her stomach clenched at the eagerness in his voice. "I hope I'm not bothering you."

"Never," he said. "How's it going down there?"

She wetted her lips. “Good, really good. Um, that’s why I’m calling. We’ve identified Brianna.”

“Wonderful news.” Caution entered his tone.

“The best,” she said. “Clay and I have been talking . . .”

“And you’re going to try to make it work,” he finished for her.

“Well, yes.” Would it be rubbing salt in the wound for her to tell him that she loved Clay?

“I could tell when you saw him that you still loved him. I’ve been expecting this, Eden. Don’t feel bad, honey. My heart is only cracked a little. It’s not broken.”

Inexplicable tears burned her eyes. “You’re a good man, Kent Huston.”

“Too bad there’s no demand for good men,” he said with a chuckle. “If you ever need anything, let me know. I’ll always be your friend.”

It was all she could do to say good-bye and hang up. Though the call had been difficult, she felt lighter, freer, as she went back to her tasks.

Her iPhone dinged and she glanced at the screen to read her text message. *On my way. Meet me in 10 minutes at your husband’s property. Be ready with the flash drive.*

Santiago was coming. He’d given her no time to prepare. Dropping the laundry, she called Julia and told her what was happening. The judge promised to mobilize the Border Patrol at the abandoned house as quickly as she could. Would it be enough? Eden suspected Santiago would show up with plenty of firepower.

She called his number. When he answered, she didn’t wait for him to put her off. “I can’t get to the property by then.”

“Ten minutes, Eden. I’m bringing the last picture I had. Be there with that flash drive or you won’t like the consequences.”

He ended the call. She ran to the door and scanned the yard for Clay. He was watching Rick and Buzz working with the girls on their horseback riding. When she shouted his name and gestured, he jogged from the back paddock to the bunkhouse.

"What's wrong?" he asked when he reached her.

She tried to maintain her composure, but her pulse was knocking on her ribs. "Santiago wants to meet at your property. We only have ten minutes."

"My house? How did he even know about it?"

"I have a feeling he's much more powerful than we know. He'll be there in ten minutes!"

He fell into step beside her. "That's barely enough time to get there. Did you call Julia?"

She nodded and rushed toward the truck. "She's supposed to be getting Border Patrol out there, but I'm not sure they'll arrive in time to do anything."

She stopped when a familiar silver Lexus rolled up the drive. "Oh no, not now. Mom is here. We don't have time for this. You deal with her and I'll tell Allie what's going on." She rushed for the house and told Allie they had to run an errand and would be back.

Clay was waiting in the truck when she got back. The Lexus was rolling away down the drive. It turned left at the road and accelerated away. "What did you tell her?"

"That we had an errand to run. I suggested she go get coffee in town."

Eden climbed into the truck and fastened her seat belt. "I have a bad feeling about this. It's much too rushed. Something is going to go wrong. Why couldn't he just take the drive and leave us alone? He could trust us a little."

"Calm down, honey." He opened the compartment between them and withdrew a gun.

"Where'd you get that?" The sight of the black metal tightened her chest.

"I borrowed it from Rick."

"Does he know what's happening with my dad?"

"Yeah, I told him."

"I wish you wouldn't take that."

His expression went grim. "We're not going into this with no protection."

She said no more but clutched the grip on the door as they sped toward their destination. She prayed as the truck barreled over the potholes.

The turnoff to the dead-end road was just ahead. Clay pulled the truck to the side of the road. "See that house?" he said, indicating a low-slung ranch home. It was stucco and had a swing set in the side yard. "I want you to wait there for me."

She stared at him, unable to believe he would even ask her to leave. "I'm going with you."

"Eden, I don't have time to argue with you. I want you to wait here for me. Please. I can't have you walking into a dangerous situation. Brianna needs a mother."

"She needs a father too!"

He set his jaw. "And what happens to her if your father shows up with guns blazing and wipes us both out just to make sure we don't do something with any copies we've made? She'll stay in foster care, that's what. And I'm not ready for that to happen."

She wasn't either. "He's not going to shoot me."

"One of his thugs nearly burned you up."

She bit her lip, knowing he was right. The situation was fraught with uncertainty. There had been no time to negotiate a peaceful outcome. There would surely be bullets flying. "I'll call him back and tell him this won't work. That he can send his henchman to pick up the flash drive instead."

"I don't believe you'll be safe until he and his people are behind bars. There is more going on than we know. He's unable to control one of his guys."

"Escalating the situation won't change that."

"We might bring down an empire today." He leaned across and shoved open her door. "If I have to carry you to the porch kicking and screaming, I will."

She could tell by his face he was serious. Every cell in her body shouted for her to stay put, but she unbuckled her seat belt and slid out of the car. "I will never forgive you if you get yourself killed, Clay Larson."

"I'll try to stay alive, Angel. Pray for me."

She slammed the door with all her might and watched as he pulled away. She stayed where she was until he turned and disappeared in a cloud of dust around the curve. The derelict house wasn't far. She could walk there in ten minutes. But should she?

What if her father really was waiting with guns? She'd feel better if she knew the Border Patrol was stationed around the property. Julia would know. Pulling out her phone, she called the judge, who answered on the second ring.

"Eden, have you arrived?"

Eden paced along the side of the road. "Clay made me get out and he's gone on ahead. Is the Border Patrol there?"

"We got lucky. Two agents were in the area and hightailed it over to hide in the barn. As far as I know, they're there now."

Her stomach clenched. "Only two?"

"There are more coming. But they won't get there for another fifteen minutes. I'd hoped you'd be able to delay your father."

"Clay didn't want both of us in danger because of Brianna."

Julia grunted in agreement. "I didn't think about that. He's right. You stay put and let him handle it."

"Where are you?" Eden asked.

"At the courthouse, ready to throw them in jail."

"Call me when you hear anything," Eden said. She ended the call and dropped the phone back into her purse. She automatically stepped off the side of the road when a car approached.

Her heart sank when she recognized her father in the passenger seat. And three other men in the car with him. There was no chance to hide. They'd already seen her. The car slowed, then stopped beside her. The tinted passenger window rolled down.

Santiago's face was impassive as he looked her over. She could see her appearance here had thrown him off his expectations. "Father," she said.

"I told you that I doubt that relationship. Has your vehicle broken down?" He stared over her shoulder at the house behind her.

There was no car in the driveway so she couldn't confirm his guess. "No. My husband was unwilling to allow me to go. He was afraid you might harm me. He has the flash drive for you."

There was a flicker of his lids, then, "Get in."

The man on the passenger side behind her father opened the door, then slid over. She had no choice but to slide into the backseat. Her pulse throbbed in her throat. What was he going to do to her? The men all had guns. This didn't look good. If she'd just done what

Clay asked, she would have been up at the neighbor's house. Santiago wouldn't have seen her.

The car pulled back onto the road as soon as she shut the door. The thick silence weighed her down. She wondered how she could get a message to Clay or Julia, but the man beside her would take her phone the minute she dug it out.

The car turned onto the dirt road. Moments later Clay's old family house was in sight. His black truck was there. Behind it was a silver Lexus.

"Whose car is that?" Santiago asked, his voice sharp.

"My mother's," Eden admitted. "I don't know why she's here."

The man grunted. "What does she want?"

"I thought maybe you knew. She's married to your brother."

"I have seen neither one of them in ten years. I would have preferred to keep it that way. Though I did appreciate her call the other day."

Was that his teeth grinding? Did he hate them that much?

"Park here," Santiago said at the end of the driveway. "I do not like the smell of this. What did you see when you examined the property, Carlos?"

The man beside Eden shrugged. "It has been abandoned for many years. Other than squatters in the barn, there was no one here this morning."

"Very well. Drive in."

The driver turned into the lane and parked behind Clay's truck. Half expecting Carlos to forbid it, Eden opened her door and got out. Clay straightened from where he had been leaning at her mother's car. He froze when he saw Eden with her father.

Eden's mother climbed out of the car and stood watching Santiago. A moment later Omar did the same.

"Mom, what are you doing here?" Eden asked.

Nancy walked to the end of her car. "I knew something was going on so we followed Clay's truck. We suspected we would find Hector here."

"What's going on?" Clay asked.

"I think I should be asking that," Santiago said, slamming the door behind him. "I arrive for a friendly exchange and find this *puta* here."

Eden's mother didn't react to the derogatory term. She had eyes for no one but Hector. "Hello, Hector," she said. "It's good to see you."

He spat in the dirt, then glanced at his brother. "Omar, I would have expected you to have more sense than this."

"You owe us, Hector. Every other attempt to collect has failed. My wife didn't have to tell you that these two have incriminating pictures of you. You should show some gratitude and pay your debts."

"I owe you nothing." Hector motioned to his men. "Guard them while Eden and I conduct our business."

He walked back toward the barn. Eden and Clay followed. At the side of the house, Hector stopped and dug into his pocket. "This is the last photograph I have of your daughter." He held out a picture.

Eden took it and Clay peered over her shoulder. The little girl in the picture appeared to be about two years old. Blond hair. It had obviously darkened since then.

There was not much time to study it before Hector held out his hand. "My property, please."

Clay pulled the flash drive out of his pocket. He dropped the device into the older man's palm. "We're square now. Did you succeed in calling off the person who has been targeting Eden?"

Eden saw his lids flicker before he shuttered his expression. "I am working on it."

"Working on it? What does that mean?" Clay's voice rose.

"It has not been as easy as I had hoped."

Santiago turned to leave, but Clay caught his arm. "I need more assurances than that. Someone nearly killed her, tried to burn her alive! It takes a twisted monster to do something like that. Give me the name. If you can't handle the job, I'll do it myself."

Santiago stared at Clay's hand on his arm, then glanced at his face. "As I said, I am taking care of it. It is not your concern."

"Anything to do with my wife is my concern. You might be fine with walking away from your daughter, but she's my life. I won't let any harm come to her."

Santiago raised an eyebrow. "You persist in calling her my daughter. Perhaps you should ask my brother how he came to be married to her mother."

Eden gaped at him. Surely he didn't mean . . .

"You appear surprised, Eden. Did you not wonder when they came here together?" He pulled out his wallet and removed an old picture. It was creased and stained and showed two young men squinting into the sun. The backdrop was a small village. "Can you tell us apart?"

She studied the picture. "No."

"Neither could your mother. We shared her."

Eden recoiled. She wanted to clap her hands over her ears at such an ugly truth. "You've never had a paternity test?"

He shrugged. "He married her. To the victor go the spoils."

"Why are they here?" Clay asked.

Santiago's expression of annoyance deepened. "You should ask them." He walked away.

Eden glanced at Clay and mouthed, "Where is the Border Patrol?"

Clay shrugged and shook his head. They followed Hector back

to the front of the house, where they found Omar and Eden's mother surrounded by Santiago's henchmen.

Eden's mother clenched her fists. "This is ridiculous, Hector!"

He kept walking toward his car. "What is ridiculous is that you expect me to cave to your demands. I should dump you both in the desert."

Eden pressed forward to hear. She had to know what this was all about. It might explain why her mother had come back into her life after all this time.

Clay restrained her. "Don't get too close," he whispered.

"Half the business is mine," Omar yelled at Hector's departing back. "I demand an equal share. It's what our father wished."

Hector turned with a stony expression on his face. "Both of you destroyed my wife. When I washed my hands of you, it was for all time."

What did he mean? Eden doubted he meant that they had actually murdered her. She watched the way her mother took a step back and dropped her head. Omar seemed to bear no shame.

"She deserved to know the truth," Omar said.

"You sent her a photo of a child that may even be your own. All in a petty fit of revenge when you did not get your way."

"How was I to know she would go berserk?" Omar shot back.

"She was fragile, hurt. You knew this woman"—he pointed at Eden's mother—"meant nothing to me."

The history these three shared was becoming clear to Eden. Her picture as a child must have been the thing that had cost Hector his wife. No wonder he had so little regard for her. She should feel blessed that he had let her live. So far.

30

WHERE WAS THE BORDER PATROL? CLAY COULD ONLY ASSUME THEY WERE REMAINING hidden until reinforcements came. Eden looked shell-shocked. Hector was walking away. A few more seconds and it was going to be too late.

"Hey!" he shouted.

Hector stopped and turned back toward him. "What now, boy?"

"I want your word that no harm will come to my wife."

"We have been over that. I will do my best."

Was that a sound from the barn? Clay wanted to push Eden to safety somewhere, but there was no shelter. No tree, no lawn chair, nothing but open yard. The house was too far and there was no door on this side. The growl of an engine came in the distance, then an SUV came careening up the dirt road with clouds of dust spewing from its tires. A van was right behind it.

"Ambush!" Hector shouted. He grabbed Eden's mother and, using her as a shield, propelled her toward his car. "Go, go!" he shouted to his men.

But it was too late. The vehicles blocked the lane, and two agents brandishing guns erupted from the barn. Doors slammed as men poured from the SUV and the van. Santiago's men brought their guns up. When the first shots were fired, Clay dived for his wife. His weight bore her to the ground and he covered her with his body. She didn't struggle, and he could hear her breathing in his ear, a frantic gasping.

"Were you hit?" he asked.

"No." Her arms came around his waist as more gunfire rocketed around them. "Can you see if he's been shot? Or my mother?"

Clay raised his head cautiously as the shots tapered off. "I don't see anyone on the ground except the driver. They're handcuffing Hector. I don't see your mom or Omar."

When the men were all in custody, he rolled off Eden and got up, then helped her to her feet. Santiago's glare held menace when he spotted them. Clay's gut clenched at the hate in his face.

Hector's wrists were cuffed behind him, but he jerked away from the grip of the agent and took a couple of steps toward them. "You will pay for this. Enjoy your wife while you can. She will not be alive for long."

The agent grabbed his arm again and hustled him to the back of the waiting van. The other men were shoved into the vehicle as well. A Border Patrol agent walked toward Clay and Eden.

"Everyone okay?" he asked.

"We're uninjured," Clay said. "I wasn't sure you were going to get here in time. Good work." But he felt queasy when he remembered Santiago's words. "When you question him, see if you can get him to tell you who has made several attempts on my wife's life."

"I'll do that," the agent said. "These guys are snakes. Dispose of one and a dozen more show up." He tipped his hat. "Appreciate your help, ma'am. We've been trying to get him for a long time."

Clay glanced to where Eden's mother stood with Omar. "You got anything on Omar Santiago? That's him over there."

The agent frowned. "Santiago's brother?"

"Yeah, that's him."

"There is no warrant out for his arrest. If he's been involved in this, he's kept a low profile. We'll be sure to question him and Hector both, though."

Eden's mother came running up. "Eden, please tell me you had nothing to do with this ambush." Her mouth was twisted and tight, and angry tears stood in her eyes.

"He had to be taken off the streets, Mom," Eden said. "And he sent someone after me. Someone who has tried to kill me."

Her mother's eyes widened. "You did set this up! I can't believe it."

Clay stepped in. "What did you expect her to do? Look away while this guy destroyed lives and ruined kids?"

"But he's her father!"

Eden's chin came up. "He says it's more likely Omar is my father. Is that true?"

Her mother glanced away. "That's a lie," she said, but her voice lacked conviction. "How could you do this to your own family? I'm disappointed in you."

Eden laughed derisively. "My family. You used me to get to Hector. You didn't come back because you loved me and wanted to make amends. You thought Hector would agree to see me, and you could contact him that way."

Her mother met her gaze. "I did no such thing!"

But Clay saw the truth in her eyes. Eden was right. This pair had used his wife. "Haven't you put her through enough? Did you have to hurt her like this?"

"How has this hurt her? She's fine. Not a scratch."

"I was actually beginning to believe you," Eden said softly. "I thought you'd really had a change of heart, maybe even found God or something. I believed you weren't the same woman who left me on my own. Now I find that I was just a tool."

Clay pointed to the van. "And according to Hector, this isn't the first time you've used her. What was all that about his wife?"

Her mother started to walk away. "This is no concern of yours."

Clay caught her arm and turned her around to face them. "Let's have the truth."

In the harsh light her mother looked older, drained. "Hector broke off ties with Omar when Omar told him we were going to marry. They argued. Hector said some hateful things about me."

"Like maybe the fact you weren't welcome in the Santiago family?" Eden asked.

"Yes. He called me names. We were desperate, though. Neither of us had a job, and we needed money. I thought maybe his wife would make him support his daughter at least."

The woman's lies took Clay's breath away. "But you'd already abandoned Eden by then."

The woman had the decency to blush. "Else didn't know that. We thought she would make Hector do his duty."

Eden shook her head. "No, you wanted revenge. You wanted to hurt Hector."

Her mother pressed her lips together. "He's skated through life without a thought for other people. It's about time he paid for some of his sins."

There was no getting through to this woman. She was blind to her warped character. "So you told his wife. What happened?"

"The silly woman was hysterical. From what I heard, she took some pills and overdosed. To this day, no one knows if it was accidental or deliberate."

"She died?"

"I have heard she lived but went a little crazy. I'm not sure, though."

The poor woman. Destroyed by this pair. "I don't ever want you to contact us again," Clay said. "Let's go, Eden."

The agents were gone, leaving only dust in their wake. The acrid taste of betrayal clung to Eden's tongue. She stood with Clay's arm around her in front of the abandoned house. The wind rolled two tumbleweeds past their feet.

"It's over, honey," Clay said. "We'll go on from here. We have each other and Brianna."

The love in his eyes brought a lump to her throat. "I'm clinging to that. It will take me a few minutes to come to grips with everything she's done." She glanced back at the house. "Can we look at it in the daylight?"

His grin came, tenderness in the curve of it. "Let me make sure there are no snakes in our path."

They went to the door. He kicked the pile of weeds out of the way, then shoved the door open. Sunlight streamed into the open courtyard between the outer entrance and the house. There were more tumbleweeds in the corners, but the hand-painted Mexican tiles on the ground were untouched. Their colors glowed in the sunshine.

"It's lovely!" She stepped onto the tile behind him. A mural was still intact on the back wall of the house. Eden studied the scene of cacti and distant mountains. Warm terra-cotta-colored paint on the other walls made her feel at home. Dead rose branches overran the trellis that covered a seating area. "Who painted this? I love it."

He stood examining the space with her. "I did. It was one of my early teenage attempts at art."

"It's really good." She pointed to the other walls. "You could do some other murals there. Ones of the mountains." She went to the French doors on the right wall. "Where does this lead?"

"Into the dining room." He opened the door and led her into the house. "Looks okay," he said.

She followed him into a huge room flanked with floor-to-ceiling windows. The light had a quality that lifted her spirits. She could see them living here. Brianna playing with her toys on a rug that warmed the tile. On one end of the room was the kitchen. It was still decked out in the eighties style, just like when it was built. Dust and cobwebs covered the counters and cabinets, but the layout and structure attracted her. There was a beehive chimney over the stove. In her mind's eye, she could see a new kitchen with granite counters and cherrywood cabinets.

"How many bedrooms?" she asked.

"You won't believe it. Six. And six bathrooms."

She gaped. "Why so many? There were only three of you kids, right?"

He nodded. "Mom wanted room for company, and she liked to

sew, so one room was set up as her craft space. It was a great house to grow up in." He took her hand. "Let me show you our room."

Our room. Eden liked the sound of that. They could make a home here with Brianna. She could hear her daughter's laughter in this place. And any other children who might come along too. She let Clay lead her to a wing that had several rooms sprouting off of it. She peeked in as she passed and saw two generous bedrooms and several bathrooms.

"The master is at the end of the hall," Clay said.

The door was closed, and he pushed it open to reveal a huge room with fifteen-foot-high ceilings. Clerestory windows illuminated the space. Eden wandered the room and exclaimed over the huge bathroom with a separate shower and soaking bathtub. The walk-in closet was as large as their bedroom back at the bunkhouse.

"I never expected anything so grand," she said.

His grin widened. "Only the best for the love of my life."

She realized the tension she'd felt was gone, washed away by dreaming of the future with this man she loved so much. "Let's see the rest."

By the time she'd seen the five bedrooms in the wing at the other end of the house, she was ready to move in. "How long do you think it would take to get it ready?"

"Depends on what all we want to do. We'll have to get it cleaned, a new roof for sure."

"A new kitchen," she said. "The bathrooms are fine. They just need to be cleaned." The expensive Mexican tile and hand-painted sinks were still in good condition in all the bathrooms. "This place is like a small village. The three of us will have trouble finding one another."

"I can find you anywhere," he said, taking her in his arms. "You can run and hide, but it will do you no good. You belong with me."

"It's the only place I want to be," she said, nestling against him.

They would fill this house with love and laughter again. "What time is it?" she asked. It felt like two days since they'd left the ranch.

He glanced at his watch. "Nearly noon. Sister Marjo should be getting to the ranch soon. We'd better go."

31

SITTING HERE WITH CLAY, IT WAS HARD FOR EDEN TO REMEMBER THAT A FEW HOURS AGO they feared for their lives. It was all over now. The judge had called to report that one of Santiago's lackeys was beginning to talk. Julia hoped to have several branches of Santiago's empire cleanly amputated in another day or two.

Eden glanced at her watch, then at Clay, who was on the porch swing with her. "She's late." She was enjoying resting in the circle of his arm. The girls played with Frisbees in the front yard.

He hugged her. "Only forty-five minutes. Be patient. We're in the boonies. It takes awhile to get here from Austin."

Allie stepped from the house. "Lunch, girls!" She held the door open while the children scampered inside. "Still not here?" she asked.

Eden nearly groaned. "Where is she?"

Allie's smile faded as she glanced at her watch. "She said she thought she'd be no later than noon. I hope her car didn't break down."

The phone rang from inside. Eden had a feeling it was going to be bad news. Her stomach muscles clenched when, a few moments later, Allie returned with a grim expression.

"What is it?"

"That was the sheriff. He found Sister Marjo's car abandoned off the road. There's no sign of her."

Clay lurched to his feet. "She had an accident and tried to walk for help?"

"Maybe. It appears that someone sideswiped her. The driver's door was hanging open like she got out in a hurry. He's got some deputies out looking for her now."

"We should help too," Clay said.

Allie nodded. "Maybe on horseback. Rick can decide. There's lots of desert to cover."

That plan ruled out Eden. No way she was getting in a saddle. "What else can we do?"

Allie glanced at her with an intent expression. "Pray."

"I have been." And God had been so faithful. Little by little, he had filled Eden's life with hope. She'd been afraid to allow herself to dream, but God had given her all she could possibly desire.

Clay rushed off to the barn to fetch Rick. Both men returned leading saddled horses. Eden watched them mount up.

"I want to go too," Allie said.

"It's brutally hot out there today," Rick said. "I'd rather you stay home. In your condition."

Eden glanced at Allie and saw a flush running up her neck. "Condition?"

"I'm pregnant," Allie said. "I suppose I'd better stay home. But I don't want to."

Rick dropped a kiss on her lips. "We'll find her. Try not to worry. And pray."

"We will."

The men mounted their horses and rode off down the drive. "Congratulations," Eden said. "When is the baby due?"

Allie smiled. "Not for five months yet. I'm not even showing. Betsy is hoping for a girl. Matthew wants a brother, of course."

Eden found her own hand had wandered to her belly. She remembered carrying Brianna. Then she'd been young and scared. What would it be like to have another baby with Clay now that the barriers between them were finally down?

She forced her thoughts back to the present. "We might as well make sure the girls are eating," Eden said.

Clay settled in his saddle. "Would you mind shutting the barn door?" he asked Eden. "I just realized we left it open."

"Sure." She glanced at Allie. "You want to check on the girls? I'll shut the door."

"Sure."

Allie headed toward the house. Eden had shut the door and turned to leave when a voice from inside the barn stopped her.

"Eden," the distorted voice whispered. "I have her."

She wanted to run, but she stepped closer to the barn. "You have who?" But she was afraid she knew. "Sister Marjo?" Who was on the other side of this wall?

"Only you can save her."

A window was nearly at eye level. She stared into the barn, but the brilliant sunlight turned the glass into a mirror and she could see nothing. "How?"

"Leave Bluebird. Today. Right now. Clay's truck is outside. His keys are in it. All you have to do is get in and drive away. I'll let the nun go."

"Did you hurt her?"

"Not yet."

The implied threat made her swallow hard. "She's done nothing to you."

"Oh, but she intended to. I had to stop her."

She doubted she could trust this guy. "How do I know that you'll turn her loose?"

"You have my word."

"The word of a kidnapper? That's hardly any guarantee."

"Brianna is next. Do you want their blood on your hands?"

She shuddered at the mental image. What could she do? If only she could summon help. Someone could sneak into the barn and find out who was threatening her. But even if she yelled for help, Allie wouldn't get here in time. Eden could run in the front of the barn, but the man was likely to escape out the back.

"What's it going to be, Eden? Your choice."

"Who are you?"

"You should know."

The voice was distant now, as though the man had moved away from the wall. Which way should she go to catch a glimpse of him as he fled? She paused a moment, then ran for the back of the barn. Nothing. She ran around the side to the front. No one there either. Did she dare go inside? She glanced at the corral and saw Buzz pulling a saddle from a horse.

"Buzz!" She waved frantically, and he dropped the saddle on the top rail of the fence and joined her.

"Yes, ma'am?"

"There's someone in the barn, threatening me. Will you go inside with me?"

He pushed his hat to the back of his head. "Ain't no one, Miss Eden. I was just in there."

She grabbed his arm and tugged him toward the barn door. "It's the person who tried to kill me, Buzz!"

He quit resisting her. "I'll get him, Miss Eden!" Detaching his arm from her grip, he stepped inside the barn's shadows.

She hesitated outside, then followed him. The darkness was an adjustment after the brilliance of the day outside. It took a moment to see clearly. She sniffed to see if the guy's cologne perfumed the air but smelled only hay and horse. Buzz was cautiously checking out the stalls. He shook his head when he saw her in the doorway.

"The haymow?" she asked.

He shrugged, then climbed the ladder to the haymow. While he searched there, she went to where the man must have stood while he was talking to her. The tack hung on nails, and metal cans of feed lined the area. Staring hard, she thought she saw the imprint of where he'd stood. But there was no other sign that he'd been here.

Buzz's feet appeared from the haymow as he backed down the ladder. He shook his head. "No one here, ma'am."

She shivered as she realized she was no closer to identifying the kidnapper. And Clay was out there looking too. He needed to be warned. Whoever this guy was, when he learned that Hector had been arrested, his venom would increase.

By dark the men had to give up. The moonless night was too black to see tracks or even the ground from their perches on their horses. Clay didn't want to admit defeat, but he had no choice. Eden would be worried as well. Lacie would have to have heard about it by now too, poor kid. Eden had left a message on his voice mail, but he'd been riding at the time and lost the signal before the message could play.

His spirits were dragging by the time he dismounted at the barn. One of the stable hands grabbed the reins of both horses and led them off to be curried. Clay's belly rumbled and he realized he hadn't eaten since breakfast. It was now nine.

"I reckon Allie will have something warm for us," Rick said.

Though he was hungry, Clay wanted to see Eden. "I think I'll have a peanut butter sandwich at the bunkhouse, then hit the hay. See you in the morning."

"Thanks for your help," Rick called, heading to the house.

Clay's steps dragged as he went back to the bunkhouse. The drone of the TV floated from the building. Canned laughter, then a man speaking. Andy Griffith. He stepped inside to the aroma of popcorn. It was like a welcome-home kiss.

He didn't call out Eden's name because he didn't want to wake the girls. After hanging his hat on the hook by the door, he kicked off his boots and padded in his stocking feet to the living room. Eden lay sprawled on the sofa, one arm flung over her head. Lacie was curled in the crook of Eden's arm. Their eyes were closed. So peaceful. When they heard the news that Sister Marjo was still missing, they'd be upset.

He thought about carrying Lacie to the bedroom, but he'd

probably wake them both that way. Rattling around in the kitchen would awaken them too. He grabbed an apple from a bowl on the table and went to the bedroom. Maybe there was something on the news about Sister Marjo.

He fired up his laptop and logged on to the Internet. Nothing on the news. Maybe a nun's disappearance in the desert wasn't newsworthy. Checking his e-mail would help him unwind. He was still wired. He launched Apple Mail and saw he had five messages, all from his superior officer. A new hot spot was breaking out in Africa. He wanted Clay to cut his leave short and come back. Clay's fingers poised on the keys. No time like the present.

He wrote an e-mail telling the captain that he would be on leave until his enlistment ran out.

Now he had to figure out what he wanted to do, but God had led him this far. There was something out there for him. He went to the national park site and studied the openings. Nothing in Big Bend yet, but it would come. He was sure of it.

His camera bag was beside his chair. He hadn't seen the pictures he took of the tornado yet. Plugging his camera into the laptop, he took a look at the shots he'd taken. The first one made him suck in his breath.

"I bet I can sell these," he said. He called up his list of publications and contacts, then returned to the Internet. It was satellite Internet, slow as molasses, but he got the best images sent off to his top-paying contact. He would go through every door the Lord opened. The future would be good as long as he had God and his family.

He shut down the computer, then went to check on Eden. She had rolled to her side. Before he decided what to do, she opened her eyes and gave a sleepy smile.

"Hi, beautiful," he said, sinking to his knees by the sofa.

"You're home," she murmured, stretching her hand toward him. He leaned over to kiss her, but before his lips touched hers, her eyes filled with alarm.

"What's wrong?"

"Did you get my message?" she whispered over Lacie's head.

He shook his head. "No signal most of the time. I saw you'd called, but I figured you were wondering when I was coming home."

She clasped her arms around their daughter. "He was here."

"Who?"

"The kidnapper."

He started to rise. "You saw him?"

"No, he was in the barn. Whispering to me through the wall." She shuddered.

His temper began to simmer. "Did you call for help?" He sat beside her and slipped his arm around his girls.

She nestled against him. "Buzz helped me look for him. I think he must have watched to see which door I went to first, then waited for me to go to the other one before darting out the back."

"What did he say?" As she told him the guy's claim that he had Sister Marjo, his gut twisted. "Did you tell Allie?"

"Of course. She called the sheriff, but there wasn't anything he could do. We have no idea who the guy is. If Hector would cooperate, we could get him. Julia said one of the other men is talking, though."

For the first time in a lot of years, Clay wanted to swear. He'd get his hands on the guy and make sure he never bothered Eden again. "I'm going to check out the barn. Maybe there's a clue you missed."

When he pulled his arm away, she grabbed it. "It's dark out there now, Clay. Buzz and I checked it out. There's nothing."

"I have to see for myself. I'll be right back." He shoved his feet back into his boots, grabbed the flashlight, then went across the yard to the barn.

When he flipped the wall switch, the lights pushed back the shadows but not enough. Eden was right, though he hated to admit it. Even the flashlight didn't help much. In the side of the barn where she said the man must have stood, Clay scuffed the loose straw on the floor with his boot. Nothing but floorboards under there.

He ran his hand along the sill and checked out the tack hanging on the walls. His fingers touched some kind of wire. He traced it up to a tiny speaker just over the window.

"What on earth?" he muttered.

The guy had rigged up some way to talk to her while she stood outside. No wonder she and Buzz hadn't seen him. He'd never been there in the first place.

32

Eden expected Clay back from the barn any minute. She'd returned Lacie to bed and gone into the kitchen to get Clay some dinner. Chili bubbled in the pan on the stove. She stirred it, then shut off the gas. She cut slices of homemade bread and got out the peanut butter.

"Miss Eden?"

She turned to see Madeline rubbing her eyes. "What are you doing up, sweetheart?"

"I heard a voice." The little girl leaned against her leg and moved restlessly. "I have to potty."

"It was just Mr. Clay. He got home. Let's get you back to bed." She took the girl to the bathroom, then tucked her back into her bed. "It's okay."

"Read me a story," Madeline said, pulling the sheet to her chin.

The night always brought a new softness to the child, but her underlying antagonism returned with the morning light.

"You've already had a story." Eden kissed her cheek. "I'll sing you a song, though." She sang the favorite "Amazing Grace" and realized how meaningful the words were to her tonight, how amazing it was that God had brought her daughter back to her.

Madeline was still awake, so Eden caressed her hair and sang two more verses. She could feel the little girl relaxing. Her gaze went to the bed where Lacie lay, but it was too dark to make out the child's features. Soon they'd be a family. The three of them could cuddle in a king-size bed and tell stories and sing songs.

"Mr. Clay was outside my window," Madeline muttered, her eyes already closing.

Eden didn't bother to explain that his voice had carried from the living room. She went back to the kitchen and glanced out the window but saw no sign of Clay. Maybe she could check her e-mail while she was waiting. She went to the bedroom and lifted the lid of Clay's MacBook. It opened to the mail program. She started to click out of it, but the message from Clay's commander was on the screen and she caught the words MIDDLE EAST ASSIGNMENT.

She felt sick as she read the captain's request for Clay to cut short his leave and head out on a new tour of duty. What had been his response? He'd talked about living here, but when it came down to actually walking away from the military, would he do it? She feared the answer was no.

No longer in the mood to check her e-mail, she shut the lid and went back to the kitchen. She picked up the plate of bread she'd cut. As she set the bread on the table, the lights in the kitchen went out.

Every muscle tensed. "Clay?" Did she hear breathing or was it her imagination? She felt along the top of the refrigerator. No flashlight. Of course, Clay had taken it. She didn't even know where to look for another. She stood in the middle of the kitchen with her heart pounding against her ribs.

She had to get help. Cautiously feeling her way, she eased toward the door. When she stepped onto the porch, a breeze lifted her hair. It was just as dark out here. There was no moon, and clouds hid the stars. She couldn't even see the steps to the yard. Her hand found the porch post, then her foot felt the steps drop off. If she didn't fear waking the girls, she'd call out to Clay from here. The thought of walking across the yard in her bare feet was daunting. There could be snakes, scorpions, or tarantulas.

After hesitating, she decided to go back and get her shoes. It wasn't as though the lights being out would awaken the girls. She retreated to the house and felt her way to the living room, where she found her shoes by the sofa. She slid her feet into them and went to the back door again. From here she should see the lights on in the barn. At least she had a direction to aim for. It was pitch black out here. She realized she still clutched the spoon she'd used to stir the chili.

She heard something behind her. "Clay?"

Half turning, she felt a hand on her arm. Then something sweet and moist pressed against her nose and mouth. Struggling, she tried to scream but only succeeded in sucking in more of the chemical on the rag pressed against her face.

Then she was falling into a darkness even more profound.

The flashlight beam probed the darkness only a few feet as Clay walked back toward the house that he knew had to be back here. But there were no lights to guide him. Surely Eden hadn't turned out the lights and gone to bed. Frowning, Clay strode in what he thought was the right direction. He stopped and shined the light higher, then saw the outline of the bunkhouse. Finally. He mounted the steps and poked his head inside.

"Eden?" He flipped the switch on the wall but nothing happened. He caught his breath. A thrown breaker or something deliberate? "Eden?" he called again.

Where was the breaker? He tried to remember. He'd seen it somewhere. In the kitchen maybe? He made his way to the kitchen. The scent of chili hung in the air. He hadn't smelled it when he came in the first time, so Eden must have been warming it for him. He touched the stove and found the pot warm. Where was she? Alarm bells were ringing in his head.

He shined the light around the room. No sign of the breaker box. Wait, wasn't it on the outside wall right here? Letting the flashlight guide his way, he shoved open the screen door and stepped onto the back porch. The electrical box was mounted on the siding. He aimed the light at the panel and opened the cover. All the breakers looked okay. Frowning, he studied them, then stared at the main. It was flipped off. His gut clenched.

He stepped back into the kitchen. "Eden?"

It didn't matter if he awakened the girls now. He had to find his wife. Room by room, he turned on lights and searched. The bright lights did nothing to lift his fear. Not in the living room. Not in the bathroom or their bedroom. In the children's room, they all slept in spite of his voice calling for Eden.

He had to get help from Rick. He went out to the living room and called her name once more, then stepped to the porch, pausing to turn on the porch light. The bulb pushed back the shadows, and he could see the swing and the chairs on the porch. No Eden.

Cupping his hands to his mouth, he called for her again. When there was no answer, he went down the steps to the yard, sweeping the flashlight beam over the area. Something glittered in the weeds. He focused the flashlight. A spoon covered with chili.

"Eden!" He raced to the main house and pounded on the door. When Allie opened it, he looked past her. "Get Rick. Eden's missing."

"Oh no!" She turned and called over her shoulder. "Rick, hurry!"

Rick came through the kitchen door still chewing on his dinner. He swallowed. "What's wrong?"

"I think someone has taken Eden." The words caused cold terror to curl in his belly. "Call the sheriff." He sagged against the door frame and wondered if he would ever see his wife again.

33

Every breath dragged in a sickeningly sweet taste. Eden tried to open her eyes and couldn't. Another odor penetrated the smell of chloroform. Mouse droppings. She managed to lift her lids and squinted in the dim light.

She lay on a dirty sofa littered with chewed paper and mouse dung. Every instinct told her to spring to her feet, but her muscles refused to obey. The most she could do was to lift her head away from the disgusting mess.

A soft hand touched her arm. "How do you feel, dear?"

She stared into the face of a woman in her late forties or early fifties. Dark hair, sweet smile, compassionate eyes behind wire-rimmed glasses.

Eden tried to smile back, but she was sure it was more of a grimace. "My head hurts."

The woman helped her sit. "You've been unconscious all night."

Eden's head throbbed so badly she found it hard to think. "Where am I?"

"I'm not sure. In a cabin somewhere in the desert. I can't make out much. The windows are boarded up and there are only tiny cracks to see out. The door is padlocked on the outside."

It all rushed back to Eden. The lights going out. The attack. She wobbled to her feet. "I have to get out of here!" Brianna and the other girls had to be okay. And Clay.

The woman grabbed her arm. "Settle down, honey. Neither of us is going anywhere."

"We're prisoners here?"

The woman shrugged. "The only power over us is what God has allowed. When he's ready to release us, nothing will stand in his way."

Her manner drew Eden. Such confidence and trust calmed her. She wished she was so quick to have faith. "Have you seen our captor?"

"Only vaguely. I could tell little through the windshield as I tried to escape being struck by the truck. I hit my head when I was forced off the road. When I awoke, I was here."

Eden eyed the woman, realizing who she was. The lady wore a black skirt and white blouse that was a little wrinkled. Where was the habit, the wimple? "Forced off the road. You're Sister Marjo?"

"Why, yes. How do you know of me?"

"We were expecting you at Bluebird Ranch. I'm Eden Larson. My husband and I are counselors for the girls."

She took off her glasses and polished them on her skirt. "Then you've been taking care of our Lacie."

"I have."

"What did you see when you were taken?"

"I was drugged in the dark and saw nothing." She could still smell the sickening odor of the chemical and wished she could have a sip of water. "Is there anything to drink?"

"Let me get you water." The nun went to a plastic jug by the door.

A sleeve of cups was beside it. There was also a loaf of bread, a jar of Jif peanut butter, and a can of nuts beside it, but Eden wasn't hungry. Her tongue wanted to stick to the roof of her mouth, so she drank the water greedily when the sister handed her the red cup.

"Did you see him bring me in?" Eden asked after she drained the last drop.

Sister Marjo shook her head. "I was sleeping, then heard the door shut. I found you on the floor just inside the door. I assume he dropped you inside."

"You carried me to the sofa?"

The nun shuddered. "I couldn't let you lie on the floor. Spiders and scorpions."

Eden shivered too. "Thank you."

She peered around the dim space. The one-room cabin held only a battered table, the shredded sofa, and a bank of open cabinets that were empty. The place smelled of dust and disuse. And mouse.

"Where did you sleep?"

"I curled up on the table."

"I'm sorry."

"It was nothing, my dear. I was quite comfortable."

Eden went to the boarded-up window on the wall by the door. She tried to slip her fingers under the board, but she couldn't even get her nail beneath it. "I think these haven't been up long."

Sister Marjo came to stand beside her. "I thought the same. They appear to be quite new."

Eden went to look into the old sink, layered with cobwebs. "If we only had something to pry them up with."

"I looked everywhere. There isn't so much as a spoon."

Eden glanced to the door. "What about the peanut butter? How are you spreading it?"

"I haven't so far. I assume he expects me to use my fingers, but there's no way to wash so I've had a handful of nuts only. I didn't want to contaminate the whole jar of peanut butter with my filthy hands."

No help there, then. "If there was even a stray nail," she said. "It's so dim in here. Can you tell what time of day it is?"

"I believe it's morning. It was still dark a couple of hours ago, then the room began to lighten a bit." She pointed to threads of sunshine coming in through cracks in the walls and the roof. "I don't have a watch."

Eden was already feeling a bit claustrophobic. She wanted out of here. If she had the nerve, she would crawl on her hands and feet along the floor and feel for anything that might be helpful. She slipped off her shoes and swept her stocking foot back and forth across the surface.

When she heard something roll across the floor, she pounced on it. "It's a nail!" she said, holding it aloft. Maybe they'd get out of here yet. She had to live, had to raise her daughter.

The first board held fast to the wall. Eden's initial high hopes began to fade when she couldn't pry the nail under the second board either. "I need something to hit it with," she said. "Maybe the nut can?"

Sister Marjo ran to get it. “Here you go.” She handed it to Eden.

Wedging the tip of the nail under the lip of the board, Eden smacked the head of the nail with the can. “It’s under!”

She knocked it again and it slipped a tiny bit more. Little by little she drove the nail under the edge.

“You need something to exert leverage now. The nail is too small to maneuver,” Sister Marjo said. She glanced around the room. “Let me see if I can get the table leg off.”

She flipped the table on its side and began to wiggle one of the legs. “It’s loosening!” The leg clattered to the floor, and she brought it to Eden. “Push on the nail with this.”

Eden wedged the edge of the nail into a crack in the end of the table leg and pushed on it. The board seemed to give a little. Patiently she repeated the movement so many times she lost track. “I’ve got it!” she said when the board came up far enough that she was able to get the table leg under it. One more hard shove and she was able to wrench the board from the window.

Sunlight streamed through the opening. There was no glass in the frame.

The nun peered outside. “Any idea where we are?”

Eden stared too. “Not really. I don’t see any other houses or roads around.” Even if they got out of here, which direction should they head? “I think I can get the rest of these boards off now.”

She grabbed the board she’d removed and used it as a fulcrum to pop the next board loose. Once it was out, she and Sister Marjo might be able to squeeze through the window sideways. But once it was free, she decided to take another board out. Then the entire window was open to the elements. The heat poured in, and she wiped her brow.

"You're very inventive, young lady," the nun said. "Shall we get out of here?"

Eden smiled. "I'll go first so I can help you out." She put on her shoes. With one arm through the window, her shirt snagged on the rough wood, and she heard the material tear. Jerking it free, she managed to get outside the building. She could toss the blouse.

"This should be fun." The sister hiked up her skirt and put one leg through.

Eden grabbed her arm and helped her onto what was left of a front porch. They were free! She turned and stared at the barren hills. There was no sign of civilization in any direction. No sound of tires on pavement. Only the caw of a crow overhead. The wind rustled through the cacti and grasses and made her feel alone and vulnerable. A lone coyote cried somewhere in the distance and the sound raised the hair on the back of her head.

"I can see you're frightened," Sister Marjo said. "Don't be. God sees us."

Eden knew that too, but there was something in the nun's voice that was more confident than a platitude. "He talks to you?"

"Not in audible words, but with impressions." The nun put her hand on her chest. "I feel it here. And we should go that way." She pointed to a distant desert peak.

It wasn't the direction Eden would have picked. They would have to climb that peak. But somehow she trusted the other woman's instincts. "Okay."

She and Sister Marjo set off across the sand. The hillside was nearly covered with cholla cacti, and she knew enough to proceed carefully. Also known as the jumping cactus, just the slightest brush would have left their skin punctured with tiny needles. The sun beat down on their heads, and she hadn't been gone from the cabin more than five minutes before perspiration trickled down her back.

They reached the top of the peak and stopped to catch their breath. The vista from here didn't reveal any clearer idea of their location. "Now what?" she asked. Was she crazy for listening to a nun she didn't even know? One who had never been here before either?

Sister Marjo peered from behind her glasses. She took her time staring in all directions. "That way," she said, indicating they should continue west.

"You're the boss," Eden said.

They trudged down the slope and hit the flat desert, which seemed to stretch out for a hundred miles. Not a single cloud softened the brutality of the sun on their heads. Eden wished she had something to cover her arms. She was already beginning to burn.

"We should have brought our water and food," Sister Marjo said.

Eden nearly groaned. "That was dumb," she agreed. "I'm already getting thirsty. I guess I thought we couldn't be far from help, but I was wrong. There are no ranches, no nothing, as far as I can see."

"God knows where we are, dear girl. 'Where can I go from Your Spirit? Or where can I flee from Your presence? If I ascend into heaven, You are there; if I make my bed in hell, behold, You are there.'" Sister Marjo smiled. "I love the 139th Psalm, don't you?"

A pang of longing clutched Eden's heart. Such confidence, such trust. If the nun's faith were a bucket of water, Eden had only a drop of the same confidence. She wiped her forehead again and glanced around. This desert was similar to hell, but Eden kept the thought to herself. She set her sights on a patch of cactus in the far distance. If they saw nothing by the time they reached that vista, she was turning back for the water.

34

Eden had been gone all night and all day. Clay leaned back in the saddle as he reached the ranch and wiped his forehead with a handkerchief. They'd found no sign of her. The sheriff had everyone in four counties looking for her and the nun.

Allie came rushing down the steps from the porch. "Nothing?"

"Not a sign." He didn't even try to hide his discouragement. "Has anyone else reported in?"

"The sheriff called a few minutes ago. He's found nothing yet. Zeke is still out. Della is taking care of all the kids."

"Are the girls worried?"

"We haven't told them, but I think they suspect something is wrong. They're a little wild today," Allie said. "Brendan is here."

Clay dismounted, and Buzz took the reins, then led the lathered horse away. "Where is he?" Clay started toward the house.

"Getting a horse so he can help with the search. He and Rick are about to go out again. Rick came in half an hour ago to get a fresh mount."

Clay changed direction and followed Allie to the corral, where he found both men saddling horses. "Thanks for coming to help, Brendan," he said.

The other man pulled the cinch on the saddle. "I did some research on that Daniel character you mentioned," he said. "He's been gone from home for two days. No one seems to know where he is."

"You think he's around here, that he took Eden?" *The slimeball.* Clay wanted to strangle him.

"It's a possibility." Brendan stopped and glanced at Clay. "You look as scraggly as a coyote."

"I haven't slept." He'd tried for about an hour, but his eyes had refused to close. "Anything else you've uncovered?"

Brendan flipped the stirrup into place. "The ransom money in that suitcase. You put marked bills in it. Some of it surfaced."

Clay had checked for a while, but the money had never turned up. The last time he'd asked about it had been a year ago. "Where?"

"In Bluebird. About six months ago."

That was a shocker. "Well before we came. But how do you connect Daniel to the money? And Bluebird?"

Brendan finished saddling his horse. He put a boot in the stirrup and vaulted onto the horse. "I'm not. Just relaying what I found out."

Rick mounted his horse. "What about Santiago? Is he giving up any new leads?" He sneezed and the horse reared a bit, but he quieted the animal with a touch.

Brendan leaned back in the saddle. "Still not talking. But I'm sure he's connected, since you believe that his influence caused the attacks on Eden in the first place."

What about Daniel, though? Clay still thought Eden's foster brother had something to do with it.

Rick glanced at his wife. "Rita back from town yet?"

Allie pointed to the truck. "I just saw her pull into the drive. Why?"

"I sent her after cold meds, and I could use a dose before I go out again." He blew his nose, then put his hanky back.

Allie called the cook as she got out of the truck. "Could you bring the medicine, Rita?"

The young woman dug the box out of the bag, along with a bottle of water, and jogged toward them. "I was hoping you guys were here. There was a man asking about Bluebird Ranch when I got gas."

"What did he look like?" Clay asked. Maybe this was their break.

"Young, maybe thirty."

"What did he say?" Rick asked, downing his pills with a gulp of water.

"Asked the way to the ranch. He wanted to know if the Larsons were still here."

"What else can you tell us besides his age?" Clay asked. One of Santiago's henchmen?

Rita shifted the bag to her other hand. "Sandy brown hair. Horn-rimmed glasses. Snappy dresser. I can't remember the last time I saw a man with shoes that shiny."

A picture formed in Clay's mind. Daniel had been missing for two days. Long enough to get here. "Daniel," he said. "I'll bet it's him."

"But if he's just now asking how to get to the ranch, he can't have Eden," Allie said.

"Unless it's a ruse," Brendan said. "I'd better talk to him."

"I'm coming with you," Clay said.

"I don't think either of you will have to go anywhere," Rita said, staring at the drive. "There he is now. I thought he'd likely be right behind me." She started for the truck. "I'll let you handle this. I forgot milk after I heard this guy. I need to run back to town."

Clay watched the blue Chevy, obviously a rental, roll up the drive. He walked toward the vehicle as the door opened and Daniel got out. He hadn't changed any since Clay last saw him five years ago. He still wore his hair slicked back. The plaid button-down shirt and the pants with the sharp crease completed the image of a man consumed with his image.

Daniel's expression was wary as Clay stopped in front of him. "Clay," he said. "I came to see Eden. I . . . I started missing her and realized I don't want her out of my life."

Clay wanted to grab him by the neck. "Like you don't know where she is." He was vaguely aware that Rick, Allie, and Brendan had stopped just behind him.

Daniel's eyes widened. "What are you talking about?"

Clay took a step closer. "Where is she?" he yelled in the guy's face.

Comprehension dawned in Daniel's eyes and he grinned. "You mean she's left you already? I knew it would happen."

Clay clenched his fists. "She didn't leave me. Someone took her." He jabbed his finger in Daniel's chest. "I'm betting that someone is you. The sheriff has a few questions for you."

"What are you talking about?" Daniel held up his hands. "I just got to town." He reached into his pocket and drew out a boarding pass. "See here? I flew into El Paso four hours ago. When did she go missing?"

"Yesterday." He didn't trust anything this guy tried to say. Clay batted Daniel's hand away. "I want to know where she is."

The paper flew from Daniel's hand. Rick caught it in the air. He opened it and stared. "He's telling the truth, Clay. He just got to town. This is his flight information and the rental receipt for the car. There's no way he was here last night when Eden went missing."

"You're serious?" Daniel asked. "Someone really kidnapped Eden?" His voice rose. "What are you doing to find her? She's been gone a whole day!"

Her lips were as cracked as the dry riverbed they'd just crossed. Eden wasn't sure how much longer she could keep going. Squinting at the sky, she realized it was midafternoon. They had been out here at least six hours. The point she'd been heading toward was farther than it looked. They should have turned around, but by the time she realized it, they'd gone so far that they decided to keep on. They thought they would find civilization soon. She missed Clay and the girls. The thought they might be in danger haunted her.

"Let's rest a minute," she told Sister Marjo when they reached a spot where limestone cliffs streaked by erosion rose in the sky.

Several caves looked inviting, but she knew better than to crawl inside to escape the sun. They could harbor anything from bats to snakes. And scorpions and tarantulas were almost a given. She dropped onto a nearby stone and wiped her forehead. Her skin felt hot and tight.

Sister Marjo still appeared to be doing all right. Her face was red and her forehead moist, but she had retained her smile. She took off her glasses and polished them on her blouse, then perched them back on her nose before joining Eden on the rock.

"Are you doing all right, beloved?" she asked, putting her hand on Eden's arm.

"Why do you call me *beloved*?" Eden asked. The sun stripped her of the inhibition that had kept that question locked behind her teeth. "You barely know me."

The nun cupped Eden's cheek in her hand. "Because you are God's beloved." She smiled when Eden shook her head. "I see from the hurt in your eyes you don't believe it."

"I know he loves me, even though I don't deserve it. But he sometimes lets his children die." She hadn't meant to say what she was thinking. She didn't want to frighten Sister Marjo, though she was beginning to think the woman would face a saber-toothed tiger with equal equanimity.

The woman dropped her hand. "There is no death for a believer. Not really. There is only this life and eternity waiting."

Eden moved away from a lizard on the rock. "I want to raise my daughter. To love Clay. I don't want to die out here. I've been asking God to let me live." With every step, she'd pleaded with God for help to arrive.

"Jacob wrestled with God in the desert when he saw the ladder with angels ascending and descending. Perhaps he brought you out here to do the same."

"Clay calls me Angel," Eden said.

"Messenger of God," Sister Marjo said.

"I'm far from a messenger from God."

"We are all his messengers. We can choose to trust and let his love shine out of us, or we can let bitterness and disappointment steal our joy. It's your choice."

Eden turned her head to stare at the limestone jutting into the sky. *Choice.* She didn't have any choices. She hadn't chosen to be abandoned. She hadn't chosen to have her daughter kidnapped. And she certainly hadn't chosen to die out here under the blazing sun. In spite of it all, she clung to her trust in God, but fear still coiled in the pit of her stomach. God had her in his hands, but there was no telling whether he might choose to take her to heaven today.

The last time she'd been in church with Clay, the preacher had delivered a message about Job. The minister had said something about trusting God when all seemed lost, because he had a purpose in everything he allowed. She'd wondered what possible purpose God had for allowing them to be deprived of their daughter for five long years.

Her vision became distorted. Was she dehydrated? She blinked as she saw a bird overhead that appeared as large as a pterodactyl. She huddled into a ball, hoping the bird didn't see her. Her head spun as she seemed to shrink to the size of a mouse. It felt as though she were in a vortex, spinning faster and faster. She wanted to fling out her arms and grasp something solid, something she could trust to hold her steady.

I am here.

God's voice wasn't audible, not like the caw of the crow overhead, but she heard it in her heart. He had never gone anywhere. Who was she to question his ways, even if he let her die today? A verse came to mind. *"Where were you when I laid the foundations of the earth?"*

"I can choose to trust," she said aloud. Her voice seemed small and insignificant, but her chest expanded with the words. Trust was hard for her. It always had been, probably because of being abandoned by her mother. She wanted to have the kind of faith Sister Marjo had, the kind Clay had. Her own seemed anemic by comparison.

A hand pressed hers. God's? Or Sister Marjo's? She closed her eyes and toppled to the sand. The grit bit into her cheek, but she couldn't move. Was God looking at her? Seeing her distress the way he'd seen Hagar in the desert? Gradually her head quit spinning, and the nausea in her belly subsided.

She sat up. The sun had sunk a bit lower in the sky. Her sense of having met with God remained. Maybe she would die out here, but if she did, Clay and Brianna would be all right. She'd glimpsed a tiny bit of God's power.

Needing water desperately, she staggered to her feet. Sister Marjo was nowhere to be found. Had the nun wandered off?

"Sister Marjo!" she screamed. The steps in the sand led toward the limestone cliffs, and Eden followed.

She ducked under a rocky bridge and entered a small valley. The sound of water came to her ears. A small spring bubbled by a tall ocotillo. Sister Marjo crouched beside it with her hands cupped together.

"Sister?" Eden said.

The nun looked up. "You're better! I was about to bring you some water," she said.

This place was a tiny bit of paradise in the desert. Eden stumbled past green sage and a few desert wildflowers. "How did you find it?"

"I heard the water."

There'd been no sound out by the rocks, but Eden didn't argue. She knew the woman would claim God had told her. And maybe he had. She stooped and plunged her hands into the pool. Gulping the cool moisture greedily, she drank her fill, and her light-headedness began to subside.

"You're different," Sister Marjo said, her gaze fastened on Eden's face.

Eden met her gaze. Of all the people who would believe she'd had an encounter with God, it was this woman. "I can trust now."

Sister Marjo's face broadened. "You heard God's voice."

"Maybe. I just know I have no control and never have had. I have tried to control everything about my life after my mother abandoned me. I realize now that all I can do is trust God." Oh, how she wanted to see Clay's face again. To tell Lacie she had a mommy and daddy who loved her. But that was not for her to decide.

35

Eden and Sister Marjo sat by the stream and rested. Eden dangled her hand in the water. The only thing lacking was shade, but the cool water made up for it. It was tempting to stay here and wait for someone to find them, but it wasn't going to happen. They'd stumbled in here by accident, so the chances of someone else doing the same were remote. Once they rested, they had to decide what to do.

"Tell me about your family," Sister Marjo said.

Eden smiled. "My husband is an air force photojournalist. He's always off documenting stories of war and combat. He's won a lot of awards."

"Out of the country?"

"Yes, quite often. He loves what he does." That e-mail. Would he leave again soon? "He's talked about getting out of the military and becoming a ranger, but I'm not sure he will do it. He loves the excitement."

"And you have a daughter?"

Eden stared into Sister Marjo's kind eyes. This woman knew her daughter better than anyone. "My daughter was kidnapped when she was six weeks old." She launched into the story and watched the nun's eyes widen and fill with tears.

The sister took a hankie from her sleeve and blew her nose. "I'm so sorry, beloved. You'll see her again someday."

"I already have." Eden leaned forward, unsure how much to tell her. Something about the nun inspired confidence. "We found out one of the girls at the ranch was our Brianna. But we didn't know which one, so we had DNA tests run. We just got the results. Lacie is our Brianna."

The nun gasped and put her hand to her chest. "M-My Lacie? You're saying my Lacie is your daughter?"

"Yes." Eden patted the nun's hand before she leaned back. "So you don't have to worry about her anymore. We want you to stay part of her life, but I'm sure you are happy to know she has a mother and father who love her very much."

Sister Marjo took off her glasses and cleaned them. Her smile didn't return. "I don't know much about DNA tests, Eden. But I do know that what you are saying is impossible."

Eden's eager smile faded. "I don't understand."

The sister replaced her glasses. "The story about her being left on the church steps? It's not the full story. My niece is Lacie's mother."

"Th-That's impossible. The DNA test was very specific. Lacie was the only match." Eden tried to think through how this could be. "Did you see your niece pregnant? Maybe she was involved in the kidnapping and passed Lacie off as her own child."

"No, dear. I delivered the child myself. I saw Lacie's birth with my own two eyes."

Eden shook her head violently. "This doesn't make any sense."

"No. No, it doesn't. But I can assure you that Lacie is no relation to you."

Eden's fatigue fell away. "I have to tell Clay. We must figure this out. I think you and I should go back to the cabin. We can hide and watch to make sure the guy isn't there. He's got to have a vehicle. We can see the direction he came from."

"I think we're close to finding the road," Sister Marjo said. "Just over the hill."

"We've been thinking that for hours." Eden took a last gulp of water and stood, drying her hands on her pants. "But we've just wandered farther and farther. I don't think we can keep that up. Right now we're not lost, but if a wind kicks up we could be. All we have to do is follow our tracks back."

She set off toward the limestone bridge, the exit from their piece of paradise. She headed toward the opening, but a figure ducked under the limestone. It was Rita.

Eden rushed toward her. "Rita! How did you find us?"

The cook was in jeans and a long-sleeved cotton blouse. She had a knapsack slung over one shoulder. "I saw your tracks at the cabin and followed them in the four-wheel drive."

"You went to the cabin first?"

Rita nodded. "I remembered it was out here. When no one could find you, I decided to check it out on my way back from town.

I saw the boards missing and your footprints out across the desert, so I followed."

Eden's hope that Clay was with her vanished. "Is Clay all right? And the girls?"

"Oh yes. Shannon took the girls with her. That big MacGowan place has enough employees to populate an army. Clay is out looking for you."

At least the girls were safe. "I don't suppose you have any food in that sack, do you?" Eden asked. "We're famished."

The young woman smiled. "I sure do." She dropped the satchel to the sand, then knelt and opened it. There was a jar of peanut butter and some bread inside. "This seemed the least likely to spoil," she said.

Jif peanut butter. Just like the food at the cabin. Eden told herself that millions of people used Jif. It meant nothing. "Thanks," she said, taking the jar. "Do you have a knife?"

Rita's smile faded. "I didn't think to bring a knife. Use your finger. Your hands have been in the water."

Eden turned her back to Rita and went toward Sister Marjo. She and the nun exchanged a long glance, and she knew the other woman was as uneasy as she was. Could it be just coincidence, or did Rita have something to do with all of this? She knelt and unscrewed the lid to the Jif, then smeared some on a piece of bread. The rich aroma made her mouth water. She handed the peanut butter and bag of bread to the nun, then licked her finger while Sister Marjo made a sandwich of her own.

Eden took her time eating the peanut butter and bread while she turned the facts around in her mind. The cabin was in the middle of nowhere, yet Rita had gone there to "check it out." It sounded fishy. She leaned over the spring and took a long drink.

She pasted a smile on her face, then stood and turned toward Rita. Her smile froze when Rita's hand came up with a gun in it. "What's this all about?" Eden asked.

"I knew you wouldn't buy the story for long," Rita said, her face calm. "Let's go."

"Where are we going?"

The other woman's smile was cold. "To a funeral. Yours."

There were few hours of daylight left. Clay urged his horse toward the ranch. He had to find Eden before darkness fell again. If he had to endure another night wondering about her fate, he would go crazy. But this horse was done in. He had to have a fresh mount.

When he reached the corral, he dismounted and ran for the house. Maybe some news had come in while he was gone. His cell coverage had been nonexistent out in the desert. "Allie!" he called.

Allie stepped out onto the porch as he neared it. Her eager smile faded when she saw him. "I'd hoped you'd found her."

He sagged against the porch post. "No news?"

"Nothing. Rick and Brendan just went out again, and of course the sheriff and his men are out. Julia came by. She brought you this." She handed over an envelope. "I think it's the court-ordered results on the DNA test. She said they would normally have mailed it, but she knew you were eager so she took a look and ruled on it."

He ripped it open. If they had a court date, he could tell Eden when he saw her. And he would find her. He scanned the paper until a word brought him upright. DENIED. He read it again.

"What's wrong?" Allie asked.

"This says there was no familial match with Lacie."

"That can't be right!"

Clay glanced up at her. "I have a DNA test that says differently. What's the judge trying to pull here? Could she be blocking the proceedings for some reason?"

"The sample collection was supervised and observed," she said. "I don't see how that's possible. Could you have mixed up the samples you sent in?"

"Eden and I did it together. We were very careful."

"You took them to the post office yourself?"

He thought back, then shook his head. "No, Rita took them for me. She was going to town to buy stamps."

Allie frowned. "Speaking of Rita, she never came back from the store, and she left hours ago."

Something screamed for Clay's attention, but he couldn't put his finger on what had made him so uneasy. "Have you tried to call her?"

"Yes, but you know how spotty cell reception is out here."

"Wasn't she just going after milk?"

"So she said." Allie glanced at her watch. "It's been four hours. Something has to be wrong."

Rita had taken the samples to the post office. And it was clear someone had switched the samples. "Could we check out her room?"

"Check her room? I don't understand. She's just late."

"Maybe it's more than that, Allie. I want to see her room."

Allie frowned. "I hate to invade her privacy like that. Maybe she had a flat tire."

Clay wanted to know the truth. Now. "Think about it, Allie. It's clear someone switched those samples. She's the only one who had opportunity."

"But what could be the reason?"

"You tell me. How long has she been employed here?"

Allie's forehead wrinkled. "About six months I think. Yes, that's right. Six months."

"Six months!"

"Does that mean something to you?"

"Brendan said the marked money from the kidnapping attempt showed up in Bluebird six months ago."

She put her hand to her mouth. "Oh, that's right!" Her lips pressed into a straight line. "All right, let's check out her room."

He followed her into the house, nodding at Betsy and her little brother. "Where are the rest of the girls?"

"Shannon came and took them for me. She and Gracie are organizing a sleepover together."

"Good. They shouldn't be witnessing all of this."

Allie stopped at a closed door at the end of the hall. "This is her room." She tried the door and frowned. "It's locked. No one locks stuff here."

"Do you have a key?"

"Somewhere." She thought a moment. "There's a master on the ring by the back door. Wait here." She hurried back the way she'd come.

Clay twisted the knob, but it didn't budge. None of this made sense to him. Unless Rita was in cahoots with the kidnapper. Maybe his girlfriend?

Allie returned with the key ring in her hand, and he stepped out of the way. She fitted the key into the lock and twisted. "Got it." She flipped the switch inside the door.

He followed her into Rita's room. It was smallish, with a double bed covered by a quilt. A dresser and chest of drawers were on either side of the bed. "Let's start here," he said, stepping to the dresser. He rifled through neat stacks of T-shirts, shorts, and socks.

He held up a bottle of men's cologne. "Does she have a boyfriend?"

Allie sniffed it. "Not that I know of. Strange."

He dug farther into the drawer and pulled out a Cowboys T-shirt. "What the heck? I've been looking for this for over a week."

Allie's eyes went wide. "It's yours?"

"Sure is." He dropped the shirt and went to the last drawer. It held high school yearbooks and other documents.

A picture lay on top. He picked it up and stared. Rita looked to be about sixteen in the photo, but he was more interested in the boy who was beside her. "Holy cow, look at this. She's beside Jose Santiago." He flipped it over and read the back. "Rita and Jose Santiago." He stared at Allie, who was rummaging in the drawer. "She's related to Jose!"

Allie was reading something else. "Here's her birth certificate. And passport. It's not from the United States. She's foreign? She gave me citizen documentation before we hired her."

Clay opened the passport. "It's Colombian. It says here her name is Rita Santiago. Jose's sister?"

Allie glanced at the birth certificate. "Her mother was Else Björn. Her father was Hector Santiago!"

The strength went out of his knees and he sank onto a chair. "What if she blamed Eden for her mother's situation?"

Allie nodded. "It makes sense. And her mother was probably blond, so that's why she doesn't look Hispanic. Even if she colored her hair, her skin is fair."

He rubbed his head, then began to flip through the pile of

yearbooks. Rita seemed to have attended several different schools. "Whoa, this is where I went to school," he said when he reached the third one. "This is my senior yearbook."

Allie looked as puzzled as he felt. He flipped through the annual. "I don't even know what I'm looking for."

"There are a couple of sticky tabs." She took the yearbook from him and flipped to the yellow slips of paper. "Is this you?"

He stared at the photography club page. A very young version of himself stood proudly holding an award he'd received for a photo documentary at the zoo. "Sure is."

She squinted at the people in the background. "This young girl looks a little like Rita. Only she's got brown hair in this picture."

Clay studied the picture. "I vaguely remember her. She was three years behind me in school. I noticed her hanging around a lot. My friends said she had a crush on me, but I don't know if it was true or not. I never really spoke to her. She was just a kid. I never even knew her last name."

"Look here." Allie pointed to handwriting on the edge of the page. "'Your words are my food, your breath my wine. You are everything to me.—Sarah Bernhardt,'" she read aloud. "There's an arrow pointing to your face."

He wanted to shudder. "It's a little creepy."

"It's a lot creepy. You don't suppose she's followed you all these years, do you?"

"I think we'd better find out," he said grimly. He took the yearbook from her and tucked it under his arm. "I'd better call the sheriff."

36

THE STENCH OF MOUSE DROPPINGS AND DUST GREETED THEM WHEN RITA TOLD EDEN to open the door of the cabin. Darkness had fallen by the time they got back, but the truck headlamps kept them following the footsteps in the sand. Eden had tried to ask her questions, but the woman had remained silent except for the occasional order to shut up.

Eden stopped just inside the door. "You can't kill me without telling me why."

Rita grabbed a lantern by the door and thrust it into Sister Marjo's hands. "Light it," she said, indicating a box of matches on the floor.

Eden watched the nun fumble with the matches before managing to get the lantern lit. Did Rita plan to leave them to die here in the cabin? She seemed to like fire. Eden prayed the woman didn't intend to set the cabin afire.

Sister Marjo adjusted the wick, then held the lantern aloft. "Where shall I put it?"

Rita gestured with the gun. "The table is fine."

"Where are your cohorts?" Eden asked. "Are we waiting for them?"

"He's dead. All because of you." Hatred laced her words, and her eyes spit venom.

"The man in the car?" Eden couldn't figure out the connection.

"You've destroyed my life. First you took Clay. Then you made me lose my mother and my brother."

"The man who drowned in the car was your brother?"

"Yes." Rita shut the door behind her and gestured to the sofa. "Sit. Both of you."

Eden looked at the gun, then at the filthy sofa. There wasn't a lot of choice. Her discarded sweater was still here, so she laid it out and sat on it, perching gingerly on the cushion. Sister Marjo settled beside her as if she didn't even notice the mouse droppings and stains.

None of this made sense to her. Rita's mother and brother? "I don't understand."

"You will," Rita said.

"I'm not to blame for Jose's death," Eden said. "His greed was the cause of his death." It suddenly hit her—Rita had to be her sister unless she and Jose had different fathers.

"Shut up!" The other woman advanced two steps and waved the gun menacingly. "You knocked his car into the river. He didn't have a chance. I don't know what you were trying to do. Didn't you care that you could have drowned your own daughter?"

"It was an accident." Eden eyed the manic light in the woman's eyes. Was she even sane? "I misjudged the distance, and the car skidded."

Rita's eyes narrowed. "I was watching. It was deliberate."

"Why did you take my daughter? You didn't even ask for that much ransom."

"It was never about the money. She should have been mine."

"I don't understand."

"Clay belongs to me. With you out of the way, we can be the family we were meant to be."

Though nothing she'd said made sense, Eden decided to humor her. "Is that why you lured us here? To kill me?"

The woman smiled and stood taller, almost preening. "I've seen the way Clay looks at me, talks to me. You're blind if you haven't noticed he wants me and not you. He'll be glad when you're out of the way. You were never supposed to come with him."

Eden decided not to discuss the woman's delusions about Clay for now. "How is this my fault?"

The woman dug in her pocket and pulled out a tattered picture of a family. "We were so happy before you came into our lives." She held it under Eden's nose. "Now one is dead, the other is imprisoned in a mental hospital, and there is only me to avenge them all."

A much younger Hector Santiago stood with his arm around a beautiful blond woman. She had her hand on the shoulder of a girl of about ten with light-brown hair and solemn blue eyes. Rita. Beside her stood a boy about a year or two older. He looked more like his father.

"You're my sister?" Eden asked, unable to look away from the photo. No wonder Santiago had been unable to call Rita off. She was bent on revenge. "Why did you ask for money if you wanted revenge?"

"It was my brother's idea. To lure you out so he could eliminate you for me. But you killed him! I hate you!" Rita aimed the gun at Eden's head.

Sister Marjo leaped between Eden and the gun. "My dear girl, think about what you're doing. Clay is a good man. He'll be torn up with guilt if you do this. You'll lose him forever."

The gun in Rita's hand wavered. Her finger left the trigger. "Why did you have to get involved in this, Sister? This is not your concern."

The nun took a step closer. "I don't believe I had a choice. It was you who ran my car off the road and brought me here."

"Only so you wouldn't tell that Lacie wasn't Brianna. I had no choice." She narrowed her eyes as she stared at the nun. "You told her, didn't you?"

"Yes," Sister Marjo said, still blocking the path to Eden.

Eden tugged at the sister's hand, and the nun sat back down on the sofa. "Why didn't you want me to know?" she asked Rita.

"It was too soon. I needed more time. Once Clay realized the results were wrong, he would have remembered that I was the only one who could have switched the samples. I couldn't let that happen."

"The results were wrong." "How do you know Clay? He didn't seem to recognize you." Eden held her breath. Maybe that was the wrong thing to say.

Rita shrugged but her lips tightened. "My hair is a different color. You know how men are. And I've changed since school. But he recognized me all right. That's why he talked to me so often. He didn't want to tell you, though. Not yet."

Rita must have generated these excuses when Clay didn't say anything about knowing her. Eden decided not to follow that train of thought any longer. “Where have you kept Brianna? If she should have belonged to you, why is she being raised by foster parents?”

“Her name is Madeline, not Brianna.” Rita’s eyes darkened. “It’s all my mother’s fault,” she spat. “She had to go and take an overdose. When she was put in the mental institution, the state took Madeline before I could get out myself. Pushy, nosy people.”

Madeline. Her Brianna was Madeline. Eden wanted to live long enough to hold her daughter, to breathe in the scent of her hair.

She soaked in what Rita had said about her mother. Hospitalized. Schizophrenia could run in families. This woman was obviously mentally ill, but Eden wasn’t educated about the different illnesses. “Who was the woman who came to see Madeline? Clay met her.”

“My mother. I had to stay in the house. She didn’t know I was there.”

“She called herself Madeline’s mother.”

Rita shrugged. “She had Madeline for three years while I was—away. She won’t be back. I’m sure my father has her stashed somewhere again.” She loaded the peanut butter and other items around the room into a sack. “Can’t leave any evidence,” she said.

Eden’s stomach clenched. *Evidence.* Whatever Rita had planned wasn’t going to be good.

Rita pointed the gun. “Enough talk. It’s time to go.”

Eden nodded, trying to maintain an open, interested expression free of condemnation. She had to save Sister Marjo somehow, but there was no reasoning with someone as delusional as Rita.

“Where are we going, dear?” Sister Marjo asked.

Rita smiled. “It has to look like an accident. I know just the place.”

The helicopter rotors were so loud no one could hear a thing. Clay sat in the back with Shannon MacGowan's husband, Jack. Rick was in the front seat with Michael Wayne, who was piloting the bird. Friends of Bluebird Ranch had scoured the desert by land and air, but it was dark now. And they'd seen nothing. Clay had berated himself for hours as they searched for a sign of the truck. Why hadn't he recognized Rita? He'd thought she reminded him of someone but assumed it was an actor, that one who'd played Heidi.

Michael glanced at Rick and made a cutting motion across his throat. They were heading back. Clay wanted to protest, but the chopper was running out of fuel. The helicopter banked and began to circle back the other way.

Was his wife dead? He rejected the thought. She had to be all right. He had to find her. If they went back without her, he would get a horse and go back out. He couldn't rest until she was safe at home again.

Desperate for some clue, Clay pressed his forehead against the window and studied the dark landscape. Was that a light? He stared, willing it to come again. *There.* A dim glimmer, so faint it could have been a reflection of the moon off water. He tapped Michael's shoulder and motioned for him to go down to take a look.

The other man's glance was compassionate, but he held up two fingers, meaning he'd circle for no more than a couple of minutes. The chopper dropped down closer to the desert. All the men pressed their noses to the glass and stared at the dark ground beneath them. Clay knew the others had seen that glimmer when Rick pointed excitedly and Jack nodded.

"Set it down!" Rick yelled over the sound of the rotors.

Michael nodded and eased the helicopter onto its skids. The

tail boom spun around until the cabin faced the light. Clay opened the door and jumped out, keeping his head down. The pulsating air nearly knocked him over. He didn't wait for the other men but headed across the desert to a dark shape that appeared to be a cabin. The light came from an opening in one of the boarded-up windows.

As he neared, he heard the engine winding down on the chopper. The other men would be right behind him. He reached the front door in a few steps and shoved it open. A lantern was set on the table, its wick sputtering. His gaze swept the room, but it was empty. Whoever had been here hadn't been gone long or the lantern would have burned out.

Rick and the other men rushed into the cabin behind him. They stopped and no one said anything for a long moment. "Guess that's it," Michael said.

Clay stepped to the sofa. "I can't figure it out. If this place is inhabited, why does it look like no one has been here in decades?"

Rick snatched up the lantern and held it aloft. "You're right. No one has lived here in years. But this lantern was lit?"

"Yeah." What was that on the sofa? "Bring that light here," Clay said. As Rick neared with the lantern, he realized a navy sweater lay on the cushion. He snatched it up. "This is Eden's!"

"Are you sure?" Rick asked.

"She had it on last night after the sun went down and the air cooled." He held it to his nose. Beyond the smell of the sofa, he caught a whiff of Eden's cologne. "It's hers. She was here. And not long ago." He strode to the door. "Bring that light with you. Let's see if there are tire tracks."

Outside, the darkness was so vast that the lantern cast little light except in its immediate circle. Rick swept it back and forth. "There!" he said, pointing at his feet.

Clay saw it too. "Tread marks." He knelt and put his hand in one, as though it would make him nearer to Eden. "They have to be close. Can we get back in the air and look?"

Michael hesitated. "I've got only an hour's worth of fuel left. I have to head back to my place in no more than half an hour or I won't make it."

Clay stood and brushed the sand from his hands. "Deal."

The men ran for the helicopter. The engine coughed to life and the *whup-whup* of the rotors began to drown out the desert's night sounds. By the time they were airborne, Clay was ready to jump out of his skin. They'd missed Eden and her captor by mere minutes, he was sure. He peered through the window, but the landscape was dark.

He realized the chopper was heading for the road. Tapping Michael on the shoulder, he shook his head and screamed over the noise of the blades. "Go back over the desert. She won't risk driving on the road."

Michael nodded and the helicopter began to bank to the right. As the craft soared low over the desert, Clay saw a moving light. "There it is!" He jabbed at the window, then realized no one had noticed. He smacked Michael and Rick on their arms and pointed. "Down there!"

Rick pointed and the helicopter picked up speed to catch the vehicle. The twin beam headlights on the truck went out.

"She's seen us!" Clay shouted. How could they follow when the night was so black? Before he could ask the question, Rick flicked a switch and lights blazed down to the desert from the helicopter. "There it is!"

Michael nodded, and the chopper dropped lower and sped up

until it was right over the top of the truck. The lights shone into the cab, and he saw Eden's face pressed against the passenger window. Her face set and determined, Rita gripped the steering wheel with both hands. Her teeth were bared. He caught a glimpse of an older woman in the middle. Sister Marjo?

How could they get the truck to stop? There wasn't much fuel left in the helicopter. If Michael put it down in front of the truck, Rita would just go around it and keep on driving. They couldn't force the truck off the road because there was no road.

"Take it down!" he yelled, his mind made up. When Michael complied, Clay thrust open his door and jumped.

37

If not for Sister Marjo, Eden would have leaped from the truck speeding across the desert. But she couldn't leave the nun behind. The sound of the helicopter filled her head. It had to be Michael with Clay and the other men. Rescue was in sight. She could have clung to that hope if a madwoman wasn't behind the wheel.

A sudden thump jarred the truck. Eden whipped her head to look out the back window and saw Clay lying in the bottom of the truck bed. He got to his hands and feet and his gaze met hers. Seeing him gave her fresh courage. She had to help, but how? The blinding light from the helicopter grew dimmer as the chopper rose and fell back.

Rita glanced in the rearview mirror and smiled. "I knew he couldn't stay away from me."

Eden glanced back and saw Clay crawling toward the window. She unlatched the window and slid it open before Rita could stop her.

"Stop the truck, Rita," he said through the open window. "Let's talk about this."

Rita smiled. "Not just yet, love. I have to take care of these women who are trying to keep us apart. Wait for me at the ranch. I'll be back soon."

"I can't go to the ranch unless you stop."

Rita frowned and shook her head, as though trying to think through the logic. "I guess that's right." She tromped on the brake, and Eden and the nun nearly went flying through the windshield. Eden grabbed the dash and hung on. The truck's rear end slewed in the sand before coming to a stop. Rita switched off the engine. The tick of the motor beginning to cool was loud in the sudden silence.

Eden whipped her head around to make sure Clay was all right. He lay crumpled at the front of the bed. "Clay!" She thrust open her door and jumped out in spite of Rita's grab at her arm.

He stirred when Eden called his name. She put her foot on the tailgate and climbed into the bed. He had to be all right. She reached him and knelt by his head. Her fingers came away wet when she touched his forehead. Blood? It was too dark to see the color of the moisture, but the coppery odor was enough evidence.

She looked up to see Rita bearing down on her. "He's hurt," Eden said.

"Get away from my Clay," Rita said through gritted teeth. "I'll take care of him. You've done enough." She pointed her gun at Eden.

"You nearly killed him!" Eden held her ground. She wasn't leaving her husband.

Clay stirred and moaned. He put his hand to his head, then struggled to sit. "What happened?"

Eden helped him. "I think you hit your head."

"I said get away from him," Rita ordered.

Eden flinched as a loud report came from the gun. A bullet slammed into the truck near her hand. "Okay, I'm leaving."

She scrambled away from Clay. At least Rita wasn't going to hurt him. Once the woman's back was turned, Eden might be able to wrestle the gun away from her.

Rita climbed into the truck and knelt beside Clay. "Can you stand, my darling?"

"I think I need your help," Clay said, his voice weak. "Can you lift me up, Rita? You'll need to put the gun down so I can take your hand."

Eden held her breath. Would the woman fall for it? She watched as Rita hesitated, then stuck the gun in her waistband. She put one arm around Clay's waist and with the other took his arm and draped it around her neck. In a quick movement, Clay reached for the butt of the gun with his free hand and plucked it from her. He wheeled away, and Rita staggered back, then fell against the window of the cab.

"Clay? What are you doing?" She got slowly to her feet.

The gun was in Clay's hand. He backed away, then jumped to the sand. "Get out of the truck, Rita."

She was sobbing. "What are you doing, Clay? I did all of this for you. We can be together, you and me with Madeline. A real family." She sank to her knees, holding herself. Rocking back and forth she began to keen, a noise filled with pain.

In spite of all the woman had done, Eden wanted to go to her and comfort her. She started forward, but Clay's arm shot out.

"Don't," he said. "She's like a venomous snake. The minute you get too close, she'll strike." He nodded to the cab. "How's Sister Marjo?"

"She's fine." Eden sidled along the truck to the cab and glanced into the open door. The lights on the dash were still on.

Sister Marjo sat placidly clutching a tiny New Testament in the wash of interior lights. "Finished, beloved? I didn't want to interfere as the three of you made peace. Though I was praying, of course. God assured me he didn't need my help on this one."

Eden held out her hand. "It's all over. We can go home now." Behind her she heard the sound of running feet. The rest of the rescuers had arrived.

The nun closed her Bible and slipped it into the pocket of her skirt. She accepted Eden's hand and slid off the seat to the sand. "This has been an experience I don't believe I'll ever forget," she said.

Eden hardly knew what to say to that. Kidnapped, imprisoned, lost in the desert, and nearly killed. It had been eventful all right, but not the kind of event she ever wanted to repeat. She and the nun walked to the back of the truck as Rick and Michael approached Rita. Michael spoke in a soothing voice and soon had Rita quieted. She wondered if he'd given her a sedative.

Clay opened his arms, and she ran into them. Home. All that was missing was Madeline.

The small group sat in the main house with a pot of coffee and a partially demolished plate of chocolate chip cookies on the coffee table. The sheriff's eyes were puffy with dark circles, and Eden wondered when he'd last slept. Even Brendan looked a little rumpled and worse for the wear. Daniel sat by Clay as if he was making an attempt to accept what he couldn't change. Eden could hear Sister Marjo on the porch with Lacie. They were singing "Jesus Loves Me."

Eden needed a shower, but first she had to hear what Brendan had to say. "So Rita got out of the mental hospital six months ago," she said, "then planned to eliminate me so she could have Clay." She glanced at her husband sitting beside her on the sofa. "Has anyone talked to her mother?"

"She's in an expensive mental hospital in El Paso," Brendan said. "Paid for by Hector Santiago."

"But she was just here a week or so ago," Clay said.

Brendan nodded. "When Hector said he was working on fixing the problem, I believe he thought his wife was behind it all. He found out she'd been released and had his goons track her down and take her back to the hospital."

"What about Brianna?" Eden asked.

"I sent one of my men to talk to Else. She showed him pictures of Brianna when she was a baby. Rita was holding her like a proud mother. Hang on, I have the picture on my computer." He clicked a few keys, then turned it around for her to see.

Eden stared into the smiling face. No trace of the insanity in those blue eyes. Just proud motherly love. She shuddered. "Anyone seeing her with the baby wouldn't have doubted anything."

"Nope." Brendan shut the computer lid. "From what we can tell, she took good care of the baby, but she had an episode at the grocery store. She lost her temper and overturned a whole aisle of food, screaming and raving. They had her hospitalized for observation.

She was diagnosed as schizophrenic and committed until she was stabilized."

"How old was Brianna when this happened?" Clay asked.

"About two. Her mother cared for the baby after that until she had another episode herself."

"Where have they lived? Not with Hector?" Eden asked.

Brendan shook his head. "Else left him when your mother told her about you. Hector gave her plenty of money and set her up on a ranch just west of here. I think he thought if she lived in a secluded spot, she'd be all right. And she was for a while."

"How old was Rita then?"

"About fifteen. As near as I can tell, she went to school with Clay that one year and became obsessed. When she found out he married her half sister, she had her first episode of mental illness. She was committed for a year, then got out. It was then she decided to get revenge and took Brianna. She appears to have loved the girl. Then she had the episode I mentioned."

Eden leaned more tightly into the safety of Clay's embrace. "We have to talk to Madeline. We're certain, right?"

Brendan nodded. "The picture of Brianna at age two cinched it. I had it compared to pictures of Madeline and it was a match. No doubts at all. The courts will want to do the DNA matching probably, but you can be assured Madeline is your daughter."

"I want to tell her now," Eden said, staring up at Clay.

"All right." His arm dropped away and he rose, offering her his hand.

She took it and they walked to the door. "We'll be praying," Allie called after her.

Eden stopped and turned. "I'll take all the prayers we can get," she said, meaning it. "God is the only one who got me through this." She saw Clay beginning to smile. Her friends too.

"What happened out there in the desert?" Clay asked as they walked back toward the bunkhouse.

"I did a little wrestling," she said. "God won."

38

EDEN AND CLAY STEPPED INTO THE BUNKHOUSE. SHANNON GLANCED UP FROM A BOOK AND smiled. Madeline was settled in the crook of her arm. "The girls are asleep except for Madeline here. She and I have been reading stories. Bible stories."

"The story is finished," Madeline said. She closed the book.

"I'll leave you all alone now." Shannon winked at them, then planted a kiss on the little girl's hair. "Remember what we talked about," she whispered to the child. "Talk to you tomorrow."

When the screen door slammed behind her, Eden glanced at Clay. Who was going to break the news? They hadn't discussed it.

Madeline's eyes were big, as though she was picking up their tension. Eden wondered what Shannon had said to the little girl. There was a new softness in Madeline's face.

Clay cleared his throat. "Miss Eden and I have something to tell you." He sat on the sofa beside her and lifted her to his lap.

"Am I in trouble?"

"Of course not. Why would you think that?"

She shrugged. "Miss Shannon made me stay up. I thought I was going to be punished for being rude to Miss Eden." Her face puckered. "I'm sorry, Miss Eden." She began to cry. "Miss Shannon said God doesn't like me to be disrespectful."

"Honey, it's okay." Eden pulled her onto her lap, and the little girl buried her hot face against Eden's chest. "I thought you were still mad at me about something. Want to tell me about it?"

The child nodded, her face still buried. "I thought you liked India better. I wanted you to love me."

Eden pressed a kiss against Madeline's hair. "I love you so much, honey. We have something very special to tell you, sweetheart. Stop crying and look at me." She pushed Madeline's head away and wiped her face with her palms. "We came here to find you."

Madeline's eyes widened. She swiped at her face. "Find me? Was I lost?"

It amazed Eden that they were here in this place about to tell their daughter the story. *Thank you, God.* She swallowed the lump in her throat. "Yes. Yes, you were very lost. And we were lost without you."

"I'm going to tell you a story about a princess, honey," Clay put in. "Once upon a time there was a king and his queen. They had a baby girl they named Brianna."

"I like that name," Madeline said, her eyes fastened on his face.

"A wicked witch took the baby and told the king and queen that their baby had died."

Madeline's lip came out. "I don't like sad stories." She laid her head on Eden's chest.

"This story has the very best ending," he assured her. "Anyway, when the baby got bigger, the king found out that the wicked witch had lied. Their baby wasn't dead. She'd just been hidden away. All they had to do was find her and they would be a family again."

"Did they find her?"

"They did. We did. *You* are Brianna, Madeline." His voice thickened, and he swallowed hard before continuing. "A long time ago, someone took you away from us, but we found out where you were and came to find you. You are our very own little girl." His eyes were wet. "And we're here to take you home with us."

Madeline's mouth gaped. Eden couldn't stop the tears from flowing. She hugged her daughter to her and kissed her cheek. "We've found you, honey. You're ours and we're never letting you go again."

Madeline's arms crept around her neck. "Is this a real story?"

"It's very real." Eden glanced at Clay and saw his cheeks were wet too.

He embraced them both. "You are our daughter, honey. We've searched the whole earth for you."

"So you're going to adopt me?"

"We don't have to adopt you," Eden said. "I carried you in my tummy."

"For real?"

"Pinkie swear," Eden said, holding up her little finger.

Madeline's tears dried up. "Can I call you Mommy?" She glanced at Clay. "And Daddy?"

"Forever and ever," Clay said. He picked her up and danced around the room with her.

Eden's heart was so full she almost couldn't bear it. She joined Clay and Madeline. He put an arm around her, and the three of them stood in a tight embrace.

"Wait until the other girls hear this story," Madeline said. Her eyes were drooping, and she put her head on Clay's shoulder.

Clay grinned at Eden. "Too much excitement."

"I know the feeling," she whispered. "I'm tired too. But happy. So happy."

His eyes filled, and he kissed her, then walked around the room with Madeline. He hummed a few bars of "Amazing Grace."

The little girl's eyes closed, and her breathing deepened. Eden watched the perfect trust as their daughter slept in her daddy's arms.

"She's out," Eden whispered. She went before them down the hall and opened the bedroom door.

Clay placed the sleeping child into her bed, and they kissed her cheek, then stood in the doorway and watched the sleeping girls before backing out of the room. Eden's heart welled as she looked at the faces of "her" girls. How could she bear to leave them?

Clay put his finger to his lips and led her down the hall. When they reached their room, he shut the door and leaned on it. "There's something else, Eden," he said.

His tone filled her with dread. "I know. I saw the e-mail. You're going out again." She didn't want to be that old Eden. The one who pouted and cried at the thought of being left alone. She had changed. "As long as you come back, we'll be okay."

He shook his head. "That's not it. I already turned in my resignation."

She gasped. "Y-You're not going?"

"Nope. You have to put up with me."

"Then what's the problem?"

"What about the other girls?"

"What do you mean?" His voice was so intense, and she wondered if he felt the same way she did.

"How would you feel about adopting all of them? Except Paige, of course. It wouldn't be fair since she has a family who loves her."

"You mean, we'd have four little girls?" She struggled to wrap her mind around it. It had been a secret dream of hers. Whenever she thought about separating the girls, her mind closed down and all she could see was the six of them around the dinner table together. Playing Candyland. Laughing and loving.

"Could you do it?"

She leaped into his arms and smothered his face with kisses. He reeled around the room and they fell onto the bed. "Yes, yes, yes! I didn't think you'd even consider something this drastic. We'll have a very full house," she warned. "And it will be expensive to raise four kids."

He hugged her close. "Maybe more if the Lord blesses us with another child or two. Maybe a boy this time. Oh, and one other thing."

"You want to adopt the whole world?" She laughed and snuggled closer.

"I want to continue to work here at the ranch. They can't pay much, but we already have enough. Our place isn't far. I could build another dorm there and expand the work here."

Her vision swam as her eyes filled. "I can't think of anything I would like more."

He lowered his lips to hers, and Eden found all thought fleeing. God was giving her paradise.

ACKNOWLEDGMENTS

I JUST CELEBRATED EIGHT YEARS WITH MY THOMAS NELSON TEAM—TRULY MY DREAM team! Publisher Allen Arnold (I call him Superman) changed everything when he came on board. Everyone in the industry loves him—including me! Senior Acquisitions Editor Ami McConnell (my dear friend and cheerleader) has an eye for character and theme like no one I know. I crave her analytical eye and love her heart. She's truly like a daughter to me. Marketing Manager Eric Mullett brings fabulous ideas to the table. Publicist Katie Bond is always willing to listen to my harebrained ideas. Fabulous cover guru Kristen Vasgaard (you so rock!) works hard to create the perfect cover—and does it. And of course I can't forget my other friends who are all part of my amazing fiction family: Natalie Hanemann, Amanda Bostic, Becky Monds, Ashley Schneider, Jodi Hughes, Ruthie Dean, Heather McCulloch, Dean Arvidson, and Kathy Carabajal. I wish I could name all the great folks who work on selling my books through different venues at Thomas Nelson. Hearing "well done" from you all is my motivation every day.

Erin Healy has edited all of my Thomas Nelson books except

one, and she is such an integral part of the team. Her ideas always make the book better, and she's a fabulous writer in her own right. If you haven't read her yet, be sure to pick up *Never Let You Go*, *The Promises She Keeps*, and *The Baker's Wife*.

My agent, Karen Solem, has helped shape my career in many ways, and that includes kicking an idea to the curb when necessary. Thanks, Karen, you're the best!

Writing can be a lonely business, but God has blessed me with great writing friends and critique partners. Hannah Alexander (Cheryl Hodde), Kristin Billerbeck, Diann Hunt, and Denise Hunter make up the Girls Write Out squad (www.GirlsWriteOut.blogspot.com). I couldn't make it through a day without my peeps! Thanks to all of you for the work you do on my behalf, and for your friendship. I had great brainstorming help for this book in Robin Caroll. Thank you, friends!

I'm so grateful for my husband, Dave, who carts me around from city to city, washes towels, and chases down dinner without complaint. As I type this, today is the first day of his retirement. Now he will have more time for those things—and more. Thanks, honey! I couldn't do anything without you. My kids—Dave, Kara (and now Donna and Mark)—and my grandsons, James and Jorden Packer, love and support me in every way possible. Love you guys! Donna and Dave brought me the delight of my life—our little granddaughter, Alexa! This year at Christmas she was interested in watching her Mimi sign copies for her daddy to give away. When I told her that Mimi wrote the books, I'm sure I saw shock in her face. Okay, maybe I'm reading too much into her little two-year-old mind, but she will soon understand what her Mimi does for a living.

Most importantly, I give my thanks to God, who has opened such amazing doors for me and makes the journey a golden one.

READING GROUP GUIDE

1. It's said a child's early experiences shape their personality when they're grown. What experience do you think was most instrumental in shaping Eden?
2. Losing a child is one of the hardest things a marriage can suffer. What could Eden and Clay have done to have been able to get through the pain of losing Brianna?
3. Clay never gave up on finding Brianna. Why do you think he was so steadfast?
4. What was the base problem in Eden and Clay's marriage?
5. At first Eden was determined to preserve her perfect image. Why do you think what other people thought mattered so much to her?
6. Why do you think Clay never got rid of his childhood home?
7. Why do you think God allows pain in our lives?
8. Why does God allow bad things to happen to good people?

An excerpt from *The Lightkeeper's Ball*

THE NEW YORK BROWNSTONE WAS JUST HALF A BLOCK DOWN FROM THE ASTOR MANSION ON Fifth Avenue, the most prestigious address in the country. The carriage, monogrammed with the Stewart emblem, rattled through the iron gates and came to a halt in front of the ornate doors. Assisted by the doorman, Olivia Stewart descended and rushed for the steps of her home. She was late for tea, and her mother would be furious. Mrs. Astor herself had agreed to join them today.

Olivia handed her hat to the maid, who opened the door. "They're in the drawing room, Miss Olivia," Goldia whispered. "Your mama is ready to pace the floor."

Olivia patted at her hair, straightened her shoulders, and pinned a smile in place as she forced her stride to a ladylike stroll to join the other women. Two women turned to face her as she entered: her mother and Mrs. Astor. They wore identical expressions of disapproval.

"Olivia, there you are," her mother said. "Sit down before your tea gets cold."

Olivia pulled off her gloves as she settled into the Queen Anne chair beside Mrs. Astor. "I apologize for my tardiness," she said. "A lorry filled with tomatoes overturned in the street, and my driver couldn't get around it."

Mrs. Astor's face cleared. "Of course, my dear." She sipped her tea from the delicate blue-and-white china. "Your dear mother and I were just discussing your prospects. It's time you married."

Oh dear. She'd hoped to engage in light conversation that had nothing to do with the fact that she was twenty-five and still unmarried. Her unmarried state distressed her if she let it, but every man her father brought to her wanted only her status. She doubted any of them had ever looked into her soul. "I'm honored you would care about my marital status, Mrs. Astor," Olivia said.

"Mrs. Astor wants to hold a ball in your honor, Olivia," her mother gushed. "She has a distant cousin coming to town whom she wants you to meet."

Mrs. Astor nodded. "I believe you and Matthew would suit. He owns property just down the street."

Olivia didn't mistake the reference to the man's money. Wealth would be sure to impact her mother. She opened her mouth to ask if the man was her age, then closed it at the warning glint in her mother's eyes.

"He's been widowed for fifteen years and is long overdue for a suitable wife," Mrs. Astor said.

Olivia barely suppressed a sigh. So he was another of the decrepit gentlemen who showed up from time to time. "You're very kind," she said.

"He's most suitable," her mother said. "*Most* suitable."

Olivia caught the implication. They spent the next half hour discussing the date and the location. She tried to enter into the conversation with interest, but all she could do was imagine some gray-whiskered blue blood dancing her around the ballroom. She stifled a sigh of relief when Mrs. Astor took her leave and called for her carriage.

"I'll be happy when you're settled, Olivia," her mother said when they returned to the drawing room. "Mrs. Astor is most kind."

"She is indeed." Olivia pleated her skirt with her fingers. "Do you ever wish you could go somewhere incognito, Mother? Where no one has expectations of you because you are a Stewart?"

Her mother put down her saucer with a clatter. "Whatever are you babbling about, my dear?"

"Haven't you noticed that people look at us differently because we're Stewarts? How is a man ever to love me for myself when all he sees is what my name can gain him? Men never see inside to the real me. They notice only that I'm a Stewart."

"Have you been reading those novels again?" Her mother sniffed and narrowed her gaze on Olivia. "Marriage is about making suitable connections. You owe it to your future children to consider the life you give them. Love comes from respect. I would find it quite difficult to respect someone who didn't have the gumption to make his way in the world. Besides, we *need* you to marry well. You're twenty-five years old and I've indulged your romantic notions long enough. Heaven knows your sister's marriage isn't what I had in mind, essential though it may be. Someone has to keep the family name in good standing."

Olivia knew what her duty demanded, but she didn't have to like it. "Do all the suitable men have to be in their dotage?"

Her mother's eyes sparked fire, but before she spoke, Goldia appeared in the doorway. "Mr. Bennett is here, Mrs. Stewart."

Olivia straightened in her chair. "Show him in. He'll have news of Eleanor."

Bennett appeared in the doorway moments later. He shouldn't have been imposing. He stood only five foot three in his shoes, which were always freshly polished. He was slim, nearly gaunt, with a patrician nose and obsidian eyes. He'd always reminded Olivia of a snake about to strike. His expression never betrayed any emotion, and today was no exception. She'd never understood why her father entertained an acquaintance with the man, let alone desired their families to be joined.

"Mr. Bennett." She rose and extended her hand and tried not to flinch as he brushed his lips across it.

"Miss Olivia," he said, releasing her hand. He moved to her mother's chair and bowed over her extended hand.

Olivia sank back into her chair. "What do you hear of my sister? I have received no answer to any of my letters."

He took a seat, steepled his fingers, and leaned forward. "That's the reason for our meeting today. I fear I have bad news to impart."

Her pulse thumped erratically against her rib cage. She wet her lips and drew in a deep breath. "What news of Eleanor?" How bad could it be? Eleanor had gone to marry Harrison, a man she hardly knew. But she was in love with the idea of the Wild West, and therefore more than happy to marry the son of her father's business partner.

He never blinked. "I shall just have to blurt it out then. I'm sorry to inform you that Eleanor is dead."

Her mother moaned. Olivia stared at him. "I don't believe it," she said.

"I know, it's a shock."

There must have been some mistake. She searched his face for some clue that this was a jest. "What happened?"

He didn't hold her gaze. "She drowned."

"How?"

"No one knows. I'm sorry."

Her mother stood and swayed. "What are you saying?" Her voice rose in a shriek. "Eleanor can't be dead! Are you quite mad?"

He stood and took her arm. "I suggest you lie down, Mrs. Stewart. You're quite pale."

Her mother put her hands to her cheeks. "Tell me it isn't true," she begged. Then she keeled over in a dead faint.

An excerpt from *Smitten*

NATALIE MANSFIELD'S HEART SWELLED AS SHE STOOD ON THE PERIMETER OF THE TOWN square and watched her niece and the other children decorate the town for Easter. A gigantic smile stretched across five-year-old Mia's face as her Sunday school teacher lifted her to place the lavender wreath at the top of the clock.

Mia saw her and waved. "Aunt Nat, look at me!"

Natalie waved back, her smile broadening. "She's growing so fast," she told her aunt, Rose Garner. "I love her so much."

Black threaded Rose's silver hair, and her smooth skin made her look twenty years younger than her sixty-two years. "I still remember the first day I laid eyes on you."

"How could you forget? I was a morose ten-year-old who snapped your head off every time you spoke to me."

Her aunt pressed her hand. "You changed our lives, honey. We were three lonely spinsters until you showed up. Now here you are providing a home for your niece. A full circle, just like that wreath. I'm so proud of you."

Her aunt's words made Natalie's heart fill to bursting. "You gave me the only stability I'd ever known. I want to do the same for Mia."

Aunt Rose wasn't listening. A small frown creased her brow. "Something's wrong."

Natalie looked at the men standing a few feet away in front of the hardware store. Their heads were down and their shoulders slumped. The dejection in their stances sent her pulse racing.

She recognized one of her coffee shop patrons, Murphy Clinton, and grabbed his arm as he walked past. "What's happened, Murphy?" she asked.

He stopped and stared down at her with a grave expression. "The mill's closing."

"That's not possible," she mumbled. Her thoughts raced. The mill was an institution and the main employer in Smitten. If it closed . . .

He finished her thought. "This town is finished."

The aroma of the freshly brewed coffee overpowered the less appetizing smell from the drum roaster in the back room. Natalie let her employee Zoe handle the customers at the bar, as Natalie took the hot beverages to the seating area by the window where she and her friends could see white-topped Sugarcreek Mountain. Spring had come to their part of Vermont, and the sight of the wildflowers on the lower slopes would give her strength.

"So what are we going to do?" she asked, sinking onto the overstuffed leather sofa beside Reese Mackenzie.

"Do? What *can* we do?" Reese asked. Her blond ponytail gleamed in the shaft of sunlight through the window. She was the practical one in the group. Reese was never afraid of hard work, but while Natalie saw only the end goal, Reese saw the pitfalls right on the path. "We can't *make* them keep the mill open."

While rumors about the mill had been floating for months, no one had really believed it would fold. The ramifications would be enormous. Natalie's business had been struggling enough without this added blow.

She took a sip of her mocha java. A little bitter. She'd have to tweak the roast a bit next time. "If the mill closes, the town will dry up and blow away. We can't let that happen." If Mountain Perks closed, she didn't know how she would provide for Mia.

And she wasn't leaving Smitten. Not ever. After being yanked from pillar to post with an alcoholic mother until she was ten, Natalie craved the stability she had found here with her aunts and her friends.

Julia Bourne tossed her long hair away from her face, revealing flawless skin that never needed makeup. "This is one of those things outside your control, Nat. I guess we'd all better be looking for jobs in Stowe."

Shelby Evans took a sip of her tea and shivered. Her Shih-poo, Penelope, dressed in a fashionable blue-and-white polka-dotted shirt, turned around in Shelby's lap and lay down on her navy slacks. "I don't know about you all," Shelby said, "but I wanted my kids to grow up here."

The women had no children of their own—and none of them was even close to thinking about settling down—but that was a moot point for Shelby. She had a storybook ending in mind that included a loving husband and two-point-five children for each of them. Natalie was sure her friend would find that life too.

Natalie moved restlessly. "There has to be something we can do. Some new export. Maple syrup, maybe? We have lots of trees." She glanced at Julia. "What about your New York friends? Maybe you could ask some of your business friends for advice?"

Julia shrugged her slim shoulders. "They know spas. I hardly think a spa is going to save us."

Reese had those thoughtful lines on her forehead. A tiny smile hovered on her full lips, and her hazel eyes showed a plan was forming. "We don't have time for exports, but what about imports? Tourists would love us if they'd come visit. We have heart." She took out her ever-present notebook and pen and began to jot down ideas.

"They come to ski in Stowe anyway," Shelby said. "All we have to do is get them here."

Natalie rubbed her forehead where it had begun to ache. "But what do we have to offer that's different from any other town?"

Julia crossed her shapely ankles. "Smitten is cute with its church and all, but cute doesn't bring tourists. I can't even get a decent manicure in this dinky town. People aren't going to pay for ambience. We need some kind of gimmick."

Reese tapped her pen against her chin. "I have an idea," she said. "Everyone jokes about the town name. Why not capitalize on it?"

"How do you capitalize on a name like Smitten?"

"What does Smitten make you think of?" Reese asked. "Love, right? What if we turn the town into a place for honeymooners?"

Shelby adjusted the bow on Penelope's head. "I went to Santa Claus, Indiana, once. Tons of people, even in July."

Natalie swallowed a groan. They'd all heard about Santa Claus too many times to count. She needed to derail Shelby before she broke into a rendition of "Jingle Bells." "We could have love songs playing as people strolled the streets."

Julia snickered and nodded toward the man striding past outside the window. "I have a feeling Carson would have something to say about that. He hated all the jokes about his name in high school."

Natalie followed the angle of Julia's nod. Her gut clenched the way it always did when she saw Carson Smitten. He was a man who attracted female attention wherever he went. He looked like his lumberjack great-grandfather, with his broad shoulders and closely-cropped dark hair.

He had all the single women in town drooling over him. Except for Natalie, of course. If the other girls knew what she knew about him, they wouldn't think he was so great.

"I'm still thinking about my idea," Reese said. "This will mean new businesses, new jobs, lots of revenue pouring in. We'd have to get the entire town on board."

Natalie's excitement level went up a notch as she imagined the town transformed with its new mission. "The town meeting is coming up. I can present the idea there."

"It's a good thing you're a selectperson," Shelby said. "People listen to you."

Natalie dug paper and a pen from her purse, a Brighton that Julia had given her for her last birthday. "There needs to be a cohesive plan. What would this love town look like? Besides romantic songs playing over speakers around town." She peered at Reese's list and copied down the items.

Shelby retied Penelope's bow. "We need a lingerie shop that sells perfume," she said. "Chocolates. Some plush hotels and bed-and-breakfasts with tubs for two." Her smile grew larger. "Maybe old-fashioned lampposts along the path around the lake. You could put outside tables on the street and white lights in the trees. Flower boxes all around town."

"And we'll need more restaurants," Julia added.

Natalie eyed her. "You said a good manicure was impossible to find. What if you started a spa?"

Julia's perfectly plucked brows lifted. She grabbed the tablet and pen from Natalie. "I don't know. I'd like to move back to New York eventually."

"The honeymooners won't spend *all* their time in their rooms," Reese said, her eyes gleaming. "We offer great outdoor activities. The skiing here is as good as anywhere in the country. People just don't know about us." She gestured toward the mountain. "And look at that view."

Natalie groaned. "The last thing I'd want to do on my honeymoon is go skiing. I'd rather sit holding hands across a linen tablecloth with a lobster in front of me."

"But I'd go skiing in a heartbeat," Reese said. "Our big draw is our outdoor beauty. We don't have an outfitters shop. We'd need that." She jotted it down on her paper. "You know how I've been saving for a shop like that for years. Maybe now is the time."

"Now *is* the time," Natalie said. "Sometimes you have to take a leap of faith. We're going to push you until you do it."

"I love it!" Shelby stood and paced by the window. "Maybe my etiquette school can be part of it too. I can coach women on how to put on the best parties and cater to the society women who come to town. Maybe teach ballroom dancing."

"And your designs," Natalie said, unable to keep her voice from rising. "Those cute outfits you make for Penelope would sell like hot cakes." She glanced at the picture of herself with Mia hanging on the wall. "I have to do what I can to save the town. I want Mia to have the security I've never had. A-And I've been thinking. I want to be Mia's real mother. I'm going to see about adopting her."

Her announcement left her friends with mouths gaping. She glanced at Shelby, whose soft heart she knew would be the first to agree with her.

Shelby's dark eyes glistened. "Oh, Nat, that's just like you! You have so much love to give. Mia's a very lucky girl."

A lump formed in Natalie's throat. "Starting the adoption is going to be my birthday present to myself. Every day I wake up and wonder if Lisa is going to take her away from me someday. I can't live with that fear."

Julia grimaced. "Lisa is never going to own up to her responsibilities, but I'm glad you're going to make sure Mia is safe."

"I'll be praying for you," Reese said softly. "There will be lots of frustrating paperwork. Let me help you with that." She flipped the page on her notebook. "And it's all the more reason for us to get this idea sold to the residents. You don't want Mountain Perks to go under."

This was not going to be an easy sell to Carson Smitten. Natalie stared out the window again and watched the man yank on the door to his hardware store in his usual confident way. She had no doubt she could convince the rest of the town over his objections. After all, what did they have to lose?